DOMINY MEMORIAL LIBRARY
A66900 46520

D1169656

RENE GUTTERIDGE
& JOHN WARD

Tyndale House Publishers, Inc.
CAROL STREAM, ILLINOIS

Visit Tyndale online at www.tyndale.com.

Visit Rene Gutteridge's website at www.renegutteridge.com.

Designed by Ron Kaufmann

Edited by Sarah Mason

Published in association with Yates & Yates (www.yates2.com).

Published in association with the literary agency of Books and Such, Janet Kobobel Grant, 4788 Carissa Ave., Santa Rosa, CA 95405.

Heart of the Country is a work of fiction. Where real people, events, establishments, organizations, or locales appear, they are used fictitiously. All other elements of the novel are drawn from the author's imagination.

Library of Congress Cataloging-in-Publication Data

Gutteridge, Rene.
Heart of the country / Rene Gutteridge ; based on the screenplay by John Ward.
p. cm.
ISBN 978-1-4143-4829-2 (sc)
1. Fathers and sons—Fiction. 2. Inheritance and succession—Fiction. 3. Fraud—Fiction. 4. Prodigal son (Parable)—Fiction. 5. North Carolina—Fiction. 6. Domestic fiction. I. Ward, John, 1970- II. Title.
PS3557.U887H43 2011
813′.54—dc22 2011032760

Printed in the United States of America

19 18 17 16 15 14 13
7 6 5 4 3 2 1

In memory of Joyce Bernhardt,
who was both the heart and the country.

R. G.

To my two children, Cali and Jack,
with a father's unconditional love.

J. W.

Acknowledgments

Rene Gutteridge:
I would like to first and foremost thank John Ward for allowing me to share in the creative endeavors of his vision for *Heart of the Country* and to be a part of his journey on this project. He's fantastically gifted and I loved working with his material. I'd like to also thank the entire Tyndale team, as well as my editors, Jan Stob and Sarah Mason, and Karen Watson, for seeing the possibilities of John's script as a novel. I'd like to thank Janet Grant, who continues to believe in me and my writing abilities. Thanks also and always to Sean, John, and Cate, who support me to no end and love me even more. The three of you are the heart in my country. Last, but not least, thanks to God—every book is a treat and I appreciate the opportunities He gives me and the gift that allows me to do each one.

John Ward:
Thanks to my grandmothers and the incredible people of Columbus County, North Carolina, for teaching me the gift of story and the value of people and character. To my parents, David and Gayle; my wife, Christy; Chris Ferebee; and Karen Watson.

1

CATHERINE

It was a strange thing to know that I was to become a memory to them. I kept searching for pain because pain means life. Instead, I smelled Lip Smackers on Olivia's pale-pink lips. I heard Faith's high-pitched giggles that still sounded childish even though she was growing into a young woman. I couldn't move my arms, but against my fingertips, I felt their hair, their shoelaces, their sticky cheeks.

I knew this would break their hearts into thousands of tiny pieces that one lifetime couldn't mend.

"Ma'am? Ma'am?"

I wished that he knew my name. I wanted somebody to know my name. The sirens wailed and screamed and I wondered if I was coming and going out of consciousness or if that's just how sirens sounded from the inside.

Above me, out of a light misty-gray that seemed like steam from a shower, I saw a man's face come into view. His eyes were frantic but gorgeous and blue. Above him I caught my reflection against a long metal strip that ran the length of the ambulance. There was a familiarity to him, but that was true of everyone in Columbus County. If I didn't know you, I knew your mom or your grandpa or your second cousin.

"Blood pressure . . ."

The words faded, just like the sirens, and his beautiful eyes retreated to a far place that I longed to reach for. I only saw the girls now, their faces passing by me like living, breathing photographs. And Calvin standing by his horse.

I wanted to be more than a memory. I hated that for the rest of their days they would only be able to touch me in their minds or set their gazes on a tiny glimpse captured by a camera.

A mother's heart cannot let go. Not even to a father who had all the love in the world to offer them. I could never be replaced.

I looked again to that long metal reflection above me. I was covered in blankets. The EMT was covered in blood, and I thought that was strange. Warm and cold sensations drifted through my body, and I searched again for any sign of pain. My face looked distorted against the metal, like in a fun house mirror, except nothing else seemed out of proportion.

"Fourteen minutes out!"

Yes, it was a long way to the hospital when you lived in the country. Only one winding road led through our neck of the woods. Columbus County did not have a well-designed road system. The state was involved in a plan to pave "farm to market" roads, the idea being to improve transportation of tobacco, corn, sweet potatoes, cotton, soybeans, and livestock to places like Whiteville and Tabor City, where the train tracks ran. But instead of designing a modern road system, they paved the old dirt roads that had generally followed horse and carriage paths. They once connected neighboring farms, working around and over the swampy areas, resulting in a system of meandering roads. I could feel the ambulance hugging the curves of the concrete. It was often on these roads where I heard the music play.

I closed my eyes, or maybe they were already closed. I told myself to live, no matter what, to live. And then I felt it, a tiny prick of pain in my heel.

2

LUKE

THERE IS CERTAIN PROTOCOL when introducing an outsider into the Carraday family. And it does not include bringing a stranger as of sixty-two days ago to the family compound, as I like to refer to it.

I watched Faith's expression as we pulled into the long drive that led to my childhood summer home in the Hamptons. Her mouth opened as she gazed upward through the tinted window of the sedan.

"Are you nervous?" I asked.

"A little, yes."

I wanted to put a hand on hers, but I didn't want her to feel my own hand shaking. Yet even as I trembled at the idea of what I was doing, I felt reassured. I knew they'd like Faith. She was easygoing, down to earth, and a way better conversationalist than any of the other girls I'd dated. I use the word *dated* lightly.

She wore a simple yellow sundress and a light-blue sweater, like she was sunlight drenched in clear sky. Ward pulled the car into the circular drive, and she let out a long, determined sigh, then smiled to reassure me she would be fine. I touched her shoulder, brushed her long hair away from her face.

"Just be yourself," I said.

"Who else would I be?" She grinned.

I'd prepared her little for what she would encounter. Faith was likable and genuinely liked other people. I figured she could hold her own with Dad. He really wasn't the one I was worried about.

Ward opened her door and helped her out. We both stood for a moment, adjusting our clothes and our nerves. I took her hand and we walked up the white concrete stairs that led to the front door.

Faith gazed up at it. "This kind of door makes you believe in giants."

"Obnoxious, isn't it?"

The door opened swiftly, before we even knocked, as I knew it would. Winston stood in his tailored suit, his warm eyes outdone only by his pearly teeth emerging. "Hello, Luke! It has been a long time since you've been here."

Christmas, to be exact. "Hi, Winston. This is Faith."

"Lovely to meet you," Winston said, graciously shaking her hand. They endeared themselves to each other almost immediately. I had a good feeling about this day already.

"Your father and Jake are on the terrace," Winston said. "I presume you remember your way there?" His eyes gleamed with a bit of mischievousness.

"We'll manage," I said, patting him on the shoulder. I guided Faith straight to the back of the twenty-thousand-square-foot estate. I knew this would be a shock to her. She'd only seen my apartment, modest by Carraday standards. I tried to play it off as we walked. "Just a little house on a tiny piece of land," I said, squeezing her hand.

"Funny," she said. Her lips trembled as she smiled. "This is . . ."

"Outrageously over the top?"

"Beautiful," she finished.

I pointed out the back window. "There they are. Trading business war stories over bourbon and Coke, I imagine."

Faith stepped closer to the window and looked out, but I noticed she was staring at the ocean instead. "Breathtaking. How can anyone not believe in a God?" she whispered.

"I suppose only if they believe they are God. And on that note, allow me to introduce you to my family." I opened the back door for her. It was a long walk to the terrace that overlooked the pool, that overlooked the gardens, that overlooked the cliffs, that overlooked the ocean. We were close before Jake finally turned around, though I suspected he knew we were coming long before that.

Dad got to his feet. "You must be Faith," he said, extending a hand and shaking hers with the mannerisms of a stoic gentleman.

Jake's cigar choked out all the clean air. Faith had lived in New York for three years, but she still had the lungs of a country girl, and she started coughing a little, trying her best to hold it in. "Hello. Nice to meet you."

"This is Jake," I said after Jake failed to speak.

At the mention of his own name, he took interest. He didn't bother to stand, but he shook her hand. "Pleased to meet you."

"You too," Faith said.

"We were just discussing some business matters," Jake said, turning his chair back to his view of the ocean. "I don't know where Candace is. Somewhere in the house."

This was Jake's way of saying that Faith should go find a woman to talk to, but I took her hand and pulled out a chair for her at the table. I saw Jake glance to Dad with his displeasure, but I didn't care. I wanted them to know this girl.

"So, Faith, why don't you tell us about yourself," Jake said, leaning back in his chair like there was nothing he cared about less.

"She went to Juilliard," I said.

Jake eyed me. "Surely she can speak for herself."

I put my hand on her back. "I'm sorry. I'm just kind of in awe of your singing talent."

"What degree did you graduate with?" Dad asked.

"I, um . . . I haven't graduated. I took some time off."

"Oh, I see."

Glad that was out of the way. A college degree or four was like a badge of honor in my family, but I knew soon enough they'd see how smart she was anyway.

"You must've dropped out to pursue some other sort of business venture," Jake said, taking a long sip of his drink while keeping his eyes glued to her. "So what is it that you do?"

"I'm hired by companies to showcase their new products. Chanel, in particular."

Jake slowly lowered his glass to the table, staring at me, then at her. "You're telling me you're a Chanel girl?"

"I'm hoping to be promoted to Chanel woman soon," Faith said wryly. She always had such a good sense of humor about what she did. She joked that if paisley came back into style, she was done. So for our third date, I gave her a small gift wrapped in paisley paper, and she laughed for a good ten minutes about that one.

Jake suddenly stood. "Dad, you want a refill?"

"Sure," he said, handing his glass over.

"Luke, why don't you help me get you and the lady something."

"Faith."

"Right. Faith."

I stood, followed Jake into the house after glancing at Faith. She looked strong and perfectly capable of handling Austin Carraday. It was time for me to handle Jake.

Inside, Winston asked if he could assist, but Jake declined and went straight to the bar.

"What's she having?"

"We'll just have some orange juice," I said, going to the small fridge behind the bar. I grabbed two glasses.

"So where did you meet this Faith . . . what's her last name?"

"Barnett. And it was at that stupid retro fund-raising party. You remember the one?"

"Really?"

"Yeah." I smiled. "I saw her at the bar. She looked like I felt."

"Not sure how to read that," Jake quipped, pouring the Coke. "But nevertheless, that was only, what, two months ago?"

"Yes."

"So you've known her for eight weeks."

"Looks like it." I braced myself. I could tell by the way he was emphasizing every syllable that things were starting to get dicey.

"And you brought her here. To the family compound? We don't just bring anyone here, Luke."

"Exactly. She's not just anyone."

"She's not just anyone?" Jake smirked. "How many Chanel girls do you think are in this city? They're a dime a dozen."

"She's different."

"Different how? She dropped out of Juilliard. That might

be your first red flag. She wants to meet your family after eight—"

"That was my idea. Meeting the family."

"She's pretty. I'll give you that," Jake said, mixing the drinks. "But pretty isn't something you've ever got to worry about, little brother. In our world they're all pretty. But pretty can be deceiving."

"I know. Believe me." I finished pouring the orange juice and angled myself where I could see his face better. "Jake, I know I've made my mistakes with women in the past. In fact, meeting Faith made me realize how many I've made." I paused as I watched him ponder. "How did you know Candace was the one?"

"First of all, we were on equal ground. Candace's family has wealth dating back a century, so I knew she didn't want me for my money."

I sighed. "Faith is different. If I were a bum on the street, she'd still like me for me."

"If she likes bums on the street, I'm going to have to wonder about her judgment."

"Come on. You know what I mean."

Jake turned to me. "You can't possibly know someone's intentions in eight weeks."

"We have a connection that tells me otherwise."

"A connection. What are we, in middle school? Haven't you lived out in the world long enough to know how fleeting emotions can be?"

From where I stood, I could see Faith. She was smiling and talking with Dad, her mannerisms relaxed.

"Why can't you give her a chance?"

"Because the Carradays don't ride on chance. The stakes are too high."

I stared at him. "This is your whole life, isn't it? The estate. The business. The family name."

"And you're always willing to risk it, aren't you?"

"Look at Dad out there, Jake. I know what he's built. I know his deep appreciation for the dollar. But is he happy?"

"I don't know if he's happy. But he doesn't have to worry about where his next paycheck is coming from, and neither of us should ever take that for granted."

"I don't take it for granted. I just can't let it define me. I can't look at that girl out there and say that she's too much of a risk because she hasn't quite found her way like we have. And truth be told, Jake, we didn't find our way. We were given it."

Jake and I watched them for a moment before he started to the door. "Just be careful. That's all I'm saying. I worry about you, Luke. I have since the day you were born. You're the dreamer of the family. You get that from Mom. And you can see where that took her."

"Leave Mom out of it."

"I don't have to. She took herself out of it a long time ago." He pushed open the back door and I watched him walk the steps toward the patio. The ocean was calm, sparkling, boasting the sailboats that glided through her waters.

I hurried after, not trusting Jake in close proximity to Faith for a second.

Faith had Dad laughing. That was a good sign. They were talking about horses. I knew Faith had grown up on a farm. And Dad had owned Arabians for a while. Faith was good at finding what connected people.

Dad got into business pretty quickly, like usual. And Jake had to pipe in with all his knowledge about what we did. I just let them talk. I wasn't interested in it right now. I was interested in the beauty before me, whose soft hair was being blown back by the ocean breeze.

I was so engrossed in watching her that I didn't realize Jake had changed the subject . . . to all the former women in my life. "Remember Leslie, Dad? I was certain that woman was going to end up on the front page of some major newspaper, and not for the right reasons."

I shot Jake a harsh look and he threw his hands up.

"Bro, only joking, okay? Settle down. Faith here doesn't seem like the kind of woman who is going to be scared off by a few flakes from your past."

He always did that. Put me in a position where no matter how I answered, I sounded like a jerk. I stood suddenly, taking even Faith off guard. "Faith," I said, helping her to her feet, "I want to show you the beach. It's amazing. It's about a fifteen-minute walk to get down there."

"That sounds wonderful," Faith said.

I guided her by the small of her back toward the steps

that led to the gardens, which would then lead us to the path to the ocean.

Jake snorted, then made some comment about the upcoming hurricane season to Dad.

Faith leaned into me. "I think the hurricane might be sitting right at the table," she said with a wink.

I laughed. That's what I loved about Faith. She could see through all the muck.

"I'm sorry about Jake. He can be that way sometimes. Overbearing."

"Maybe just protective of you." She put her face into the wind as we walked, taking in the gardens and then the cliffs. "I can't imagine waking up to this every morning," she said as I helped her down the stone pathway.

"The truth is, you take it for granted."

"Human nature, I guess."

We got to the beach and both tore off our shoes. We walked quietly along the water's edge. I'd been amazed in the first week I met her how comfortable she was with silence. She sometimes seemed to crave it. In turn, it calmed me.

There is something about being at the edge of the vast ocean that causes an instant examination of one's life. I felt completely in the moment as we walked side by side, but at the same time it was as if glimpses of my future rolled in with the tide. She was in every wave.

I stopped her, turned her to face me. She smiled and I wasn't sure I'd seen anyone look at me with that kind of . . .

what was the word? Delight? Her eyes sparkled against the high afternoon sun.

I swept the hair out of her face and took her hands in mine. Then I knelt. My knee sank into the wet sand.

The sparkle of her eyes vanished, replaced by shock. "What . . . are you doing?"

"I've been raised to never make an impulsive decision, so you need to understand that in no way is this impulsive." I pulled out the ring from my pocket and held it up to her. I felt energy tremble through her fingertips. "Faith, there are many things in life that require time and thought, and marriage is one of them. But I've thought so much of you and about you since the hour we met—enough to fill weeks if not months—that I believe this is a well-thought-out question. Will you marry me?"

"Luke . . ." She fell to her knees so we were face to face. She cupped my hand in hers and we both stared at the ring, a simple, elegant solitaire that glinted dynamically against the light. Tears welled in her eyes. She tried to speak several times but nothing came out except three or four half words I couldn't decipher.

I wanted to beg. Badly. But I figured I was taking a big enough risk by asking her to marry me two months after we'd met. So I waited.

She made me wait, glancing out at the ocean like it was going to confirm some gut feeling she had.

Then she looked me square in the eyes. Her features tensed and her eyes grew fierce. For a split second I thought maybe things weren't going to go my way. But then she said, "Yes!" and sprang into my arms, squeezing me so hard I almost toppled over. I laughed and held on to her.

In the distance, standing on the ledge of the cliff, was Jake. He sipped his drink, watched us for a moment longer, and then turned to walk away.

3

FAITH

To the lightest of applause, Luke formally announced our engagement to his family a week after he'd proposed to me. I had to look hard for one approving smile. Candace, Jake's wife, seemed oblivious to the rest of the family's disapproval, so I smiled back at her and kept her in my focus as I tried my best to not look sick to my stomach. Whatever Austin had felt for me before was gone. I suppose he didn't expect to meet me and then instantly become my father-in-law.

Luke, however, didn't seem the least bit fazed by the lack of response. I asked him why he didn't tell his dad and brother the day we were engaged, and he explained that there were just certain ways Carradays did things. The announcement of an engagement had to be more of a formal affair, a proper gathering or some such. I warned him of the enormous learning curve I was embarking on, but he told me not to sweat it. I kept getting the impression he wasn't all that fond of his world anyway. There was something restless in his eyes, detached from it all.

After drinks and "light" hors d'oeuvres fancier than anything I'd ever tasted, we returned to the city in his limo. I'd grown fond of his driver, Ward. He was an older gentleman with a wry sense of humor. I got the feeling he always knew more than he was saying.

In the very back, we snuggled against each other and watched the beauty of the Hamptons fade into the roaring life of the city. After some time of comfortable silence, Luke sat up and said, "Have you been thinking of the wedding? What you want? The sky's the limit."

"The sky seems impossible to fill."

"What have you always dreamed of? Every little girl has her wedding dreams, doesn't she?"

Sure. Olivia and I used to spend hours in the barn, setting up our weddings. The horses were our guests. We'd trade off being bride and groom. But if I had to admit it, dreams had lost their luster for me. The pomp and circumstance of dreams—and their ugly cousin, hope—had led me to a place where I'd stopped dreaming. I'd made a deal with myself that I wouldn't let dreams and the hope of what could be ever rule my world again.

"You know," he said, "Candace knows Vera Wang. They do some charity thing together every year."

A Vera Wang wedding gown? I felt breathless at the thought. I looked at this man I was to marry, the one I'd felt I'd known my whole life. It seemed he wanted nothing more than to make me happy. I had seen this kind of love only once in my life and had believed I'd never see it again. How could I have been fortunate enough to find it?

I turned my attention to him. "Luke . . . I can't be one of these people . . . one of you people."

"I know. I would never want that."

"Then what do you want from me? There's nothing that I can give you. You have everything."

"This isn't everything," he said, gesturing around us. "You are everything. I don't need another second to know I want to spend the rest of my life with you."

"Are we really doing this?"

"Yeah." He touched my arm lightly, like he was making sure I was really there.

"I have a wedding to plan!" I squealed for the first time since I'd left the country. It sounded good.

Luke laughed at me. "Anything you want! Do you want it in the city? Or back in North Carolina?"

I stared out the window, my hand in his, contemplating my options, envisioning myself in a white gown, long and shimmery. Beside me was my dad. At the front of the church stood my sister, holding a white bouquet. But they vanished right before my eyes.

I had a new life here.

I turned to him. "Let's go away."

"A destination wedding . . . I like it! Hawaii?"

"No. I mean, you and me. Just . . . you and me."

"It will always be about you and me," he said.

"Let's do it now."

I could see it in his eyes. He needed no convincing. We gazed at each other and nothing else needed to be said. This was real.

Luke leaned forward. "Ward, take us to MacArthur. And have the plane ready."

"Sir?"

"Now," he said with a smile. "Bermuda?" he asked me.

I laughed. "Actually, I was thinking of the courthouse." I looked down. I didn't dream big anymore. I hadn't in years.

"Nothing is off limits," he said. "Anywhere in the world."

Funny. I just wanted to be where he was, and the rest of the world could come and go as it pleased.

4

LUKE

She pulled at each of the sleeves on my jacket, tugging them so that the material sat close and tight atop my shoulders. Her smile gave glimpses of both pride and hesitation. Her calm eyes held mine. "I don't completely understand why you're doing this," she said, "but I know that I completely trust you."

"That's all I need," I said, kissing her on the cheek. "Wish me luck. Wife."

"You know I don't need all this," she said, gesturing around our Central Park West loft. "You don't have to build an empire."

I nodded. "I know. Empires have never appealed to me."

"Do you think this will be the hardest thing you'll ever do?"

"It'll be fine," I said. "I promise. My father is a reasonable man." A difficult swallow following that statement probably betrayed my confident demeanor, though Faith had a way of seeing through all my guises. After a year of marriage, I'd finally given up on trying any of them.

Ward picked me up downstairs and the drive was quiet. I'd turned off my phone and everything else that might be a distraction, using the twenty-five minutes to focus and go over all the important things I wanted to say.

I arrived at Carraday Towers—the place *Money* magazine had described as a palace to capital, with an old-money touch—a little after 9 a.m. Far from the gaudy gold of Trump, it reeked of staid power. I took the private elevator to the seventieth floor. Even after working here every day since graduating from college, it never felt comfortable to me. As the door swooshed open, I stepped out and turned right, walking the long hallway that felt more like a corridor, my steps quiet against the burgundy carpet.

I have very few childhood memories of my father. He seemed to look the exact same way since I was kid. Never aged. But never young. His hair was always white, like a snowdrift. His skin, baby smooth with ever-pink cheeks.

As I walked silently, hesitantly, a single thought rolled through my mind. I was there to break his heart. It was under the guise of business and life opportunity, and we would both play along as if that were the case, but I was done. I had never fit quite right into the family. I was the perpetual cockeyed glance. I was the backroom conversation. I was loved but not seen. Not like Jake.

I checked my watch. Right on time. I turned the corner and walked into an office that required double doors to keep the world out. Or in.

"Luke," he said without looking up. "Please, sit."

I sank into a leather chair that felt more like a throne, adrift in his massive city. I was surprised Jake wasn't joining us. He typically never left Dad unattended.

What I'd figured might take ten or so minutes to explain took only two. I'd made the tactical mistake of handing over my documents too early, a distraction to Dad as he tried to listen to me and read what was before him.

I held my breath but tried to look relaxed as I watched my father peer through his reading glasses, looking the sheet that I had handed him up and down. I started to fill the heavy silence that had come upon us, but Dad waved me off and demanded quiet. He then slid his glasses off his face, folding them carefully as he looked at me.

"And you say you've thought this through?"

"From every angle."

"You've already met with the Michov Brothers?"

"Yes."

"This term sheet is final?"

"It's a done deal."

At my words, I saw my father's expression change. I'd only seen that look one other time, years ago when my mother announced in front of the entire family that she was divorcing my dad. Dad had never remarried and never would. Dara was the love of his life. But money was the love of Dara's. When my father hit a rough patch and lost millions, she left.

"Why would you want to leave us, Son?"

I'd expected the question but not the tone, which was not harsh or angry. His steel-cut eyes looked dreadfully . . . disappointed? No. Sad.

"Honestly?" I asked, biding my time a little.

"Have you not been honest so far?"

I put my hands on the armrests, felt the leather under my fingers. Most people would go their whole lives and never feel leather like this. But it meant nothing to me. Because it wasn't by my own hand.

"There's nothing I can accomplish here." I looked him right in the eyes like I'd practiced in every mirror in the house.

"What are you talking about?" His hands pressed against his desk and I thought he might stand up. I hated when he stood up. "You have the entire world at your fingertips here!"

"No, I don't. I have your world," I said, my voice more urgent than I intended. Why did I need him to understand this so much? "Dad, I am checkmated on all sides of this company."

I stood and began to pace. Another thing I hated because I did it when I was nervous, but I wanted him to hear me. "First, no matter how much success I have here, everyone will always say it's because of you."

He lowered his eyes, staring at nothing on his desk.

"Second, Jake is the first in line. There is no way I can ever run this company."

His stoicism returned and he folded his fingers together. "You think you'll be running Michov Brothers?"

I walked to his desk, put my hands on it, leaned in, a little ways across. Even so, I was still far away from him. The desk was so massive that when I was a kid, I got in trouble for lying across it to see if I could touch both ends at the same time. The rumor was it weighed four hundred pounds. Probably the marble.

"No. But, Dad, I'll be making a name for myself on the Street. This is just the first step." I tapped my finger on the sheet that lay on his desk.

"How much is enough?" he said, almost to himself.

"This isn't about money," I said, retreating to the leather chair.

"You're certainly asking for much."

"That's to buy in. I'll pay that back. With interest." I gave a short nod like two men would who trust each other in a business deal.

Dad leaned forward, his eyes sharp as ever. "Just about every person who has sat in that chair and said those words to me has left with my money and never come back."

I didn't know what to say to that. I knew my dad had been burned many times. Part of it was his position. It just happened at that level. Part of it was, as I always suspected, that my dad was a champion for the underdog. He really did believe in hard work and a little bit of luck. He'd never admit it, but he did. I hoped he believed that for me.

"I can't sit in this building for the rest of my life." I felt heavy suddenly. It hit me: I'd felt like this my whole life, and it was the first time I'd said it out loud. "I just can't, Dad."

"So you're going to quit and take my money with you?"

I shook my head. He wasn't getting it. He was hurt. Growing angry. Which made me angrier because he never seemed to hear me. "No," I said evenly, "I'm going to quit and cash out equity that was going to be my inheritance."

"Your inheritance?" He breathed it more than said it.

"If I lose it, I lose it."

"Hmm." He leaned back in his chair, almost disappearing into the shadow of the massive bookshelf behind him. "That's a dangerous game."

"Life's about taking risks." I also leaned back, crossed my legs. "They don't actually teach that at Harvard. In a class, anyway. But it's not a bad philosophy."

"Sure. Until you lose."

Dad's secretary, Mona, came to the door, her long legs the center of attention. "Mr. Carraday, they're waiting on you."

"Thank you, Mona."

I glanced at my watch. Dad had scheduled me in for a whole fifteen minutes. Unbelievable. In the old days, I would've walked next to him, fighting to keep up with his pace, talking fast to get all my points in. But instead, I remained seated. That, perhaps, was the most powerful statement I could've made. I watched Dad stand and gather his materials for his next appointment. I stayed quiet. So did he.

He walked past me. I didn't turn. But then he did, which surprised me. All he said was "Okay, Son. Okay." And he left.

I expected my heart to be broken, but it had never felt more glued together in my life.

I took a moment to compose myself and close my briefcase. Mona smiled warmly at me as I left, assuming business was as usual. I returned to the corridor that took me to the private elevator.

At least I could have Ward drive me one more time.

But no sooner had my feet hit the concrete sidewalk than Jake was on my tail. Dad had to have called him right away.

"Have you lost your *mind*?" he yelled behind me.

There was no use running. I had to face him.

He hadn't even caught his breath when he said, "You didn't even tell me? You just march into Dad's office and blow up our family?"

"I couldn't tell you, Jake. I knew you'd tell Dad. And I needed to be the one to do it."

"I don't understand this at all." His eyes searched me as though he might find the answer in my expression.

"I know you don't. That's because you're the firstborn, Jake. You're never going to understand what it means to be second."

His shoulders slumped a little. "Is second so bad?" he asked, gesturing up toward the skyscraper that held our offices. "Is this so bad?"

"No. But I have to make my own way."

A pause in our conversation was filled by the busyness of the street. Sounds of traffic swallowed both our heavy sighs. Streams of people filtered by without a moment's notice of our strife.

Then Jake said, "It's her."

"No."

"It is. It's her. I told you from the beginning to U-turn it right around."

"This was not Faith's idea," I said firmly.

"You bought a *rental.* Do you not understand this, Luke? She's the kind of girl you rent—not what you buy."

"Why are you making this about her?"

"She is not good enough for this family. She never was. She never will be."

"This is *not* about her."

"Oh yes it is." Jake spun, almost walking circles around me. "I'll give her credit. She may be hillbilly trash, but she's not stupid."

I'd never seen Jake like that. He'd never stooped so low. That morning I'd told myself to keep my cool no matter what. But I really couldn't have predicted this. Jake was losing his mind right before my eyes.

"She is my *wife.*"

"And she knows that as long as you're with the family, as long as we have influence, she's in jeopardy. So she sells you garbage about standing on your own—being your own man—and the next thing you know, you actually think this is your idea."

"It is my idea."

"Right. You've ostracized the family that's been nothing but good to you, taken millions from us, and handed it over to that wife of yours. Real smart."

I stood there on the sidewalk, watching my older brother sweat like a pig, his eyes shadowy with contempt, and all I could think of were our days as little boys on Dad's yacht, soaking up the sun. We were close then. He was always taller, bigger, but he never pushed me around. I could tell he thought of me as his equal most of the time. It made me stand taller next to him, and I found myself listening to his advice as we got older.

But then we both were indoctrinated into the family business. We were allowed a week off, to move back home from our universities. And then we started.

It seemed like eons ago. I stood my ground as I pushed my foot hard into the sidewalk. "Don't talk to me like that. Don't talk about her like that."

"The truth hurts, kiddo."

I wanted to slap that smug look right off his face. "One year," I growled.

"What's that supposed to mean?"

"In one year I will yield more than you've ever done in your career."

"You're burning a bridge, Luke."

"Watch your clients."

He stormed off. I turned and walked to the idling car at the curb. I got in, told Ward to take me home. I stared out the window, remembering hazy sunsets on the beach, finding clams and swording with sticks. Two bronze-skinned boys playing endlessly, until the sun hid from them.

But Faith was my life now. I had to do anything to keep her.

5

FAITH

I STOOD LOOKING at it for a long time, hardly able to tear my gaze away, though all the excitement of the New York social scene was behind me. Music thumped in my ears and conversations tickled them, but all was drowned out by this single, simple painting.

A bump against my shoulder caused me to turn. My friend Maria grinned wildly at me, the thrill of people and power evident in her soft-brown eyes. Her hair, spectacularly elegant with shiny curls bouncing lightly around her face, was outdone only by her magnetic, gleaming smile.

"This is amazing!" she said, managing her typically high-pitched voice. "Did you see? Graham Deveroe is here!" Her excitement faded as she looked at me. "Of course you didn't see. You've been staring at this dumb painting, haven't you?"

"Dumb? It's brilliant. It's impressionistic," I said, ignoring her skeptical eyebrows. "It's layer upon layer of every kind of yellow under the sun."

"The sun? Every kid paints a sun. How hard is that? But it's lopsided. And that's one thing the sun is not. Lopsided."

"It's not *the* sun. Maybe it's the interpretation of our spirits."

"My spirit isn't yellow." She gestured toward the painting. "It's a smiley face without the smile. My vote is actually for mustard gone wild."

I studied it for a moment. "It's pure delight, imagined by the genius painter Ramsey Selles."

"Oh, brother. It's *a* sun, reimagined by a guy who has probably also done disservices to the ocean and possibly the moon."

"I really wish you got art."

"I do. In the form of men. See that one over there? Dark haired, brooding, perfectly proportioned? I've had my eye on him since I walked in the door." She wrapped her arm through mine. "Too bad you're already married to the very rich and highly independent prince of popularity and prosperity."

I turned her to face the painting. "I like it. It's striking. You wouldn't miss it in a room, that's for sure."

"You cannot buy that and put it on your wall."

"I think my living room would never be the same."

"Yes, because no one would ever visit you again."

"Think bold."

"I'll just think taste. How's that?"

I wanted to admire the painting more, but I felt him in the room. I always did. He was like a magnet. I turned and he was breezing toward us. The suit jacket parted as he walked. He was wearing the tie that I bought him. I loved to watch him walk. He had a confidence that I always wished I had.

Luke touched my arm as he flashed the smile that had probably brought him as much success as his mind for business. I still liked his touch, and I liked that he was mine.

"Ladies." He pecked me on the cheek and looked at Maria. "How much of my money has she spent?"

Maria, always with a drink in one hand and an agenda in the other, as Luke put it, rolled her eyes as she sipped her martini. "It's not your money. It's your dignity she's destroying."

"I didn't know I had any of that left," he said, grinning at me.

I wrapped my arms around him. "It's important to cherish what you have, not crave what you don't."

"See that?" He pointed at me with a large gesture. "Love of my life, mother of my future babies right here." I noticed him notice someone in the crowd. His eyes grew intense and focused. He patted Maria on the shoulder as he started to walk off. "Watch my wallet?"

Her finger traced her glass. "Don't look at me. Graham Deveroe is here. I've got better things to do."

"Happy hunting!" I said to Luke, then returned my

attention to the painting. "He's tracking down a two-billion-dollar pension fund for a big buy-in. The CFO is here."

"Nice. Close that and you'll have a place big enough to hide that hideous painting."

Before long, a man with elegant movements and theatrical eyes approached us, slipping up beside me almost unnoticed. "Brilliant, isn't it?"

"I love it. I have to have it."

"Allow me to help you. Give me a moment to check on the price—"

"No need. I'll take it."

"Yes, Mrs. Carraday. Thank you."

"Wow, must be nice," Maria sighed. "I must find my own Luke."

I glanced sideways at her. "Marriage isn't all bliss, you know."

"Oh, really?"

I grinned. "Okay, 99 percent of the time it is."

"I knew it. You guys are the fairy tale, aren't you?"

I grabbed a drink off a passing tray. "I love that man. All the perks are worth nothing unless you have trust and love."

"You're coming up on the four-year itch."

"It's the seven-year itch."

"Not by New York socialite standards."

"I'm not a socialite."

"I know, and it drives me crazy. Embrace your role, woman!"

I laughed. "Maria, we really must find you a rich man to cater to your every need."

"Believe me, I've tried. Your method doesn't work for me."

"My method?"

"You know, sitting at a bar looking lonely and miserable. It's like you were catnip to his inner feline. How does that attract a guy?"

I smiled, remembering the day I first laid eyes on him. I was at a party that Maria had dragged me to, wishing I were anywhere else, when he sat next to me at the bar. I figured I'd get the usual "Can I buy you a drink?" line, but instead he bemoaned having to be there. "You look like I feel" was his pickup line. Soon after, he managed to get me to the outdoor patio on the roof. Two hours went by in five minutes, it seemed.

We left tonight's party early, much to Maria's dismay. When we got home, he poured us wine and I observed him. I couldn't imagine we'd ever have that seven-year itch Maria talked about.

We sat on our lavish couch, staring at the yellow painting leaning against the wall above our mantel. I could tell Luke loathed it. His face clouded over as he saw it. His mood hadn't been good since we returned home.

I was still engrossed in the painting when I heard the pop of a wine bottle. "Another one?" I asked as he returned to the couch.

"This could be a three-bottle night."

"Did something go wrong at the party?"

"This is good," he said, leaning forward, pretending to engage the painting as he quickly sipped his wine.

"Is that the California cab we bought yesterday? Luke, that was supposed to be for the party tomorrow night."

"Why waste it on our friends?" He grinned, and I felt a little relief. At least he still had his sense of humor.

"You're bad," I said, toasting him.

"Am I?"

"Very."

I raised my glass to the painting, then sighed and put it down. "It's too much for the living room, isn't it?"

"It's horrible."

"Come on, let's move it."

"To the trash?"

"No," I said, elbowing him in the ribs. "Let's try the bedroom."

"Now?"

"I can't let you sit around and pout all night about this painting."

"I like pouting."

"I know you do," I said, patting him on the shoulder. "Come on."

We lifted the painting off the wall. "This is soooo heavy!" he said.

"I told you that you should be going to the Pilates class with me."

"Very funny."

We managed it into the bedroom. Luke took down the

picture that hung over the fireplace and I got the stepladder. Together we lifted it and got it hung. I adjusted it so it was perfectly straight.

Luke kicked his shoes off and fell onto the bed. "Maybe the bathroom?"

"Maybe your office?"

"Okay, okay . . . I surrender."

I hopped onto the bed with him. "I really like this painting."

"I know you do. And it's a good thing I really like you. I can live with the painting, but not without you."

"That's the sweetest thing you've ever said to me."

"This is the biggest sacrifice I've ever made for you."

I laughed. That man always made me laugh. We sat there on the bed for a while, both looking at it.

"You know," I finally said, "I think it goes better in the living room."

I expected a slap on the arm, but instead there was silence. I looked at him. He was staring into space.

"Hello?"

"What?"

"I just made an outrageously irritating statement and you're not returning it with an outrageously insulting comment."

"Sorry," he said with a small smile. "I hate when I miss a chance to outrageously insult you."

I sipped carefully, trying to choose my words. "Is everything okay?" I finally asked.

"Yeah."

I set my wineglass down on the bedside table and turned to him, giving him my full attention.

He glanced at me. "What? You've got that serious look."

I gathered my courage. I'd been hearing rumors. For months now. I had ignored them. But tonight, I couldn't do that anymore. I had been in the bathroom at the party when I'd first arrived and overheard two women talking. They never mentioned Luke, and maybe it was a stretch for me to think they were talking about him or anything to do with him. But my gut had filled with an unusual dread. "Luke, what's a Ponzi scheme?"

There are many great things that happen when two people get married, one of them being that they learn to read each other like a book. And I saw it flash across his face, so fast that had I blinked, I would have missed it. His eye twitched and his lips quivered and then he maintained his expression with such force that I held my breath.

"Why do you ask?" He poured more wine even though his glass was nearly full.

I let out a breath. "I was having lunch with Rachel Cohen, and she started—"

"What does Rachel Cohen know about a Ponzi scheme?"

What did Faith Carraday know about one either?

I kept my voice even-toned. "It's just that Howard said something to her about the Michov Brothers being *Ponzi*."

"Howard said that?" Luke's face flushed. He set down his wineglass. "Howard is an idiot! He sells one tech venture, and suddenly he's Warren Buffett." He got off the bed, loosened his tie. "Tell Rachel to keep her mouth shut. Tell her that talk like that can kill a stock on the Street."

"I was just asking," I said, watching him walk to the bathroom. He shut the door. "What is wrong with you?" I yelled.

It was quiet, and a few moments later, Luke opened the door and sat next to me on the bed.

"I was just asking." My voice quivered and I hated it. I looked away.

"I'm sorry." He patted my hand. "Look, a Ponzi scheme is when a fund like ours takes the money from new investors and uses it to pay off existing investors' returns on investments. It gives the illusion of profit when there isn't any."

"Like musical chairs."

"Yeah. And it works great until the music stops."

"It's illegal, right?"

"Very."

"Luke," I said, touching his arm. Tears rushed to my eyes just talking about it.

"Baby, listen to me. Michov is not a Ponzi scheme."

"Swear?"

"I promise."

I laid my head against his chest and felt his breathing. His heart was racing, but even so, I knew he was telling the truth.

6

LUKE

THE AIRY, OPEN CAFÉ typically caused me to lose focus on work, which was good. Faith and I met here, often just the two of us, to get away from it all, even though the vastness of the city loomed everywhere we looked. But today, Maria wanted us to meet her new and slightly older boyfriend, Walter, who seemed to thoroughly unimpress her, so I wasn't sure why we were here.

"So . . . are you gonna take it?" Maria twirled her fork over a pasta and shrimp lunch, batting her false eyelashes at everyone but Walter.

"I don't know," Faith sighed, glancing at me for my reaction. I just smiled, tried to seem engaged. "It's a way bigger mortgage. But it is amazing!"

"You have to take it!" She jabbed her fork in my direction. "You hear that, moneybags? Buy this place for your wife."

"And her best friend," Faith laughed.

"Oh yeah, you know I'd be hanging out there all the time."

"You hang out at our current home all the time anyway," I chided.

"It's her *dream* home," Maria said.

"Hey, don't look at me. I say we do it." I looked at my food, losing my appetite by the second. My mind was engrossed with a run-in I'd had with Jake, a run-in that was haunting me more and more.

Walter chimed in, "Not like prices are dropping in the Village, you know?" He threw his napkin on the table. "I'll be back." He pecked Maria on the cheek.

Faith whispered, "I like him."

"Walter? Oh, please. He's gone as soon as he picks up this lunch."

The conversation continued about Maria's inability to keep a boyfriend for more than one season, but my thoughts disappeared into a noisy benefit party where I'd run into Jake a few weeks before.

I'd just left Faith standing before that hideous yellow painting that she'd somehow found the beauty in, and was squeezing and slipping my way through a crowd toward Mitchell Wellington. He was tall, so easy to track in the packed room. Paunchy but well dressed, except his hair shone with oil like it was on a beach trying to get a tan.

"Hey there, little brother." His deep voice held so much

that the everyday ear would not pick up on. Arrogance. Piousness. Self-righteousness. I turned around, smiling politely, extending my hand. He shook it with a firm grip. It had been months since I'd seen him.

"Jake, what're you doing here?"

He returned my smile cautiously, eyeing me pretty heavily. I remembered exactly how he looked that night, with a dark fitted suit pressed perfectly against his tall frame. He was at least four inches taller than I was, but often it felt like a foot because he had a long-reaching presence. It was part charisma, part intelligence. It boiled down to the fact that he was a likable intellectual who could speak on many different levels to many different people. He always found a common interest with a person he wanted to get to know.

I wanted to get to know Mitchell Wellington, but Jake was standing in my way.

"Duty calls," he replied, stuffing a hand into his pocket, jingling some loose change. "Met a corporate pension guy down here. It was painful, believe me." He lifted his gaze like he'd whiffed something foul. "How do you do this all the time? The loud music. The obnoxious personalities."

And then it hit me, as if he'd stood right there and punched me across the cheek. Kicked me in the gut. Thrown me to the ground.

"You cut me off!" I knew I sounded like we were young again, but the words just flew out of my mouth, louder than the music. "You got to Wellington! That was my fund, Jake. I've been working on that for six months."

Jake's voice was lower, controlled. "Six months?" He snorted. "If that doesn't tell you something, nothing will."

I stepped closer to him, my fists balling and heat rising on my neck. "Is this city just not big enough? Is there no way we can both make money without having to do this?"

Jake looked at me for a long moment, his eyes tracing me, then the room. His voice grew even softer. I had to strain to hear it. "The word on the Street is that you guys are three to one liability to asset at this point."

I hurriedly replied, "That's an overrated index and you know it. We're the only fund on the Street to return over 9 percent last year. You and Dad were down, what? Two and a quarter?"

His face was nearly expressionless, and I knew mine was filled with every emotion I'd ever felt for this man, all the way back to childhood. I'd loved him once. Idolized him. Thought he would always protect me.

"The mortgage thing is done, Luke."

"We're diversified."

"Not enough. Not enough." Those tough brown eyes that used to have a soft spot for me looked worried. "Luke, I can talk to Dad if you want to come back—"

I stepped back. "We're fine."

He sighed, shook his head, looked around the room, then back at me. "Don't say I didn't warn you . . ."

"You're being quiet over there, Mr. Diplomat."

Maria's voice snapped me back to the outdoor café. I

could've used a breeze to blow away Jake's words, echoing in my mind, but the day was windless.

I glanced at Faith, who smiled but also seemed concerned. Walter was returning to his seat just as my BlackBerry buzzed to life with a text.

I read it. Reread it. My temple throbbed.

"Hey. Everything okay?" Faith asked.

"I need to get downtown." I threw my napkin on my plate. "I'm, um, sorry. I'll . . . I'll call you . . ."

"But wait . . . what . . . ?" Faith reached out for me.

"Jake," I mumbled.

"Be nice," she said, touching my arm.

I took a taxi, arriving ten minutes later. I threw some large bills over the seat and slid out, looking for him. He'd said to meet at the statue of George Washington. I found him immediately, his hands coolly in his pockets. I hated that. He knew he'd be met with my frantic fear and sometimes I swear he relished it.

I marched up to him. "You text me about an investigation? Faith was sitting right beside me."

"You haven't told her."

"I'm not telling her anything right now. There's no reason for her to worry." I scraped my hands through my hair, remembering how she'd asked me point-blank about a Ponzi scheme. "You better have something real this time."

"The Feds are closing in on Michov. It's all going down. Tonight. Tomorrow at the latest."

I didn't say it, but I wondered how in the world Jake

could have this kind of information. I mean, yeah, we were the Carradays, but did that really mean we ruled the world?

I glared at him.

"Wake up, kid."

"Dad sent you, didn't he?"

"Listen to me!"

"I am not coming back!"

Jake grabbed my arm, pulled me close. His face lost the tenseness and now looked sad. And it wasn't even pity. It actually calmed me.

He let go after a moment and then pulled out a business card, sliding it into my hand. "This guy, Tony Wright—he's SEC, but he's a friend of mine. Call him. Call him right now, Luke. Tell him what you know."

"I don't know anything."

"You don't have much time. You understand?"

I watched Jake walk away, disappearing into the stream of people who continued on with their lives while mine crumbled, one little piece at a time.

My phone vibrated in my pocket. I knew it was Faith. I had to snap out of this. I felt like the world was moving in slow motion around me. I could hear. I could smell. I could see. But I didn't seem to be able to react.

Pull. It. Together.

I reached for the phone, a lump of regret filling my throat as I prepared my lie to her. "Hello?"

"Luke, why were the police just here?"

"What?" I breathed.

"The police! At the café. They asked me—"

"What did you tell them?" I could've sworn a giant was walking across my chest.

"What is going on, Luke?" Her voice climbed high with panic.

"*What* did you tell them?" My tone was too stern. I would never normally use it with her, but I had to know because as I stood there, I noticed two darkly tinted, unmarked cars pulling up. Four men in suits got out.

"Faith?"

"Tell me what is going on!"

They walked swiftly toward me. One of them, with the thick mustache and the extra-dark sunglasses, flashed his badge at me. His lips were pressed tightly together. The one next to him, bald and tall, said, "Luke Carraday?"

"Yes?"

I dropped the phone to my side. I heard Faith's voice, distantly. "Luke? Luke?"

"Tony Wright. Securities and Exchange Commission. You are under arrest for conspiracy to commit federal securities fraud." He cuffed me and it was the most surreal moment of my life. I wanted to look around, see if anyone was noticing this. But I could only stare at my hands, cuffed, still holding the phone. Faith's voice could be heard. Something snapped me to attention. Maybe it was the Miranda rights being read to me.

"Listen, that's my wife on the phone. Let me at least tell her that I'm okay. She's scared to death."

Mustache continued with my right to remain silent, what could be held against me in a court of law, that I'd have a court-appointed attorney should I need one. And as he did, he took the phone from me and punched the Off button.

A small crowd gathered. Staring like I was some kind of freak show. I was whisked into one of the black cars, now grateful for the tinted windows. But through the window, I could see that the camera phones were out, and I wondered who ended up getting my picture. I wondered if any of them cared at all about what I was arrested for. Cared that this was the unraveling of my life, a heavy wooden spool falling to the ground, unwinding its string with blurry speed. And done within seconds.

It struck me, as we rode in silence, that all I had asked Faith on the phone was what she told them. I should have reassured her. I should have done something other than try to protect myself.

Inside that stuffy black car, I stared out the window, looking up at the skyscraping buildings, and thought of the first time I met Faith. I'd been dragged to some trendy benefit party by Jake, who indulged in a few here and there.

"Please. Come on, have some fun," Jake said, shooting me a sideways glance. "This is a theme party. And the theme isn't humdrum." Jake excused himself, abandoning me to my own social devices, which weren't many. I was kind of like my dad. He wasn't ever that social, either, and relied a lot on Jake. He always sent us both to do his work, which was to shake hands and make contacts, as many as possible. But somehow I always ended up at the bar, to drink and try to avoid human contact.

As I ordered a Scotch, my avoidance of anyone in the crowd was undone by a woman with shiny black hair, tousled to look awfully unkempt. She slid up next to me.

"Luke Carraday, right?"

"I'm almost afraid to say yes."

"Maria."

"Maria . . ." I hated these moments. They happened so often. Too many people assumed I knew them, and my family knew so many people that I couldn't fit them into a stadium. But my mother, before her abandonment of the family, had raised me to be polite. So as my Scotch slid toward me, I chatted lightly with her as she explained she worked in one of my dad's buildings.

Then I noticed the woman sitting next to her. Hadn't even realized she was with a friend. She seemed to be people watching as she sipped a martini, but now all I wanted to do was watch her. She was pretty with no effort. Her hair was plainly styled but looked like it belonged on a princess. Her skin glowed through the smoky haze of the room.

Maria droned on. ". . . I work with a number of companies, developing their customer service procedures . . ." When she realized she didn't have my full attention, she tugged at my arm and asked me to dance.

"Don't dance. Sorry." I snatched my arm back.

"There's a first time for everything."

"No, really. I don't dance. Ever."

"Your loss, then." She rose, carrying her martini between her middle and forefinger, dangling it almost like it was a cigarette. She never looked back but beelined it to a tall guy in the corner.

I raised my glass to her back. "See you Thursday."

"Don't take it personally."

I glanced sideways to her friend. She shot me a short, polite smile. "She gets that way when she doesn't get what she wants. You should see her at a Barneys sale."

That made me laugh. I settled onto my barstool and faced outward so I could watch the crowd too. "So, friend of yours."

"Best of friends."

"Sorry."

She laughed, one of those deep, throaty laughs that seems to come from the soul.

"Luke," I said, sticking out a hand.

"Faith." She shook it, her hand retreating too quickly. But not before I felt her skin. Warm and soft.

"Faith . . . I gotta be honest. You look about as uncomfortable as I feel. . . ."

"Watch your head." The polite caution from Mustache returned me to my harsh, unrelenting reality. I was at the jail, in the parking garage. I'd gone from standing under bright-blue skies to the entombing darkness of underground concrete.

No Carraday ever spent a night in jail, but that didn't mean I wasn't going to be living in a nightmarish prison.

7

FAITH

MARIA HAD ASKED me repeatedly what was wrong, but I didn't answer her. I told her to leave me alone, I had something to handle. The problem was, I didn't know what, exactly, I was handling.

I didn't even know where the jail was.

The voices had cut in and out through the wind, but I knew what I *did* hear. *"You are under arrest."*

I returned to the apartment, then literally walked in circles and chewed through every nail I had. My fingers, bloody to the quick, raced through our Rolodex for our lawyer, but I didn't even know his name. Luke handled all of that. Everything.

Should I call his work?

What would I say?

I'd just explain it was a mistake.

Except his voice sounded so . . . guilty.

Hours ticked by. I sat on the sofa and stared at my phone. Maria called, but I didn't answer. Maybe they hadn't let him call anybody yet.

The sun was silky orange in the late-afternoon sky. I'd wandered to the window, stared blankly, unaware of time.

I've got to do something.

I got on the computer to try to figure out where the jail was. After making some phone calls, I found out he was at central booking, in the basement of the courthouse.

"He hasn't been arraigned," the lady said over the phone. "Check back tomorrow after 1 p.m."

"Tomorrow?" I gasped.

"No visitors until then. It's a long process, lots of people here. Call back." She hung up.

I spent a sleepless night avoiding Maria's phone calls and trying to figure out what to do. I couldn't call Jake, could I? Or Austin? I'd never known anyone who got arrested. I wished I knew what Luke would want.

This had to be some terrible mistake, some misunderstanding. Our last conversation played over and over in my head. . . . Why had he asked me what I'd told the police? He sounded so angry.

As the morning dragged, the furious angst in my soul built. I decided to call a lawyer out of the phone book for some advice. "Once he's arraigned, bail will be set," said the man, Juan Torres. He went on to recommend a bail bondsman and his own services. "He'll need representation when he enters a plea."

I thanked the man and hung up.

I got into our safe and took the thousand dollars. I stopped by the ATM and withdrew the largest amount it would let me, five hundred dollars. I hailed a cab from the bank to central booking. By then it was afternoon.

The cab dropped me at the curb of the courthouse. I drew in a breath, trying to feel steady like Luke.

He'll know what to do.

I'd barely left the curb when I looked up and saw him trotting down the steps. My heart soared. But right behind him were Jake and a man I'd never seen before, both in dark suits.

I hurried toward him. "Luke!" I said, waving my hand. His eyes were so startled when he saw me that I wondered if he was looking at some catastrophic weather event behind me. He whispered something to Jake, who gave him and then me a long, drawn-out look. He, in turn, whispered to the other man and they started walking the opposite direction.

I rushed into his arms and cried. He held me tightly, but there was something reserved about how he did. I touched his face, searched his eyes. "Are you okay? I've been so worried!"

"I'm fine."

"I thought you were supposed to get a phone call from jail?" A thousand questions were lined up, one after the other, halting right at the tip of my tongue.

"I . . . I called Jake."

I looked down the sidewalk. Jake was stepping into a car with the other man. He glanced back at me once and then disappeared inside it.

"I knew he'd know what to do," Luke added.

I nodded, trying to understand it all. "He'll get this straightened out, won't he? I mean, this is some big mistake."

Luke let go of me, took a small step back, which on any ordinary day would've meant nothing to me. But today it meant everything.

A blink.

A breath.

"Luke? It's a mistake, right?"

"I didn't do anything illegal," he said.

And then I stepped back.

We took a cab home in complete silence. My breath kept catching in my throat. Six inches separated us, but it felt like an endless chasm.

At home, he went to the fridge, took out a beer, sat down. He did not seem to be inviting questions.

"Are you hungry?"

"I guess," he said, answering with a vague hollowness to his voice indicative of not even hearing the question.

I delivered the turkey and avocado on rye, his favorite, and then sat across from him. His sandwich went untouched.

I gathered the nerve. "Are you going to tell me what happened?" I tried a small, white-flag-waving smile.

"I don't want to talk about it."

"I don't think that's an option."

His eyes, tired with dark circles under them, darted upward, his gaze boring through the thick heaviness between us.

"There must be," I said evenly, "a reasonable explanation."

His hands tore through his hair. He stood. "It's complicated, Faith. Okay? It's not as simple as an explanation. I can't explain this to you."

"Too much for a simple country girl to understand?"

He looked at me. "That's not what I said. Or meant."

"Then you better tell me what's going on."

He looked at me resentfully. My presence was no comfort to him. He turned his back and looked out the window. The dim light of the late sun cast a golden glow against him.

"They're going to say that I knew something."

"Who?"

He didn't answer.

"Did you know something?" I finally asked.

His shoulders slumped and his hands plunged deep into his pockets. "You won't understand . . ."

He was right. I walked to the bedroom and pulled my suitcase from beneath the bed. I could barely see as I threw clothes and toiletries into the bag. What was I doing? Even as I went from the bathroom to the closet to the suitcase, it felt surreal. Every few seconds, I'd glance to the door, expecting his shadow to be crossing the threshold.

In fifteen minutes I'd finished. The zipper sounded ominously final. The suitcase was so heavy I barely got it off the bed. It thumped to the ground, landing on the tip of my big toe. I cried out in pain, but I don't think it was my toe that hurt that badly.

I rolled it out into the hallway and to the front door. I turned the knob and pulled it slowly open. Was this what I wanted? But how could I trust him? I didn't even know who he was anymore.

I didn't dare look back, but I knew.

He wasn't coming after me.

8

LUKE

She probably would've never guessed that every time I came into a room, I looked for her. She was the first thing I looked for. She was the last thing I saw when I closed my eyes at night. But I doubted she would believe that now.

I stared out my apartment window at Central Park. I'd lived my whole life here, in the heart of New York City, the Upper West Side. I was raised by nannies who walked me to school, then walked my dog for me while I was away. Still, I never got tired of the view. My father had once told me that I should never take this view for granted. That most people would never get a chance to stare down on this shining city, this beautiful park.

As beautiful as this fall morning was, with the orange, yellow, and brown leaves rocking gently through the air, I couldn't admire it. I barely noticed it. Instead I watched a little boy in a bright-yellow slicker walk with his mom below.

Yellow. I turned to stare at the painting, which we'd moved back to our living room.

"Senor Luke?"

I blinked. The little boy in the raincoat was gone, but the city moved without pause and I was back to my grim reality.

"Yes, Rosa?"

"Would you like me to take your clothes to the dry cleaner's?"

I smiled because the words stung and I didn't want Rosa to see it. But we both knew that Faith normally took care of that. She loved doing it. She said it reminded her of her mother, how she always took great care to make sure her father's laundry was properly done.

"That would be terrific. Thank you, Rosa."

"Will Senora Faith be returning for the weekend?"

I stepped forward, away from the window and the sounds of the city. "You know what, Rosa? Why don't you take the weekend off."

"Are you certain?"

"Yes, yes, take the weekend off with pay, okay?"

"Senor Luke, thank you. And thank Senora Faith as well."

I nodded and watched Rosa gather her things and leave. The apartment was so quiet, I heard it creaking against the wind that always blew harder this high up.

Nearby, from a shelf I hardly ever regarded, I picked up the framed picture of Catherine. It had sat there for years, unobserved most of the time, quietly watching over me.

I didn't know much about her. Not her middle name. Not her favorite food. But what I did know was that she looked so much like Faith, it was eerie. Her eyes danced like Faith's, sparkling with life and love. Her smile looked generous, as though she never had a complaint.

Faith hardly talked about her, but when she would, there was a certain reverence in her voice and deep emotion that I rarely saw.

"Are you watching over her?" I whispered to the picture. "She won't let me anymore."

I turned and sat down in the leather club chair we'd bought a week after our honeymoon. It was once comfortable, but now irritatingly low to the ground. The leather felt too slick. How did it not feel like luxury anymore?

I stared at our home, full of space, full of silence. My eyes rose to that bright-yellow painting that I'd come to adore. She'd been right all along. It was perfect . . . once you got to know it.

I took a good long look at it. If I could take one thing to jail, that would be it.

9

FAITH

I NOTICED RIGHT AWAY that my mind had not drifted to memories, which told me that I could not drive this road anymore without a good deal of concentration. I once could. Probably blindfolded.

This road, like most here, curved. But there were no big hills, no rocks or boulders. Instead, the land was fertile from centuries of leaves and dying animals decaying into the soil, on top of the sand that the retreating ocean had supposedly left. Daddy used to tell us that where we lived had once been the bottom of the Atlantic Ocean. "As the crow flies," he would say, "we're practically still in the ocean. It's only about twenty-five miles away!"

The land itself seemed to form gentle waves as rises and ridges alternated with low-lying, sometimes-swampy areas. Houses were built on higher land. Cemeteries too. The other land had been cleared for fields, pastures, and barns. Or, if we were lucky, left wooded as God had created it.

The asphalt was once new, black and smooth, bright-white paint marking the boundaries. Some initiative of the state years ago to bring Columbus County into the right decade. But drought, heat, and years had taken their toll. I watched carefully for the potholes that had already nearly claimed the underside of my SUV. I was kind of regretting not renting a car. The last thing I wanted to do was pull up in the BMW X5 and give the wrong impression. But I had to be honest with myself. It was going to be nearly impossible not to. For many more reasons than the stupid car I was driving.

A lump filled my throat. I knew it would, as soon as I saw the flashing yellow stoplight up ahead, cautioning drivers of a dangerous intersection. The corn was high. It would be hard to see from the cross street. I slowed down and noticed my knuckles were white. I let my hands relax a little. I was incredibly high strung lately, and that was another impression I was going to have to try hard to nix. But who was I kidding? People would think what they would think. Hadn't I learned that lesson yet?

I accelerated through the intersection, not another car in sight. The road stretched straight now, a postcard snapshot of quintessential North Carolina. The leaves of the maple, oak, gum, and hickory were already turning. The majestic pecan, taller, bigger and more prevalent, filled places where old houses and shacks used to be. They seemed infinite and immortal. I gazed out, searching for those familiar, dilapidated farmhouses that I loved to find as a kid. You could practically hear them creaking from the car. Dark and hollow, they sparked a sense of imagination inside me. I'd wonder about who lived in them. They were sometimes so small.

My favorite was coming up. I smiled at the thought of it. It was a two-story, abandoned since 1954, according to my father. My friend Amanda's father owned the field next to it. We'd ride the tractor with him, then hop off and go explore, nearly always making our way to the house. It was nothing more than wood, with nails exposed and broken glass from windows that had been shattered by storms. That made it all the more fun.

We'd pretend, for hours, to be cowgirls or sisters or whatever we wanted to be. I was ten when Amanda's parents finally banned us from the upstairs. If you drove by, you could see why. The whole thing leaned perilously to the left.

Soon we outgrew it. And then they lost their farm and had to move. By then I was interested in boys anyway.

I shielded my eyes from the glaring sun, trying to find it in the overgrown field. I slowed and pulled to the side, wondering if I'd missed it.

No . . . there was the old iron gate that we used to sit on. I glimpsed the road that led up to the house. I pulled into the short gravel drive and got out.

There it was. Or had been. I stared at the pile of wood,

collapsed in on itself. It looked pathetic. What had finally caused it to fall? Hail? A hurricane? Did it matter?

I turned away and watched the wind snake through the corn, parting it like it was water in a riverbed.

And then I couldn't help it. I cried.

I pretended it was for the house.

I wiped the tears. Up ahead, the wooden sign still stood, welcoming anyone who might be interested into Columbus County.

I got back into my shiny SUV and continued my journey. It was almost over, and that was the part I dreaded. We all have something we fear. A flash in our minds. An image that haunts the empty corridors of our hearts.

There was one moment that I had worked so hard to make never happen. It was the thing that I had run from for years.

And now it was here.

So I rolled down my window and let the wind tear through my carefully styled hair. I let the lingering tears wash back against my cheeks. I didn't look at how fast I was going. I didn't care.

My mind was being flooded with a million regrets, and I couldn't be bothered by anything else. The wind stung my face but didn't block the images that forced themselves into my mind's eye. There was nothing I wanted to think about less, yet there he was, filling my mind.

I noticed I'd slowed my acceleration unintentionally. I decided that it was because I wanted to admire this beautiful country. Tidy farmhouses popped against the lush fields in which they sat. Trailers held their ground, too, anchored to soil that had most likely been in the family for decades. A little boy waved at me, his dirty shirt hanging against his sweaty skin. No shoes. Matted hair.

I tried to wave back, but my hand wouldn't release the steering wheel. It didn't matter. My windshield was tinted, a way to shield me from peering eyes. I'd never noticed before, but it was my safe place. I always retreated to my car when I needed time, space, restoration.

This time, though, I felt no relief. I had no future to dream about, so my thoughts turned to better times, which I guess is what thoughts do when they have nowhere else to go.

"Cow!" My car came to a screeching halt as I jammed my foot on the brake. I stopped inches from the animal, and that burning rubber smell instantly cleared my mind. "Cow . . . ," I whimpered. The animal just looked at me from the side, as cows do, blinking nonchalantly as it moseyed across the road. If a heart could break out in a sweat, mine would be soaked. Instead it thumped hard against my chest, causing pain that on any ordinary day might strike me as a possible heart attack. A little young for that, but with the life experience of a fifty-year-old, it was a maybe. I waited to see if I dropped dead, but I didn't.

Suddenly a pickup truck, old and dented, pulled next to me, its motor rumbling like it might be ready for the old folks' home. An old man in denim overalls reached over and cranked the passenger-side window down. "Little lady, you got awfully lucky there. Didn't you see that cow?"

I wanted to reply that no, I had not seen the cow thanks to the fact that my mind was doing anything to keep me from thinking about what was in front of me. Or behind me . . . But this guy didn't strike me as the kind who wanted to listen to personal problems.

"I, uh, was admiring the beauty of these parts." I threw in *these parts*, hoping I sounded like I might fit in. I could tell I wasn't doing a good job. He was eyeing the car. Then me.

"You all right?"

If by *all right* he meant unharmed by the cow, then yes. But I was crying at torn-down farmhouses, so *all right* needed a stronger definition.

"You're not from round here?"

"That's a hard question to answer." I tried a short, polite smile . . . the kind that worked in the city to shut people up.

"Noticed your tags. New York."

"We don't have a lot of cows crossing the street."

"I can think of a few choice words for what you do have crossing the street."

Oh, boy. "Is that your bull or someone else's?"

He smirked. Tobacco bulged from beneath his lip. "Tim Dibble's. Fence came down in the storm last night. Be on the lookout. He's got twenty or so cattle that he can't account for yet."

"Thanks for the warning."

The cow finally made his way to the other side. Pickup Man pulled to the shoulder and whipped out his cell phone. I wasn't sure if I'd ever get used to cowboys and farmers with their cell phones. Even in this technologically saturated world, it seemed Columbus County was frozen in time. It was a snapshot of what America was at its core. Lovely and rich with heritage.

I slowly continued on. Ahead the blood-orange sun settled toward the horizon. Haziness hovered over the countryside, ushering in memories of long summer evenings spent carelessly enjoying life.

I was less than five minutes away now, and with each passing second I was losing what little nerve I'd had.

10

OLIVIA

"It'll be just a minute there, Liv," Roger said. He looked disorderly this morning, like he could use a good hair combing and maybe even a shave. I stood there trying not to look impatient, even though I was. I know that about myself, the impatience thing. I kind of hate it, if I'm telling the truth, but it's what makes my world go around. If I didn't snap my fingers, things wouldn't get done.

"Nell," I said to my oldest daughter, "for pete's sake, stop touching the merchandise!"

"But—"

"Don't 'but' me, sister. I will make that butt of yours sting like it's being fried in a pan."

"I'm nine. You can't really spank me. You know that, right?"

I narrowed my eyes. "I can keep you from going on that fishing trip you and Grandpa got planned. We'll call it a spanking of the soul."

Nell's eyes grew wide and she stepped away from the kitchen gadgets they had hanging on the wall next to the laxatives and then the rat poison. I was going to have to talk to Bernie about how his store was set up.

Roger had the phone cradled against his shoulder, immersed in some conversation. He was probably talking to Martha Dixon, who had to be the neediest woman in all of Columbus County. I checked my watch. *Come on, Roger, I don't have all day.*

Nell stood next to me, wiggling. "Momma, I'm bored."

"Nell, we've been standing here for ten minutes. Why don't you go over the multiplication table in your head. I'm testing you on that this afternoon."

"I thought you said we were done for the day."

"No ma'am. I said we'd take a break, go get Grandpa's pills, stop by and see him."

"Maybe today Grandpa will let us ride."

I sighed. "Don't count on it."

Nell continued to wiggle. Victoria was stooped, looking for pennies on the floor. Probably not sanitary, but it was saving my sanity at the moment.

Roger gave me a desperate one-more-minute signal.

For crying out loud. I decided to go have a talk with

Bernie about the laxatives and the kitchen gadgets, not to mention the shotgun pellets by the greeting cards. He had condoms by the baby diapers, which might've been by design, but still. From what I could tell, his arrangement got thrown off when he had to start carrying car chargers and long-distance cards. But really, the whole thing ran better when Belinda was alive.

I stood at the counter, waiting for him. He was in the back somewhere, no doubt smoking a cigarette. I started feeling sorry for him. His whole life had been wrapped around Belinda. They'd known each other since birth, and when she died of cancer, he kind of fell apart. Now he ran this place like it was a junkyard.

Kind of like Dad was keeping the barn these days.

I sighed for a moment and realized that I was probably going to come across as harsh because I was having to wait on Roger and his one-man pharmacy. I really preferred Walgreens—an extra twenty-five minutes away but well worth it—but Daddy wouldn't hear of it. Said we had to support the local business.

Bernie came out of the back room, smelling like an ashtray. He managed a smile. "Sorry about that, Liv. Thought you were back at the pharmacy."

"Was. But Roger's got his hands full with Martha. At any rate, I wanted to talk to you about your greeting cards."

"What about them? I ain't carrying those ones that you open and they sing to you. I have to listen to these kids open and close them and it just 'bout drives me insane. I say you shouldn't let a card sing—you should sing yourself."

I put a gentle hand on the counter. "Bernie, look, what I'm trying to say is that I'd like to help you with your store."

"I ain't hiring."

"No, no. Volunteer." I gestured around us. "It needs a makeover, wouldn't you say?"

Bernie eyed the place like he'd never noticed.

"See? Where the greeting cards are? Why not move 'em over there, by the window? You and I could have this knocked out in a weekend."

He tapped his fingers against the counter, seemingly fixated on the motor oil. Then he looked at me. "You'd do that for me, Liv?"

I smiled. "Of course I would, Bernie."

"You're right. This old place needs a pick-me-up."

"Let's plan to get it done before Thanksgiving. Just in time for Christmas. Sound good?"

"You are a darling, Liv. Your daddy raised a mighty fine daughter."

I nodded. Nobody mentioned my momma much anymore, but it was Momma who was always doing things for other people.

I glanced around for the kids, hoping Vic wasn't setting the place on fire and hoping Nell wasn't fingering the—

"Nell, put those down!" I gasped. I looked at Bernie. "Maybe they should go behind the counter?"

Bernie nodded but said, "Maybe. It kinda embarrasses

me to hand them out, to tell you the truth. Bel used to have 'em here, and she'd lecture any kid who had the guts to come in and try to buy a package."

I walked to the front window, glancing at my watch for the twelfth time. I was momentarily distracted by a fancy car driving slowly by. Sleek and black. Shiny like it hadn't driven a mile on the road before. *Just wait till it hits some of these unpaved roads out here,* I laughed to myself. But I wondered who it belonged to. Nobody around here drove that kind of car. Few people had the money to. And if they did, they'd buy a bigger, better truck. Or maybe a new tractor.

I watched it creep forward. The windows were darkened so I couldn't see the guy. It looked like a fancy hatchback.

Nell looked up at me. "Who was *that*?"

Vic walked up beside us. "Somebody rich and famous."

"The rich and famous don't come to Columbus County, kids. And that's a good thing."

"Liv, I have the prescription ready!" Roger called.

I checked my watch again as I strolled to the back of the store. There was never enough time in the day. But I tried to catch my second wind. I thought I had just enough time to stop by the market and grab Dad some of that sweet corn he liked. And maybe a pumpkin.

My feet were killing me.

11

FAITH

We could always tell when somebody was coming to the house. A large dust cloud announced their arrival as they drove down the quarter mile of gravel that led to our house. Even with the windows rolled up, it caused me to cough.

The red mailbox that had been knocked down a dozen times by the postman was standing but leaning a little to the left. And after that, the long, winding road that led to the house.

I stopped my car and watched the dust cloud lift into the air and away from me, sitting in silence, with the air conditioner off. I could barely see the red barn and part of the roof of the house. I kind of wanted to burst into hysterics. Just cry. No . . . sob. Sob and tremble and bury my face.

But what a mess that would be to encounter. I didn't want him to see me like that. I didn't know what I wanted him to see. I was returning to all the hopes that had ushered me off in the first place. I left here swearing I'd come back a somebody. And here I was, broken and half the person I'd been when I left.

I checked my hair, my makeup, because that's what I did in New York. I had to look the part. But here, I wasn't even sure what my part was now. How was I going to explain myself? Would he even want to see me? I'd made the occasional phone call, but Daddy wasn't much of a phone talker.

My hand rested on the gearshift, but I couldn't get myself to put it into drive. And I couldn't help the tear that ran down my face, probably streaking right through my blush. I couldn't help any of it. I was facing my own worst fear, and driving toward it, I'd found my confidence and ordered my excuses. But now, with the dragon lurking restlessly behind the beautiful rust-colored maples, I'd lost every ounce of courage I'd mustered.

I stared at the glowing R on the dashboard. And with one swift motion, I backed up, causing the dust to rise again, like smoke from the dragon's nostrils.

I only got ten yards or so before I stopped myself, though. Because I realized, with great dread, that I had nowhere else to run to. It was here or there. And *there* was gone, like the dust from the road when caught in even the mildest wind. *There* had crumbled under the weight of reality.

I caught another tear with my finger. I noticed my hand

trembling. I noticed my heart skipping beats. And then I noticed him.

He was far away, but he was wearing that bright-red shirt he liked so much. Sitting on the small bench that looked over the fields and pastures he loved. His back was facing the road, so maybe he didn't notice my car.

I pulled to the side. For some reason, I needed to walk this out. Some of my most cherished memories were along this road, walking to get the mail, with my mom, my dad, my sister, or sometimes by myself. Wildflowers, purple and yellow, grew alongside it in the spring. I must've picked a hundred bouquets for my momma. And she'd put each one in a vase, as if it were the first time I'd ever given her anything. She was so good at gushing.

The road leading to our house was dirt, with some gravel and oyster shells thrown in holes here and there to keep down the amount of mud created when it rained. Daddy was not keeping it as pristine as when Momma was alive. Bradford pear trees lined the drive on both sides. In the spring, they were virtually covered with white blossoms, but in the fall, the leaves turned deep orange and red, each forming the rounded pyramid shape that made them so popular in this area.

One of the trees had died, hunching under the weight of its dead limbs. I wondered if it had grieved to death after Momma died.

One foot in front of the other, I walked. I wrapped my arms around myself even though the air was pretty warm for this time of year. I realized I was chilled by my own guilt. For all of it, I might as well be a blizzard inside.

I kept my eyes on him. Without him, I would stop. He was all at once what I feared and what I hoped for. What I hoped for more than what I feared. So I was able to keep walking. Dust settled against my ankles. I wondered when the last time was that I walked on dirt.

A few yards away, he sensed me and turned. My heart stopped as I watched him get to his feet. I was taken aback by how he'd aged.

I realized as I walked, faster now, that he couldn't see me well enough to know who I was. I watched him fish his glasses out of his pocket, put them on his face. By now I was close, twenty feet away. I stopped because I didn't know what else to do. His eyes widened.

"Faith?" He stepped forward. "Is that you?"

"It's me, Daddy," I said, my voice choked and weak. "I'm home."

12

CATHERINE

"Ma'am? Can you hear me?"

There is a dirt road that leads to my house. It's spectacularly unspectacular, except it's our road. Calvin had it named. I saw Olivia bounding down it, her floral skirt tangled between those lanky legs. Her curls bounced around her head, like they were square-dancing. She was my serious one. Always on task. Always together, confident in her decisions. Like her daddy.

She was smiling today, running fast in those new cowboy boots she'd saved up her allowance for. I loved that rare smile.

Behind her came Faith, little, maybe three, with her

matching skirt. She wanted to dress like her sister. But the skirt came down to her ankles. Beneath the hem I saw she didn't have shoes on. I could never get that girl to wear shoes.

"Blood pressure is fifty-two over thirty-five . . ."

I felt my eyes open, even though I thought they already were. I stared up at this boy. How old could he have been? He looked so young. Terrified. His sharp blue eyes opened wider as he noticed mine.

And then searing pain through my legs. I almost laughed, except I'd never felt pain like this in my life. I'd delivered both girls naturally, but it was nothing like this. I tried to move my hand, tried to find his. I needed a hand.

There it was. His found mine. Squeezed it. I couldn't squeeze back. I couldn't move anything. But I felt pain.

"I'm alive!"

The young man lowered himself, put his ear close to my mouth. It was strange. I thought I'd shouted it, but it appeared he could barely hear me.

"Her blood pressure is rising!" he said, sounding relieved. He looked at me again. It seemed maybe he realized I could see him, and so he smiled a little. "You hang in there, ma'am. Do you hear me?"

But I felt his hand trembling inside mine.

He let go and put his hands on my stomach. Heavy, like a brick. Just holding his hands there.

Then the pain faded again. I tried to grab for it, willing it back.

"Momma . . ."

Her voice. Her sweet, sweet voice in my ear.

"I heard that music you're always talking about."

I swept her around in a circle, holding her tiny waist as her legs clung to my hips. "You did?"

"Yes, I did. When I was in the pasture."

"What did it sound like?"

"I don't know. It smelled."

I laughed. "Smelled?"

"Yes. Like you and Daddy." She dropped to the ground, placing her arms around my waist. "I want to be like you someday, Momma."

"Me?"

"Everybody tells me I look like you."

"You do."

"And so I am going to sing like you, too."

I knelt down and smoothed her hair out of her face. "You just remember that the music comes from here." I put a hand on her heart. And then she ran, wrapped in the bright light of midday.

It enveloped her, and I couldn't see her any longer. "Faith? Faith?"

"Ma'am, calm down. I'm right here. Right here with you."

His hand slid into mine again. I felt the rubbery latex. I wanted to feel his flesh. Something wet dribbled down my arm. Warm.

The pain was there, but it was distant, as if someone else were feeling it. *Don't let it go. Don't let it go.*

"Don't let go."

His face was near mine, his eyes like beacons of light.

"Okay." And then I heard the music.

13

OLIVIA

My back ached for some of that ointment that turns hot after it touches your skin. Sometimes I just want to rub that all over my body. But I guess that's what old people do. Sometimes I had to remind myself I was thirty, not eighty. I stood in line at the grocery with just a few items, but behind the one woman in town who liked to buy three weeks' worth at a time.

"Sorry about that, Olivia," Teresa said, hoisting a two-pound bag of okra onto the conveyer. "I'll be done here in a sec."

"Mommy, can I have a—"

"No, you cannot, and if you'd like to know, the man

who invented the candy display at the checkout aisle died of candy poisoning."

Victoria's eyes widened. "He did?"

Nell snorted. "Of course he didn't. She just says that because I guess it's easier than saying a plain no." She glanced at me with those wise eyes she got from her grandfather.

Finally Teresa and her three carts of groceries were done. Angie sensed my agitation and checked me out quickly.

"Ah. Your dad's favorite," she said as she slid the pumpkin over the scanner.

"Oh yes. I probably toast six or seven pans of pumpkin seeds this time of year."

"Oooo, I love 'em too. With salt and a little olive oil."

I thanked Angie and hurried the kids to the car. We still had the afternoon science lessons for Nell, plus multiplication, and I figured Dad was going to want to chat a little like always.

I was driving too fast, hoping a rock wouldn't pop up on the windshield and crack it. It had happened seven times and Hardy was getting tired of replacing the windshield.

I saw it as I came over the hill . . . that black, shiny city car I'd seen from the corner store. It was parked on the side of the road, near the mailbox. It made me feel funny inside. Why hadn't they pulled into the drive?

I pulled around it, eyeing it carefully. As best I could tell, nobody was in it. I turned onto the dirt drive, creeping along, watchful for anything suspicious.

Everything looked in order. I could see Silver near the fence, his tail twitching, his eyes calm.

I parked and waited for a moment.

"Mom, what are you doing?" Nell asked.

"Stay here," I instructed and got out of the truck.

"But the sack—"

"Just stay here."

The front door was open and the screen was shut. I climbed the steps to the porch and tried to see into the house. I never knocked at Daddy's, but then again, there weren't ever any cars out front that I didn't recognize.

I opened the screen door. It let out its typical screech.

"Daddy?"

The front room was empty and the house was particularly quiet as I stepped in. Usually at least the television was on. "Dad?"

Nothing.

I hurried to his bedroom. But it was empty. His bed made. Everything tidy.

"Dad?"

I went to the kitchen and then saw out the back door. There he was. With a woman. They were looking out at the pasture and didn't see me.

I dusted my hands and smoothed my jeans, tugging at the flannel shirt that seemed to have shrunk over the past few years. I wondered about getting the kids, then decided I'd do that in a minute.

I opened the screen door and smiled pleasantly. "Hello?"

Dad turned around first and I gave a short wave, then looked at the woman. The pleasant smile dropped straight off my face. "Faith?"

"Hi, Olivia." She stuffed her hands in her pockets. Looked apprehensive. And not like herself at all. Fancy hair. Fancy clothes. Apparently fancy car.

I glanced at Dad, who gave me a look that said I should pick my smile up off the porch and put it right back on.

I walked down the steps, stretching that smile hard across my face. "Faith. My goodness. How unexpected."

Dad looked like he was about to burst with excitement and tears all at once. He walked with her as we met halfway. He had a hand on her back. A grin on his face. A spring to his step.

We hugged, but I let go of her because frankly I'm not much of a hugger. Never have been. At least since I was a kid. I tried not to stare at her, but it was hard. I mean, she looked like she'd run into a paint truck with that lipstick and eye shadow. And if her orange shirt got any louder and crisper, it might be a Cheeto.

Suddenly the door flung open and Nell and Vic were bounding toward us.

"I told you guys to stay in the truck."

"Who's that?" Nell said, pointing to Faith. "Here's your medicine, Grandpa."

"Girls," Dad said, "this is your aunt. Faith. This is Nell and Victoria."

Good grief, could this get any more awkward?

"Well, listen," I said, huddling the girls and pushing them toward the house, "I know you two have a lot of catching up to do. Years' worth, really. I've got to get home and get the schoolwork done. Faith, you just stopping by or are you here for a while?"

"Not sure yet."

Of course you're not. "Okay. Boy, wish I could be as whimsical as that. 'Course that'd throw Hardy for a loop, you know, me just up and leaving. Dad too, for that matter." I let out an unfortunately timed laugh, which sent awkward ripples through the breeze.

"Daddy, pharmacist says that's the same medication, it just looks different. New manufacturer or some such. Faith, I'm sure we'll catch up soon. You might want to move that fancy car of yours. That gravel can put some real dings in even the nicest of paint."

I heard Dad say something, but I pretended not to hear it. I let the back screen slam and continued to whisk the girls out front and toward the truck.

"I thought you said we'd stay for a little bit," Nell whined.

"Not today. Busy, busy." I hoisted Victoria into the truck and shut the door, then went around the back to try to catch my breath. My hands were shaking. It was like I'd seen a ghost or something.

I climbed into the truck and started it up.

"I didn't know we had an aunt," Nell said.

"'Course you did. I told you."

"We never seen her," Victoria said.

"Yes, well, she's very busy with her life in New York." So busy that she couldn't pick up the phone. Told us she was married after the fact, on a postcard from someplace I'd never heard of. Eloped. I think I still had her present in a closet somewhere.

We drove up the dirt road. I cranked the air just to keep the kids from jabbering. The pumpkin sat there on the seat next to me.

After a while, Nell leaned forward from the backseat. "She looks like your mommy."

I might've seen a ghost after all.

14

FAITH

"DON'T WORRY ABOUT LIV. She'll come around. Just shock, that's all. I was getting ready to ask you if you'd called her to let her know you were coming."

I looked at my feet. Pedicured toes peeking out of designer stilettos. Just didn't fit the scene here. "No. I, uh . . . I wasn't ready for that." I lifted my head as a gentle breeze rustled the leaves. "Can we walk to the barn?"

Dad shrugged. "Sure."

We walked in silence for a while. There was too much to say, and that was the problem with coming home. At least like this. But the simple walk to the barn brought me a comfort I couldn't explain. Took me back to my roots, I guess.

It's easy to underestimate your roots until they're all you've got left.

Beside me, Dad limped a little, like he had a bad knee. I'd have to ask him about that later. Every time I looked at him, he'd smile. Part of me wanted to just observe him without his knowing. His temples were gray. The skin over his eyelids sagging just a bit.

I had hoped the sadness would be gone from his eyes. But it was still there.

Dad unlocked the large door. I pulled one side; he pulled the other.

At the barn's smell, I was instantly taken back to my childhood, memories bulleting through my mind so fast they were almost blurry. My mind wasn't the one really seeing them, though. It was my heart.

I could see her atop Lady, blazing through the fields, racing Daddy. She was looking back at him, laughing, racing Lady harder.

Olivia and I would cheer, one of us for Momma and one of us for Dad.

I followed him through the empty barn out into the pasture, where the horses must've been. "Silver," I said, smiling as we approached him. He was standing in some mud, twitching his tail. He used to be a beautiful white, with a hint of gray undertone that caused him to shimmer. He was dirty white now. I couldn't go all the way to meet him because of the mud. Didn't stop Dad, though, and he looked behind me like he expected me to be there, then noticed my shoes.

"Where's Lady?" I asked, glancing down the fence line.

"Lady died. Couple of winters ago."

A hard knot formed in my throat. Dad didn't look at me but instead seemed interested in the graying sky. He then gave Silver a hearty pat-down. "Silver over here's been hanging tough, though."

"Liv and I always said he was the son you never had." I smiled and looked at the horse. He looked so old, so worn out. Lonely. He blinked at me and I wondered if he remembered me. My smell. My voice.

"Has anyone taken him for a ride recently?"

Daddy didn't answer, but he looked at Silver and the answer was obvious. "He's still got it in him."

"Let's saddle him up, then."

We started toward the barn. I noticed just then how the paint was peeling and how the equipment wasn't tidy like he'd kept it before. It was sort of a picture of my dad's life. Maybe mine too.

"You're not going to ask me why I'm back?"

"We don't have to talk about anything. Ever. If you don't want to."

I nodded, helped him with the saddle, and appreciated more than ever this simple man. It was perhaps his simplicity that drove me away, at least in part. He didn't grieve like me, and I couldn't ever get him back where I wanted him. But now I appreciated it because I understood the complications of life more than ever. I'd learned more of its complexities and its deep disappointments. I had a better grasp on heartbreak.

Silver without Lady was like Daddy without Momma. Watching that lonely old horse being saddled up for the first time in who knew when caused the threat of tears. Daddy buckled and strapped, seemingly not having missed a day of it.

"He's all yours." He pointed to my feet. "Except you're not gonna go far in those. Heck, you might just impale his sides if you're not careful."

"My riding boots still in there?"

"'Course."

I hurried to the barn, slung off my shoes and found the boots in one of the storage closets. They still fit perfectly. I marched toward the horse, my boots plodding through the mud.

I stroked him on his jaw, where he liked it the most, and patted him hard against his still-muscular frame.

"Don't worry. He remembers you." Dad helped hoist me on. And it was like riding a bike. "I guess you'll be staying for dinner?"

I nodded.

"I just have some TV dinners around. Maybe we'll go get some fried chicken, okay?"

"Sure." I winked at him. "I promise. I'll be home in time for dinner."

He snorted. "Yeah, where have I heard that before?" He slapped Silver on his hindquarters and the horse leaped forward. We were off to the fields.

I sank low, let my hair come undone, let the wind snap at my face.

"Whoa, buddy," I finally said to Silver, pulling up on his reins. We were walking along a line of trees. The sun was setting and I loved how the light filtered through the trees, streaming through the gaps and illuminating patches of dying grass. Fingers of heaven.

The warmth of the sun saturated my skin, and I turned toward it, closing my eyes. I missed him. I missed his touch already. His lively eyes and killer grin.

". . . it works great until the music stops."

Out in this part of the country, people lived by faith alone. They had to. The soil of the earth and the clouds of the heavens collided in prayer. And I felt it too. It was peaceful and void of the frantic noise that washed away any hope of quiet solitude in my life.

Except I couldn't pray. Shame washed over me. My momma had taught me many simple prayers, but for the life of me I couldn't utter one.

I stroked Silver's mane. "Come on, buddy. It's time to go back . . ." I wanted to say *home*, but the fact was I didn't know where that was anymore.

15

LUKE

I PRESSED THE PHONE to my ear so hard that I felt the cartilage crunch against it. "Pick up . . . come on . . ." I waited impatiently. Filling in the infinitesimal seconds of silence were haunting voices. Jake's, Faith's, my father's.

"Hello?"

I gasped at the sound of his voice.

"Jason, hey . . . hey, it's Luke."

"Yeah, I could see that on my caller ID."

"Listen, I've left you a few voice mails, just wanted to see if we could get together and maybe—"

"I can't be seen with you, Luke. Okay? You get that, right? I mean, that'd be instant career death."

"Oh, come on, Jason. Don't you think you're overreact—"

"No, I don't. I saw it that day."

"Saw what?"

"I was getting a hot dog, saw you standing on the street corner, looking around like something was really wrong. I was just about to go ask you if you needed help when . . ." He cleared his throat. "When they came and took you away in handcuffs."

"So guilty until proven innocent, eh?"

"You know what kind of world we live in, Luke. This is nothing new to you. We eat our young and everybody knows it, and so do you. And if the tables were turned, you wouldn't even take my call."

Click. I held the phone there for a moment, hoping it was just a glitch and that he was still there.

I took in a deep breath. And another. I dialed Steve. Voice mail. Then Kelly. Voice mail. Then Richard. Voice mail. I wasn't even sure why I was calling people, but it seemed a good idea to maintain some contacts . . . some normalcy.

I leaned against the counter, listening to the hyper flow of air in and out of my nostrils.

It was the village, and I had leprosy.

I set the phone down and my mind drifted away again. Where had Faith gone? She wouldn't answer my calls, which I expected, at least temporarily. But it was a strange feeling not knowing where my wife was.

My doorbell rang, sucking me back into my present circumstances. I'd been expecting Darmon but hadn't realized what time it was. I quickly opened the door and greeted him with a hug and a few slaps on the back.

"Come on in," I said, ushering him in and closing the door. "No trouble getting up here?"

"Not like last time, that's for sure. I swear your doorman really works for the Secret Service."

"He takes his job very seriously." I smiled. "Come, sit down. You want a drink?"

"No, I'm good." And he didn't sit. "Listen, we need to talk."

I glanced at him from the kitchen, where I was opening some seltzer water. "I know. I've got to catch you up on a lot of things. I know you've heard some stuff."

"Luke, I can't stay."

"What are you talking about? You just got here."

"Yeah. I know." Darmon looked like he was being crushed by every second that went by. "I wanted to talk to you in person. You deserve that."

I set the water down. Put my hands on the counter. "Sounding kind of ominous, Darmon."

"You're in a big mess. A world of trouble, Luke. You know that. I don't have to tell you."

"What's your point, Darmon, because I called you over here for that very reason. I am in a world of trouble. That's when you call your friends. Your best friend."

"I don't know what you've gotten yourself into. I couldn't believe it when I saw you on the news." He shook his head and fingered his watch. "I can't help you out. There's nothing

I can do. And standing around defending you is only going to make me look like I know something or at the very least vitiate my reputation."

"Just get out!" I shouted at him. The suddenness startled us both.

"Luke, look—"

"Get out!" My voice turned sarcastic. "Why should I expect any more from you than this? We've only known each other since we were thirteen."

"I never understood it."

"What?"

"Why you left your dad's business. I had to work for everything I ever achieved, but it was handed to you on a silver platter. Yet you wouldn't take it."

"Let yourself out, you self-righteous . . ." I couldn't finish the sentence, even though a hundred crude words sat on the tip of my tongue, ready to be spewed. I couldn't disrespect him, even though he'd abandoned me at my darkest hour.

I heard his steps and the door shut quietly. I wanted to sob into my hands and scream and throw something, but I suddenly went completely numb and couldn't even feel the pain of my own predicament. Only one thought wandered through my mind: *How can I stay this way?*

16

CATHERINE

I SAW A GLIMPSE of yellow and realized suddenly how much I loved color. I noticed it more than other people, I think.

I was kind of shy as a kid. Not bursts-of-red-up-my-neck shy, but reserved, way more than the rest of my family. So to get attention, I wore a lot of bright colors. When neon was all the rage, I thought I'd died and gone to heaven.

When I was eleven, I finally caught the attention of my family when they heard me singing one time in my bedroom. I didn't realize it, but they were all in the hallway with their ears to the door. Suddenly I was like a superstar or something.

"I didn't know you could sing!" Ma said.

"Don't know where that comes from," Pa had exclaimed.

"Nobody in this family, that's for sure. Ever heard your mother sing at church?"

And that's exactly where I ended up, too, the very next Sunday, singing a solo of "A Mighty Fortress." Pretty soon I was a regular at church, in the choir, at the county fair, and certainly at any picnic or party I attended.

I relished the attention. I hadn't had much of it until that point, and so I soaked it in and took every opportunity that was afforded to me. But what I didn't realize at the time was that somewhere along the way, I started defining myself by my talent. Easy to do when your family has nearly their whole identity wrapped up in you. I made a name not only for myself, but for them too.

They never took advantage of it or used it wrongly, but I'd stand up on that stage, belt out a song, and watch tears come to Ma's eyes. I'd walk past Pa and he'd be talking music with his buddies. I knew I had something special and didn't want to waste it.

But then I met Calvin, and as much as he loved my singing, he seemed to see music in my soul instead. He saw me. Really saw me. If I couldn't carry a tune, he wouldn't have cared. He always said we made our own music. And he said that whatever I sang first started in my beautiful soul. Looking back, he was kind of a deep guy for being so young. But he'd worked the fields, just like generations before him, and I think it does something to you when you're out there in the quiet, with time to think. Calvin told me he watched lots of sunsets by himself, and I always imagined his soul saturated with light.

"Ma'am? Ma'am? Wake up!"

"Catherine . . ."

He leaned over me again, and I swore either he was deaf or I was imagining that I was being heard.

"Catherine . . . ," I repeated. Were my lips even moving? I couldn't tell.

"Glad you're back with me. I need you to stay with me . . ."

Okay. Stay with you. Boy, he had pretty eyes. My Faith would like those eyes. She was drawn in by old souls. I knew that when she came home and announced Rupert Stewart was her boyfriend. In the third grade.

"Rupert?" I asked. The kid was nice but had thick glasses, a bowl cut, and nearly always mismatched clothes.

"He's read all the Judy Blume books."

It lasted about a week, but I knew my girl looked for substance, and in those blue eyes that kept my gaze, I saw substance.

I was drawn to my metal reflection again, and this time I told myself that I had to look. Not just glance. But look.

"Blood pressure is rising again," he said.

I stared at it for a long time. The pain was coming back. It made me want to scream, but I couldn't move. His hands were still over my belly.

Blood on his gloves.

Yellow here and there.

A moment of clarity interrupted the pain and the terror that I felt, and I saw it clearly. I saw *me* clearly. And I knew I'd made a mistake. The metal wasn't distorting me. It was perfectly capturing me.

"Her heart rate is . . ." His voice trailed off. I don't know why. But I couldn't look at myself any longer. Maybe I trailed off.

I had to ask myself, was I better off dead? And maybe at that moment I was because I felt nothing at all. No hope. No love. No peace. No memories. Complete emptiness, except for the flickering of my soul against a harsh, dreadful wind.

17

FAITH

"You're far away . . ."

I gasped, turned. Dad had crept up on me while I was lost in my thoughts of Luke and our life before. "Hi. Sorry. Was just . . ." I didn't have to say it. He knew. I hung the saddle up and grabbed the brush.

"Good day for a ride. Nice weather."

"It was perfect."

"How was he for you?" he asked, nodding toward Silver.

"The best. A real gentleman." I nudged Dad. "Mom used to say the same thing about you."

He stared off into the horizon. Then he turned back toward the house. "Well, your sister has fixed dinner."

"What?"

"It's a special day."

"She didn't have to go to that trouble."

A wry smile crossed his face. "That's what your sister does. She goes to the trouble. It'll be better than anything I come up with, that's for sure. I'll meet you back up at the house."

He ambled toward it, taking his time, and I took mine. What had I done, coming back here? I was already a huge inconvenience. And I could tell Olivia didn't approve. How could I explain the last few . . . ten . . . years? How could anyone possibly know how I got here? Why I came here. Why I left, for that matter.

My mother's face rippled in my mind as if it were laid against water. She told me that no matter what, I'd always have home.

But I don't think she could've predicted what a mess all of us would become.

I spent a little while with Silver, brushing his coat. Used to be that the shine came back when I did that, but no matter how much I brushed, the sheen didn't return. It was okay, though. We understood each other.

I walked back to the house in my bare feet, feeling the grass between my toes. I loved being in my bare feet. Luke and I used to go to Central Park and I'd always kick off my shoes, which inevitably led to a much-loved foot rub from the man of my dreams.

At the back door I slipped on my shoes and walked in. Dad was in the recliner. Just the top of his head peeked over the worn leather. A football game droned into what was otherwise a silent house. Off the kitchen was their bedroom. I slipped in there quietly. I didn't know why, but it just felt like I needed permission to wander this home I'd grown up in.

The familiarity of the room greeted me, but the warmth was gone. I'd spent hours in here talking with Mom about boys, horses, singing. The arrangement hadn't changed. A soft layer of dust was at first the only indication a woman wasn't keeping the room. The pictures were still around. But it had been stripped down to simplicities, serving a man with simple needs. I stepped quietly, carefully, my hands clasped behind my back as I wandered from picture to picture.

I noticed Dad's Bible on his nightstand. Well worn. A bump in the middle. I wondered what it was and walked over, carefully lifting the cover. Between the pages—Leviticus chapter 9 to be exact—was Momma's wedding ring. Silver. Thick but a little hard to get a grip on. I picked it up carefully and held it close to my face. I knew by heart the tiny inscription on it but read it anyway. *C & C. May the music never stop.*

I studied it for a moment, then looked at mine. Massive by comparison. Platinum. The diamond stretched from the bottom of one knuckle to the top of the next. It had taken a whole week to get used to the weight of it.

"Hey."

I turned, embarrassed by the private moment he'd stumbled upon. I quickly slid the ring back into his Bible.

"Hi there."

"Sorry 'bout that. Must've fell asleep in the recliner."

"No problem."

He looked at his watch. "Your sister's not exactly the type to keep waiting, so we better go."

"Sure. . . . Dad?"

"Yeah?"

"When did the music stop?" I looked at him, catching his startled expression. But I had to know. "Was it before or after she died?"

Dad took a long look at me. An uncomfortably long look. "It never stopped. I still hear it. Every day." He walked out and I trailed behind him as if I were a little girl again.

We got into Dad's pickup truck, the same one he had when I left, and got on the main road. I realized I didn't even know where Olivia lived.

18

OLIVIA

"I THOUGHT WE were having grilled cheese," Nell said, hanging on the counter like it was some sort of jungle gym.

I shooed her off it. "We were. Now we're not."

"'Cause Aunt Faith is coming over?"

I glanced at her. "You don't have to call her Aunt."

"But you said she's my aunt."

"Technically, but you kind of have to earn the right to be called that."

Victoria, coloring at the table nearby, pointed to the pumpkin. "What about Grandpa's pumpkin?"

"He's got everything he needs over there. Nell, hand me the eggs, please."

Nell hurried to the far end of the counter and carried them to me. But the next thing I knew, she'd dropped them. Bright-yellow egg yolk oozed out from the container, spreading quickly across the floor.

"Nell!"

"I'm sorry, Mommy! I'm sorry!"

"Go to your room!" I screamed, dropping to my knees to see if even one egg survived. I carefully opened the carton, but there was not a single one left.

Victoria stood over me, crayons in each hand. "Momma?"

"Victoria, please, just go away. Just go."

I knelt there over the eggs with my dish towel. I heard Nell crying in her room.

Then the back door opened. Hardy. His heavy boots, which I always asked him to take off, tromped down the hallway to the kitchen. Was I crying? I didn't even realize it. I tried to dry my tears quickly, but it was no use. I knew my face was blotchy. I was not a pretty crier. Faith could cry her eyes out and they wouldn't even get red.

"Olivia? What the heck are you doing down there on the floor?"

"Nell dropped all these eggs. Now I can't make a cake."

"Why don't I just run down to Kevin's, see if they have any."

"It's too late. I won't have time to make it before they get here."

"Are you crying?"

"No . . ." I glanced up at him. "You wouldn't understand."

Hardy bent down next to me with a rag, started cleaning it up.

"I'll get it."

"Now, there. I'm the kind of man that can get down on his knees and clean up an egg or twelve."

I laughed a little. "I just wasn't expecting company tonight and I have a lot to do."

"Well, you didn't have to invite them over, you know."

"Daddy eats TV dinners except when he comes over here. He would've had nothing for her to eat."

"I bet they could've managed."

"It's family. It's what we do."

"I know. You keep telling me that." He winked, and before I knew it, the eggs were cleaned up.

"You want me to go talk to Nell?" he asked.

"I'll do it. Can you get the plates out?"

"Sure."

I walked down the hallway, batting at my eyes to keep them from watering again. Nell was lying on her bed, her knees pulled to her chest, blubbering with the best of 'em. I sat down next to her.

"I'm sorry . . ." Her face dripped with tears and I held her head against me. "I didn't mean to."

"Of course you didn't mean to. Why would you drop a bunch of eggs on purpose?"

She wiped her eyes and smiled at me. I grinned back at her, patted her little head, and sat her up. "I'm sorry I got so upset."

"You were going to make a cake with them, weren't you?"

"Yep."

"Is that why you were so upset?"

"Well, I like cake an awful lot."

She smiled. "Me too."

"But there's always another day." I tried to remain calm, but how could I serve a big dinner with no dessert?

"Mommy?"

"Yes?"

"Can I call her Aunt Faith if I want to?"

I stroked her hair. Avoided her eyes. "Yep."

"I've never had an aunt before."

"She's been gone for a long time."

"Where does she live?"

"New York, I think. Last I heard."

"New York? Wow."

"Don't be too impressed with that hoity-toity city. We here in Columbus County are the heart of the country."

"Did you see her shoes?"

"Fancy, huh?"

"Yeah. She's pretty."

"Always has been."

"Now you're like me."

"How's that?"

"We both have our sisters."

I rose from the bed. "I have to finish dinner. Will you help Victoria pick up her crayons? You two get washed up, comb your hair, and wash the bottoms of your feet. Hear me?"

"Yes ma'am."

I returned to the kitchen. Through the back door I could see Hardy grilling the meat. It smelled good. I turned my entire focus to the meal. Everything had to be just right. Even if we had to live without dessert.

They'd be here in twenty minutes.

19

LUKE

In the evening I took a walk. The leaves were starting to fall, brilliantly colored if life was good. If not, just brown and dying. Faith and I loved this time of year. We'd sit for hours in Central Park on the weekends, on a blanket, eating goat cheese on brown rice crackers and sipping wine. We had the whole picnic basket and everything. She'd wear amazing dresses that flowed around her legs, showed off her shoulders in a way that always caught my attention.

I stared at the spot under our favorite tree. I could practically see her, in her favorite white dress with a sweater around her shoulders when it got colder, leaning against me as we talked about everything under the sun.

A girl skipped by and I lost the image like a leaf blown away. I had so many memories, but they were fleeting. I couldn't hold on to them for long.

I could call her. I knew I should. But what would I say? What was there to say? I doubted she'd take my call anyway. She'd hear details soon enough, I guessed, through the media maybe.

Dread filled me from head to toe as I thought about what my future held. A certain regret danced around that dread, that I'd left my family's business to pursue what I saw as a more exciting endeavor. I wasn't surprised by the regret. Long before I was in trouble, I had the same regret. I just kept trying to ignore it.

The day I told my dad I was leaving, it was like a weight had lifted off me. I felt unchained from something I was literally born into. For years I didn't even realize there was an option. Nobody ever gave me a choice. And I didn't realize until I was older what "second child" really meant. It seemed like a curse.

Not always. I still had memories of chasing the wind through the Atlantic waves. Building sand castles. Climbing the rocks on the small cliffs. I couldn't have known then how prophetic my words would be. I was eight, and the ocean's waves were being stirred by a coming hurricane. Jake and I were building forts out of sand, trying to beat the storm that was coming. I hollered over the wind, "I'm going to build mine bigger and better than yours!" He just smiled, like he was happy for my effort but knew it wasn't possible.

Those words echoed in my mind as if I'd said them moments ago. I sat down on a lonely bench in the park, feeling the hatred of recent days still burning deep in my bones. I remembered the day Jake chased me down after I told Dad I was leaving.

I was young. Too young to articulate what I wanted. What it meant to me. I'd told him to watch his clients, but it's not what I meant. I'd drawn a line in the sand when I should've just walked away and proven myself with my actions.

But Jake always did have a mouth on him, especially when it came to defending his family. You'd rather cross paths with the devil than Jake Carraday.

I pulled the phone out of my pocket. I wanted to hear her voice. But I knew she wanted nothing less, so I slid it back into my pocket and sat.

20

FAITH

THEY'D BOUGHT A HOUSE a few years ago, a big step up from the tiny rental they'd started in. Olivia was married and pregnant at twenty, like most girls from around here. The wedding was small. I was the maid of honor.

It took only five minutes to get to her house. It was brick, modest but pretty. A beautiful flower garden framed the porch, and wooden wind chimes hung near the front door. A stone frog was perched in the mums. The grass blades looked soft, deep green, perfect for running barefoot in. I hopped out of the truck and threw off my shoes, walking through the grass as if it were sand on the beach. Oh, that felt good. Was that fescue?

Suddenly the screen door flew open and out came Nell in a beautiful blue dress, way fancier than I'd expect for just a dinner. "Hi!" she said as she ran up.

"Hi there."

She leaned into me. "I'm going to call you Aunt anyway."

Didn't know what that meant, but I smiled. "You can call me anything you'd like."

"Where are your shoes?" she asked, her eyes wide.

"Back in the truck. Don't you go barefoot around here?"

"'Course. All the time. But I liked your shoes. They had jewels on them."

"They're my favorite," I told her with a wink.

"Maybe sometime you can spend the night with me. I got two sleeping bags."

"You do? I'd love that."

"Do you like princess movies?"

"Definitely."

Nell grinned. "You're my new favorite toy."

I laughed. "And I don't even need batteries!"

Dad walked up, smiling as he ruffled Nell's hair. "Hey, kiddo."

The door opened again and Hardy came out. He had a beard now and was a bit gray around the temples. His kind eyes were unchanged. "My goodness! Faith, welcome. I'm so glad you're home." He greeted me with a warm hug.

"Hi, Hardy."

"Olivia's in the kitchen, fixing dinner like we're feeding an army."

"Your house looks so beautiful."

"Aw, thanks. It was quite a fixer-upper when we first got it. I'm a fan of mustard on my hot dogs but not on the walls and carpet. At any rate, come on in."

Nell took my hand and we walked in. Behind me Hardy and Dad got caught up in some conversation about tractors.

Inside, I could smell the comfort of the home-cooked meal. Olivia turned, apron on, wiping her hands with a dish-rag. "Hi there!" Her voice chirped with politeness but not yet with kindness. Still, she smiled and beckoned me closer. "Come on in."

"Thanks," I said. "You didn't have to do this, Liv."

"Nonsense. Anyway, there's no cake. Sorry about that."

"Cake? Gosh, no worries. I don't eat cake much."

Dad trailed in behind me. "Hey, Liv."

"No cake, Dad."

"What?"

"Sorry. We had a mishap with the eggs."

I glanced at Dad, surprised to see genuine disappointment on his face. Maybe I had underrated the power of cake. "Your table looks beautiful." It was decorated with a pumpkin and some fake fall leaves, with two orange candles in the center.

Someone tugged on my shirt. I looked down to find Victoria staring up at me. "I'm going to be a Ninja Turtle for Halloween."

Olivia laughed. "That's my tomboy right there. Climbs trees. Has sword fights. Would die before she wore a tiara."

"You sound tough," I said to her.

"I can lift a bowling ball."

"Wow. That is tough."

"Dinner's served," Olivia called.

"Not eating on the TV trays?" Dad asked as he walked into the dining room. Again, he was kind of pouting like a kid.

"Dad . . . ," Olivia said in a chiding sort of way. "We have a special guest with us. She deserves more than a TV tray."

The word *guest* stung, but I figured Olivia already knew that.

We sat down and Dad said grace. When was the last time I'd prayed? At least this kind of prayer. Yeah, I'd thrown up some desperate prayers lately, but nothing calm. Nothing meaningful.

I looked up after the "Amen" to find Olivia watching me. She glanced away as she passed the potatoes.

"Been meaning to ask you when you decided to grow your hair out so long," Olivia said.

I tucked my hair behind my ears.

"Saw in the tabloids at the grocer that a bunch of celebrity types were wearing it the same way. Guess that's the thing." She handed me the radishes. "You always looked better with it shorter, I think. Better for your face."

"Looks real nice, Faith," Hardy said.

That created a perfectly awkward moment, saved only by Nell, who said, "I think you look like a princess."

Victoria piped in, "If she's got muscles, she could be a pro wrestler."

Nell glared at her. "She doesn't look like a wrestler, Vic."

"I'm just sayin', she could be one if she wants."

"Girls," Olivia said.

"Okay," Victoria said, not skipping a beat, "maybe not a wrestler. I know! A rock star!"

I smiled at her. "Not in this lifetime." But I was kind of dying. I didn't want to be the topic of conversation.

Luckily Dad bailed me out. "Hardy, I heard you guys got in a little hunting yesterday."

"Got a five-point buck."

"Did you really?" Dad set down his fork. "Whereabouts?"

"Down in the runs—about a quarter mile from Jeffrey's crossroads."

"They're running down there this year?"

Hardy nodded, and I enjoyed my meal and the conversation. When I was a kid, I hated all the talk about hunting. But now it soothed me, like gentle thunder rolling across the plains.

Olivia sliced her meat, but her eyes looked sharper than the knife. "Hardy tried a new marinade. Like it?" She left my gaze and glanced around the table, I guess so she wouldn't look inappropriate.

But I was sure she wanted to see my expression when I realized I was eating deer meat.

"Tender," Dad said.

"I tried to put in a little more lemon juice this time . . . added a teaspoon."

"That's a good idea."

I nodded my agreement but pushed the meat to the side. Wasn't a big meat eater anyway. And Olivia knew *Bambi* was my favorite movie. Man, she was stooping low.

"So where's Luke?"

Or maybe lower. I measured my response. "He's in New York."

"Has he ever been down here? I realize he hasn't been to Columbus County, but I meant North Carolina in general."

"No. Never been." It was getting harder to stay measured. I kept my knife in my hand even though I was just eating the mashed potatoes now.

"To each his own." Olivia shrugged.

I set down my utensils and stared at her.

"No insult intended," she said, slicing her way through her own bull. "I mean, it'd be great if Luke visited. I just think family's important, that's all."

"And I don't?"

Olivia looked at me. Her expression said everything. *This is my turf. You ran away. I wish you'd never returned.* She sat straighter, her eyebrows raised like she was lecturing a child. "I don't know, Faith. I guess actions speak louder than words in my book."

I glanced at Dad. He looked as wounded as the deer we were eating.

"Funny how family can be a pain and you just think, *Why bother?* Then you get fed up with your snotty Yankee husband, and here you are."

"That's enough, Olivia." Dad threw his napkin on the table.

Now Olivia looked wounded. Her eyes swelled with held-back tears. "She hasn't been home in what, ten years?"

"Now listen to me. You are sisters. We're gonna sit here and have dinner. And tomorrow we're gonna go to church together. And that's it." Dad picked up his napkin, folded it, and continued eating. Hardy did the same. The girls looked like they'd never seen anything like this before.

"Ole number nine won Richmond again." Hardy had put a gentle hand on Olivia's shoulder. She shrugged it off.

"Saw that, Hardy. I'll tell you, that's the best team in racing."

"It's not the driver. It's the car."

"You still gotta get in there and press the gas, though."

The two men went on to talk. Olivia stared at her plate, cutting food she never intended to eat. I did the same. We were as far apart as two people could be. Except for maybe Luke and me. But then again, Luke didn't hate me.

21

CATHERINE

"She's back!"

I felt air fill my lungs. I heard a harsh wheeze near me.

"I got her. Get there, Angie!" His face bent close to mine. "I'm right here. Stay with me."

"She's conscious?" A woman's voice.

"Just drive," he said. He raised a bloody glove to his forehead, wiped some sweat droplets clinging to his skin.

Music suddenly filled my ears, but I realized it came from a memory. It was the band playing at homecoming. I could almost feel the taffeta in my fingers as I remembered that day. I'd never felt prettier in my life. My dad had sprung for me to get my hair professionally done, and they did it up like a princess. Curls and beautiful, sparkly bobby pins.

We were all lined up on the football field. I was shivering in the November air as I tried to look poised. The stands were crowded, people huddled in twos and threes under blankets. I'd sung the national anthem earlier—the biggest thrill I'd ever had. I got a standing ovation!

Then, there he was. I knew him. Everybody did. He was the quarterback for our football team, and as handsome and tall as you could imagine. We ran in different circles, but in our community everybody knew everybody.

The band hit its cue . . . I can't even remember exactly what they were playing . . . but we walked across the field, met halfway, and I locked my arm around his. He grinned at me as I did, and I felt my whole body tingle. I sure didn't want to show it, though. I smiled at him and then focused on the walk we had together, and his biceps, as they announced our names.

I held my shoulders back, my head up high, and hoped I'd be picked for homecoming queen because that would mean I'd get to kiss Cal Barnett.

I was maybe holding on a little too tight as we took our place, watching the other homecoming candidates come down the field. He patted my hand and whispered, "It'll be all right."

And then it's kind of a blur. They called our names and I took his lead. We walked forward, the two of us, and stood under this metal archway that had been decorated with streamers and balloons.

Everyone was cheering so loud I couldn't hear myself think. But he stared at me like we were the only two people in the universe. He leaned in and I closed my eyes because I'd never kissed a boy before. But I didn't want it to look that way. I'd been practicing in my bedroom—me and my mirror.

And then I felt his lips. On my cheek? I opened my eyes and he pulled back. He'd kissed me on the cheek? The roar of the crowd died down a little bit because people expected a good kissing show, I guess. I looked into his eyes and they sparkled, and I realized he'd given me a kind of gift that you just can't buy . . . respect. He respected me enough to not make a show of it. We held the gaze for a moment, and then he turned and waved, and the crowd went crazy. I followed his lead, clinging tightly to him.

And from that day forward, I never let go.

"Don't let go!" His frantic voice jolted me. I didn't understand why he sounded so scared. I was alive, wasn't I? I could remember things. Why was he yelling at me?

I imagined one of my daughters with this good-looking kid. I had to see them get married. I had to. Olivia was dating a good kid named Hardy, and it was looking to get serious. Calvin really liked him, said he was a man of character. But Faith, she had a more fragile heart, and I knew it was going to have to be someone who understood that.

Waves of pain took my breath away. My body felt like it was exploding from the inside out. I clenched my teeth.

I didn't want to let go. I didn't. But I was certain people didn't live through this kind of pain. I thought my body was supposed to go into shock. And then maybe it did because I saw Cal's face, smiling at mine, even though I knew he wasn't there with me.

22

FAITH

COLUMBUS COUNTY COMMUNITY CHURCH had been standing since 1872. All the original pews were in their places, and firmly planted in each pew sat the descendants of those who'd built it. If you were in the choir, you still sat with the congregation; otherwise the attendance would look awfully sparse. According to Dad, the choir didn't even sing every Sunday anymore. I walked in with Dad and took a deep breath as I smelled the pine.

Dad sat us in the fifth row on the right side, the same place he'd been sitting since I was born. Mr. and Mrs. Fischer were next to us. Boy, they'd aged. Mrs. Fischer had a cane, and both of them wore glasses now. They didn't seem to recognize me. I smiled, but maybe they couldn't see well.

I noticed Olivia behind us on the left side, with her family. The church still seemed to struggle with membership, like always. I remember my parents being some of the youngest members, and Olivia and I being two of only a handful of children.

I didn't attend church, not once, while I was in New York. Life was busy. Sundays were for catching up on rest or anything else that you didn't get done during a week that more times than not was just a blur. But I often noticed the gorgeous cathedrals that marked some of the busiest corners in Manhattan. I loved stained glass. It reminded me of this church's. I sat quietly next to Dad, admiring the filtered light that glowed through the glass like the air had been watercolored.

I glanced back at Olivia once, and she gave me the stink eye. Essie Mae, one of my favorite women from the church, had an ongoing feud with Adeline Starks, and it was all because Essie Mae felt Adeline always gave her "the stink eye." Hard to define, but when you saw it, you knew it. Just as I chuckled at that memory, I saw Essie Mae ahead, talking with another parishioner.

It felt good to be here, even if I had Laser Eyes behind me.

"Your sister's bark is worse than her bite."

I glanced at Dad, startled. What, had he read my mind? "Olivia is Olivia," I sighed.

"She does love you."

"I'm not so sure about that, Dad."

His rebuttal was cut short by the sharp moan of the organ. Everyone abruptly stood. Was that Eliza, still on the organ? She was so hunched her nose nearly hit the keys.

Dad smiled at me. "Yep. That's her."

"How old is she?" I whispered.

"Nobody knows for sure. She keeps lying and saying she's in her eighties."

I sang the hymns. Knew most of them by heart. Dad didn't even bother opening the hymnal. I had the voice, but you would've thought Dad had the microphone. He was belting it all out, his voice just a decibel under the entire church combined.

The pastor was new. It didn't surprise me. This church rotated pastors in and out every two or three years. The young ones came, did their time, then went on to bigger and better. Drove my dad nuts. I still remember Sunday dinners and Dad ranting about it.

Ironically, or maybe not, the sermon was on forgiveness. My mind wandered a lot, back to Luke, where I really didn't want it to go. We had a lot of fairy-tale moments. Our first anniversary was in Africa. We'd attended galas and openings and benefits all over the world. I'd never had money before and swore I wouldn't get attached to it, but it was a strange thing to not have to choose between this and that, or to not weigh the cost of anything. I'd grown comfortable in life for the first time since Momma died. My life was protected on all sides, so I thought.

"You just going to sit there all day?"

I snapped my attention upward to find Dad standing over me, waiting for me to exit the pew.

"Sorry." I quickly stood, grabbed my purse, filed into the center aisle. Outside, the sun was bright, washing white light over the brick stairs, where Dad stood shaking hands in his weekly ritual. I liked watching him. He was kind, sincere, not just shaking the hand but taking in the whole arm, starting at the elbow.

"Last time I saw that dress, it was in a SoHo window."

I turned, first glancing down at my dress to see what in the world I was wearing. It was a Tory Burch, with chunky colors and a bit too short for this crowd. I looked up.

"Lee?"

"Here it is in Columbus County. Small world."

"How are you!" I hugged him and stepped back. I hadn't seen him in . . . years. I longed to see a friendly, fish-out-of-water face. But I wasn't sure I wanted it to be Lee's. He reminded me of so many things I wanted to forget. I tried to keep my wide smile. We were never more than acquaintances—his aunt went to our church, and he was a few years older—but sometimes lives collide in unexpected ways, as ours had.

"What have you been up to?" I asked, trying to fill that awkward silence that seemed to follow me everywhere.

"I'm a doctor now. Just started in the ER over in Whiteville."

"You're kidding!"

"Is that a shock?"

"The same guy who couldn't manage to make time to study in high school?"

"Turns out you can't make much of a living coasting on old football glories." He shoved his hands in his pockets. "So . . . where's Luke?"

"Still in New York . . ." I didn't know what else to say, but thankfully Dad seemed to sense my predicament.

"Dr. Lee! Good to see you!" He waved from a few feet away, then pointed to his foot. "I got a thing on my toe. Can I talk to you?"

Lee smiled. "Duty calls." He walked over to Dad.

I'd barely caught my breath when another person stood between me and the sun, casting a shadow over an already dark-side-of-the-moon me. "Essie Mae," I said.

She took my chin in her wobbly hand. "You look just like your momma. I'd swear she was standing here right now if I didn't know better. But I am getting up in age, so maybe I'm having one of those dementia streaks."

I grinned and hugged her. Before we could continue our conversation, Olivia was by our sides.

"Hi, Olivia," I said, hoping that stink eye was going to cut me some slack.

Essie Mae patted Olivia's shoulder. "Don't you look pretty in that new coat."

"Hardy got me this from that new outlet down in Myrtle Beach the other day. No occasion. Nothing. Just came home with it."

"Now that is something."

"He's a good man."

Essie Mae might have been having a dementia streak, but nothing was lost on her. She knew Olivia was sticking the knife in. I could see it in her eyes.

"Isn't it wonderful to have your sister back with us?" she said, now patting us both on the arms. "I'll tell you what, nothing is as special as family."

"Absolutely," Olivia said, and she cast a glance at me. For once, it didn't look like it wanted to pierce and mutilate my soul. "Absolutely, Miss Essie."

"Well, you two, I better get myself to the kitchen. Sunday dinner to make."

"You're still cooking?" I asked.

"Every Sunday, right, Essie?" Olivia asked.

"They keep eating it. Don't know why. That last roast was so tough that I told it to go try out for the football team."

We laughed and watched her maneuver down the steps with her cane, stopping to say hi to Dad, who was still talking to Lee.

"I love that woman," I said.

Olivia said, "Hmm," and nodded slightly. "I hate to see her so sick. I don't know how much longer we'll have her."

"She's ill?"

"That's what happens, Faith. We don't just freeze in a time capsule while you're living it up in New York. People get old."

"Listen," I said, trying to cool the waters a little. "I know. We need to talk."

"Do we?"

"You're my sister, Olivia."

"You and Daddy are coming over for Sunday dinner. We can talk then." And she was gone, skipping down the steps and joining her family. Nell waved at me and I waved back. Victoria showed me her muscles. I laughed as Dad walked up to me.

"Have you met our new preacher?"

I looked at him across the lawn, a circle of blue-haired women surrounding him. "He seems to have a way with the ladies."

Dad laughed. "Yeah. Well, these ladies see anything younger than fifty and they start batting eyelashes that fell out a decade ago."

"Dad!" I said, hitting him on the arm.

"What?" He smiled. "Pastor Jim's a good man. You should talk to him. He's pretty good with problems, stuff like that." Dad wasn't a man of many words, and with that, we walked toward his old F-150. I opened the door and was surprised to find an array of red roses, at least a dozen, on the seat.

"What is this?" I asked.

"They were on the altar. In memory of your mom."

I stared at them for a moment, then picked them up and put them on my lap and shut the door as Dad started the truck.

"Did you put them there?"

"Every year."

And that was the end of the discussion. I rolled down the window and let the breeze take the strong scent away. I remembered my mom smelling like roses. It was her perfume.

I knew it. Everybody knew it. But nobody had said out loud that it was Mom's birthday. And most likely, nobody would. In New York, I never celebrated it with anything like roses on the altar, but it never passed without me sending up a thought to her. Here, I felt closer, like maybe she was just one block over or something.

I held the roses in my lap as we drove away.

23

OLIVIA

I OPENED THE OVEN to stick the thermometer in the chicken. The heat hit my face, but my insides were already broiling. Crispy and burnt, as a matter of fact. I pulled the chicken out of the oven and stared it down like it had something against me. But really, I was picturing Faith's face. It had to set for ten minutes, or believe you me, I would've started slicing right into it.

Instead, I was going to have to put on my polite face and get out the nice place mats. I checked my watch and started setting the table. Hardy came in, squawking about the squirrels eating the pecans.

"I don't want to hear about it right now," I said.

"What's wrong with you?"

"You wouldn't understand."

"You always say that."

"Because it's true."

"No, it ain't. You got lucky with me, Liv. I am one of those guys who listens to what you're saying, even if I don't understand it. And sometimes just talking about it helps."

"Just keep the girls busy. I gotta get this dinner finished up. Dad and Faith'll be here any minute."

He leaned against the kitchen bar. "So this is about Faith."

"What makes you say that?"

"Maybe it was the fact that you watched her like she was some kind of wild animal, all the way through church. I mean, if her skull had eyes in the back, it might've worked, but I don't think she saw you."

I sighed, adjusting the place mats so they were all spaced equally apart. "Hardy, you just don't get it, okay? How could you? I don't expect you to."

"I know that you don't talk about her much."

"She left. Don't you see that? She left us. Me. Dad."

"Was there a rule saying she couldn't?"

"I'd expect you to take her side," I said, glaring at him over the half-set table. "Everybody does. She's got that Midas touch. She really can't do any wrong. I mean, she shows up here, after this many years, and wants to just pick up where we left off? Where we left off was Mom was dead, she disappeared, and I was the only one to try to put Dad back together." I put down the forks, leaned against the table, trying to keep the tears from starting. "Do you know that I never got a chance to . . ."

"To what?"

I shook my head. I didn't want to be a blubbering mess when they arrived. Sunday dinner wasn't about that. It was about family, which she hardly appreciated. Sure, she wanted us when things got bad, but what about all the other times?

I nodded toward the backyard. "Victoria is calling you."

He didn't have much to say usually, so I didn't expect him to say much now. Besides, I could tell Faith had already bewitched everyone, once again. She had that effect on people. They instantly liked her within seconds of meeting her. But they didn't know what I knew. And she certainly wasn't going to fool me. Dad, now, that man was easily fooled. He had to grieve Momma and then Faith's leaving. It was no wonder he was making such a big hubbub about her return.

I finished setting the table and went over to ice the cake. Double fudge, her favorite, on request again from Dad.

"I just want her to feel welcome," he told me over the phone last night.

Maybe I could get a banner and some balloons too. Heck, let's throw her a parade.

The girls bounded in, dirty in their Sunday clothes.

"Girls, I told you to change before you went outside to play."

"Sorry, Mom," they said in unison.

"When is Aunt Faith going to be here?" Nell asked, jumping up and down.

"Soon enough. Go change, okay? And wash up."

I stepped back to look at the cake. Perfection. And I knew secretly that although Dad had requested the cake on Faith's behalf, it was really just because he wanted it himself. Thank goodness for cholesterol pills.

The front door opened and Dad came in, changed from church and in his favorite flannel shirt.

"Just finishing up the cake." I smiled.

"Smells good."

"Where's Faith?"

"She's not coming."

I turned, wiping my hands on my apron. "What do you mean?"

"She didn't want to come," Dad said, looking me directly in the eye. "Said she didn't want to upset our tradition."

I turned and seethed, the whole of my wrath boring right into that chicken. That was just like her, to get the pity pouring on stronger. Setting herself up like some kind of martyr. I picked up the chicken, carried it carefully to the table. And the green beans too. Poured sweet tea for everyone and sat down for the family blessing. When that was done, I promptly excused myself.

"Where are you going?" Hardy asked.

I didn't answer. But I knew.

24

FAITH

THE SMALL HOUSE sat between two giant pecan trees and nestled along the edge of a sprawling sea of corn. It still was so quaint but could've used a new coat of paint. I got out, my shiny BMW an eyesore among such natural beauty. The yard was a bit overgrown, but still tidy, and I noticed she'd managed to plant some mums in pots along the porch steps.

I remembered coming to Essie Mae's house with Momma. She made tea for the adults, but lemonade for us girls. We'd play out back on a tire swing and sometimes make our way to a creek about half a mile away. When we'd return, she always had sugar cookies waiting for us.

Before I reached the porch, Essie Mae had flung open the

screen door and was waving me in. "Faith, oh my goodness, what a blessing, what a treat! You just missed a big dinner!"

Inside, it smelled like always, like all old people's homes. Hints of mustiness. Baby lotion. Vitamins. And leftovers. At least that's how it smelled to me. It was like the warmth of my childhood had wrapped its arms around me.

Floral was all the rage then, and as Essie Mae offered me a seat on the wingback with the largest floral print in the room, I gazed around the sitting room, at the dried flowers and the country baskets. Nothing had changed. Even her knitting needles and yarn sat in the same corner.

She poured coffee from a carafe with a shaky hand. "Guessing you prefer this stuff to that lemonade I used to make you?" she said with a smile.

"Maybe." I winked. "But that was awfully good lemonade."

"Made fresh." She beamed and pointed to the coffee. "Still grind my own coffee beans, so I guess this is fresh too. Cream and sugar?"

"Just black. Thank you."

She sat across from me, balancing her coffee on her lap with a small plate underneath. "Boy, have you seen how those leaves are changing? Absolutely beautiful. My favorite time of year."

"Miss Essie, you're as lovely as ever."

"May be. May be. But you didn't come here to tell me how lovely I am, did you, girl? You ready to tell me about that fancy life you've been living up in New York City?" She dropped two cubes of sugar into her coffee. "Been singing?"

"I haven't sung in a while. But it's okay. Really, it's fine."

"Hm." She twirled a tiny spoon around in her coffee. I could feel her stare as I pretended that somehow my drink was particularly interesting. "Why'd you come back home?"

I looked up at her, tried a small smile. She was feisty as ever. "Too much drama," I said with a shrug.

She set her coffee down and shuffled to the sofa near my seat, taking my hand in hers. "Baby, I've known you your whole life. And I knew your momma since she was a girl too."

I nodded, but the tears came.

"Honey, you have your momma's soul."

"No. I don't."

"But you do."

"I look like her. I sing like her. But I cannot live like her."

"Maybe it feels like a burden right now, but your momma will always be a part of you." She tapped a crooked old finger against the air. "But. You are not your momma. You hear me? When you sing, it's your voice. It's you showing the world Faith Barnett—"

"Carraday," I said softly.

Essie Mae smiled and patted me lightly on the hand. "Of course." Then her eyes grew big. "My heavens, look at that rock on that tiny finger of yours!" She lifted my hand. "Let me see that thing. What a dazzler!"

I laughed. "It is beautiful."

"Mrs. Carraday. A fine name indeed." She rose again and beckoned with a shaky hand. "Come now. Come with me, honey. I want to show you something."

We walked to the next room over, the living room, which separated the sitting room from the kitchen. Doilies covered the arms of the chairs, light streamed through the windows, and country dust, the kind that liked to find the sunbeams, floated in the air. The crisp white trim on the furniture and walls had aged to the color of vanilla pudding.

She wobbled over to the old upright piano—the very piano I'd taken four years of lessons on—picked up a frame, and held it out for me. I took it in my hands and recognized it immediately. The same picture was in my dad's bedroom. It was me, twelve, a mouth full of braces and limbs so long and gangly they'd dubbed me "Puppet." Olivia stood next to me, her arm wrapped around my neck. Her black curls were blown up by the wind, and her face had a fun, surprised look on it, like she'd just been splashed with cold water. Next to her was Mom, as delicately beautiful as she ever had been, wearing a floral summer dress and her hair pinned back in a loose bun. Her arm stretched over Olivia's back and to my shoulder, and it was so true that her arms were always long enough and her reach wide enough for anyone in our family who wanted to be embraced.

It seemed like a lifetime ago. Yet I could remember the exact moment it was snapped.

"That's how I remember you. All three of ya." Essie sat down on the piano bench, grabbing its arm for guidance.

"Your momma gave me this picture one Mother's Day. I love it. But you know, I've always wondered, what on earth made y'all crack up like that?"

I held the picture closer to me, studying every detail. "Daddy. He took the picture. We all posed so perfectly and had nice smiles on our faces, and Daddy said we looked way too stuffy, like mannequins at Walmart." I grinned as the memory ran through my head. He'd started singing—at the top of his lungs like usual—"I Feel Pretty" from *West Side Story*. It did the trick. Liv and I almost died from embarrassment. And that instant was captured perfectly with one click of the camera.

"Good to know," Essie Mae said.

"What?"

"That you can still smile after all."

I hadn't even realized I was smiling. "Come on. I'm not that bad."

Essie Mae's face lit up. "And there is that accent! I knew you still had it."

I glanced over the pictures and then noticed a postcard, propped up next to one of the frames. I picked it up. It was the New York City skyline. I didn't even remember sending it, but there on the back was my signature and lots of exclamation points proclaiming how much fun I was having. The exclamation points had been replaced by commas now. Ellipses maybe. Long pauses with no conclusion.

I set it down. "I better get back to Dad."

"He's fine."

"I know. He is. Thanks to Olivia."

Essie Mae stood, her knobby fingers slipping between mine. "I want you to sing in the choir Sunday."

"But—"

"Your butt can come too, but it doesn't sing nearly as well. And bring your father. He was banned a couple of years ago because he's awful and awfully loud, but he does love to sing and maybe some of your talent will rub off on him." She patted my cheek. "Okay, honey? And there's a fair coming up—they like singers to enter. Your momma sang in that, back in nineteen . . . eighty-four, was it?"

"Okay, Miss Essie."

We walked to the door, said our good-byes, and I got in my car. Her screen door shut, then her wooden door. I stayed in my car a long time, gazing forward.

Olivia was wrong. Life did freeze here. I was in the time capsule. Just like then, everyone wanted me to pick up where Momma left off. Just like then, I still couldn't fill her shoes. She had that thing about her, that light in her eyes that made you feel like you were the only one in her life who mattered. I couldn't even stay in Juilliard, a place Momma dreamed of going. I'd barely gotten out of the gate and I'd failed.

I gripped the steering wheel. What did these people want from me?

25

OLIVIA

It cost almost four thousand dollars to bury Momma. I was old enough to know what a strain that put on Daddy, so I gave him some of the money I was saving for college. I'd only been out on my own for a year. I'd decided I'd start at a community college and then go to nursing school. At the time, I was just starting to date Hardy, too.

Lots of reasons nursing school didn't pan out for me. I regretted it. But I guess I got my share of caretaking in.

The day of Momma's wreck, I got the phone call from Daddy, who was sobbing and telling me to get to the hospital. Hardy drove me and I found Dad and Faith in the waiting room. The doctor was just coming through enormous automatic doors, pulling his face mask off, drenched in sweat.

"I'm sorry," he said. "She has died."

It is the anguished cry of my father that I still can't get over. He fell to his knees and screamed. It sounded primitive, and I knew I'd witnessed the bloody mess of his soul. My father was tall, and to see him crumpled against the ground, screaming like he was on fire, was more than I will ever be able to bear in this lifetime. Daddy never showed much emotion. Mom had enough for the both of them. I'd never seen him cry. Or raise his voice.

I'd looked across at Faith, who was shaking so much I could hear her bracelets rattling. I stumbled to her and she fell into my arms and sobbed. Hardy excused himself because he didn't know us well enough at the time.

There I was, and there was not a single person to hold me up, so I stood with one hand on Dad's shoulder and my other arm wrapped around Faith. I knew I was going to have to take care of them. I could hear Mom's voice telling me that.

I don't know how much time passed. It could have been hours or minutes. But someone from the hospital, who didn't look like a doctor, came into the private room we were allowed and said that we needed to identify the body. I stood up with Dad, but he waved me away and followed the man through those large doors, disappearing as they swooshed closed.

Hardy found us. He brought us each a cup of water. I stared at Faith. She was pale, her eyes watery, and she looked more terrified than I could possibly describe. Like she'd been left alone in this world. Totally alone. Like she was left to die.

The slight wind stirred the trees of the graveyard. It sat on a hill and was shadowed by large trees, so it was always cold, even in the summer. "Hi, Momma." I bent down and put a white rose on her grave. Daddy always got her red roses for the church memorial, but Mom told me once that she liked white roses. I had to special order it through the local florist.

I liked this time alone with Mom. Dad never wanted me to come along when he'd come on her birthday or the anniversary of her death, so I just learned to come out here by myself.

"Faith's back in town." I shrugged, then sat cross-legged on the grave. Crisp, freshly fallen leaves blew around the headstones, dancing over the dying grass. "Guess she and Luke had some sort of falling-out." I went on to tell her how Victoria and Nell were doing. I updated her on Dad. But as I knew I would, I got back around to Faith.

"She's unpredictable, and I don't know what to do with her. Dad's all glad she's back, but at the first sign of trouble, I'm sure she'll run again." I picked at the prickly blades beneath my legs. "It must've been something awful to bring her back here. I mean, we all said if we could get out of here we would. I just didn't think any of us meant it." I sighed, my gaze hovering over her headstone. "Not that there's anything wrong with here, Momma. I know that was your choice to stay. Mine too. But it doesn't stop me from wondering what it might've been like. What the rest of the world is like. I guess it's not that great, is it? Maybe that's what Faith found out."

I let the wind talk for a while. Sometimes I ran out of things to say. And sometimes I felt stupid talking to a headstone. But sometimes I just needed my mom. "I'm thinking about changing my hairstyle. Nothing crazy like you see in the magazines, but maybe some bangs. Or a few highlights—"

I heard the crunching of leaves against the small gravel road that led from the church to the cemetery. I didn't have to look. I would've recognized the sound of those fancy shoes anywhere. I got to my feet, dusted my pants off and took a deep breath.

"I was just leaving."

I expected her to speak, but she just had her arms wrapped around herself, as if the wind were colder than it was. She was looking at the grave, a few feet behind me.

"You've never been out here." I realized it just then. She hadn't come since the funeral. The last time she saw it, it was a gaping hole in the ground. She wouldn't know it took four months for the dirt to settle. She wouldn't know the headstone cracked and we had to have it redone. She didn't know these things because she wasn't here.

"So we're going to do this. Here." Faith stepped past me and walked up to the grave.

I stood there, wanting to shove her like I did when we were kids and I'd get aggravated with her. But instead, I walked up next to her, stood beside her as we both looked at the grave.

"Which conversation do you want to have, Olivia? The one where you 'told me so,' that I shouldn't have married the man that I did? Or the one where you lay on all the guilt because I left you and Daddy after Momma died?" She glared at me. "Or how about the one where I've forgotten my roots and I don't belong here anymore?"

"Take your pick. You left, not me."

"You are unbelievable. When did you turn so mean?"

I laughed a little, studying the pair of our feet at the edge of Mom's grave. "Do you remember the night that she died? We were at the hospital. Hardy took you home."

"Yes, I remember."

"I had him take you home because Dad had to go identify the body."

"What's your point?"

"I had to be there for him when he came out. And I've been there for him every day since."

She glanced at me. "I know that. And he's better for it, Liv. Truly. I left Dad a heartbroken wreck. I just couldn't lose Mom and watch Dad. I'm not strong like you."

"Don't patronize me, Faith. This isn't about me. Or Dad. It's about you. It's always been about you, and it always will be. And you know what really irritates me? You travel all the way to New York, and then you go and quit on your dream. I mean, if you're going to run, at least make something out of your indulged self." I caught my breath. I hadn't meant to say that.

Faith started crying.

"I see how he looks at you," I said.

"Who?"

The words stuck in my throat. I was being nasty and mean and I knew it. But it didn't stop me. "You know, I fill Daddy's kitchen with groceries so he'll eat something other than a TV dinner every night. Hardy drives Dad's trash to the dump. The girls and I clean his house every week, and then on Sunday he always brings them a flower for their good work. I drive him to Whiteville for his doctor appointments because he doesn't like to get on the highway. I know what his favorite ice cream is and how he likes his coffee. But no matter what I do, he never looks at me the way he looks at you."

Faith's eyes snapped to me. "What are you talking about?"

"To answer your question, about when I got so mean, I think it was the day that Lady died and one more piece of Dad did too. Or maybe it was the day that I realized no matter what I did for Dad, I was never going to be enough for him."

Faith held her hands against her cheeks, brushing off tears, staring at me wide-eyed like I'd just made some sacrilegious comment. "Daddy loves you, Olivia."

"Maybe he does. But I had to work for it, and you get it for free." I left her there, standing over the grave, her long, shiny hair blown sideways by a wind that had suddenly picked up.

26

CATHERINE

IT FEELS STRANGE to imagine your world without you in it. I don't know if we do it often or not. Maybe we do, when we're feeling underappreciated. Or overwhelmed. But we don't dare imagine it with any real consideration.

I dared.

When the waves of pain would cease, I found myself flipping through the images of my life as if it were a photo album. It was, I guess. Most of what I saw were snapshots of what I held most dear to me. Olivia twirling on the tire swing. Faith singing "Over the Rainbow." Calvin feeding the horses.

There are some who resign themselves to dying. But my

guess is that hardly any of them are mothers. I thought of my girls, how they loved to wrap their arms around my waist, still to this day. How Faith always put on too much lotion and Olivia liked bright headbands. I'd raised them into fine young women, but now life really started for them. Now mistakes could cost them a whole life's happiness. How could I leave them so vulnerable, for the world to teach them all the lessons I was supposed to?

I tried to find comfort. I didn't think I could pray because I didn't want to ask God what His will was. When the pain came, there were glimpses of heaven so vivid that I wondered if I was there. But when it washed away and the voices around me withered against the noises of my mind, I thought of my girls without me.

They'll be all right, I whispered in my head. *They're the best of friends. They've always been there for each other.*

But Calvin. Calvin could not be all right. We were soul mates. We were one. He was a strong man, but what every beloved wife knows is that much of that strength comes from her. He could be strong because I was strong.

I wondered if I would get a chance to say good-bye. If I was going to die, then that was what I wanted, a chance to say my final words. To bless each of their heads and wish them a happy life. To tell them that all of my life's happiness was wrapped up in them. That my happy life was because of them.

"Allow me that," I said to God. "And then You can have Your way."

27

FAITH

I'd parked in the church parking lot so I could walk the long path to the cemetery. It had its own lot on the other side, but I liked the walk. It was a pebble path. I'd walked it before. But never all the way. I could never get myself to go stand over her grave.

It was different this time, though. The walk was easier. Maybe because I'd seen more of the world, realized all of its stumbling blocks. Maybe I knew where it was my mother rested, and it wasn't a hilly gravesite underneath an oak tree.

I'd not planned on seeing Olivia there. I thought when I saw her that it might be our moment to reconcile, but I was wrong. As usual.

Still, after she left, I was able to try to make some peace for myself. Talk to Mom out loud instead of just in my heart.

The wind got colder, so I walked back to my car. But I wasn't quite ready to go home. I was kind of fragile, and I wasn't sure at what moment I might burst into tears. So I sat on the curb and took the moment that I needed.

"If it makes you feel any better, it does get easier."

I turned to find Lee behind me, wearing gym shorts and holding a basketball.

"What?"

"Being back here." He set his basketball between his legs as he sat down next to me on the curb.

"What's with the basketball?"

"New activity center," he said, pitching his thumb toward the black building on the other side of the church. "Not quite the competition I got on the courts at 114th and Broadway, but it'll work."

"You *lived* in New York?"

"When I was in med school at Columbia."

"You went to Columbia medical school and came back to be an ER doctor *here*?"

He twirled the ball underneath his hands. "Summer after my second year they sent us down to Peru to assist some doctors giving aid there. Before that, I thought I was at least partly in this for the money. Doctors are rich guys, right? But down there . . . it was real medicine. And it was about helping the people who needed it the most." He nodded toward an old farmhouse across the field. "There's a lot of need here."

"New York's a different kind of world."

"Yeah." He wiped his forehead on his sleeve. Reminded me of a little boy. "You here long?"

"I don't really know."

He looked at his watch. "Well, duty calls." He stood, bouncing the ball a couple of times. "One thing you have to remember is that time stands still around here. A year in New York is like a day here, you know? Things that happened five, ten years ago seem prehistoric to you, but they're yesterday to these people."

I nodded, but I wasn't sure I was comprehending all that he was trying to say to me. Olivia had reminded me that time didn't stand still.

"And," he said as he walked off, "you know it's going to be all right, don't you?"

He didn't wait for an answer, and frankly, I didn't have one for him.

I drove back home and found Dad in the barn, doing the chores. Through the big doors I saw Silver, all alone in the pasture.

"I'm thinking of getting another horse," Dad said, putting the old blue feeding bucket back in the corner. He dusted his hands off and joined me in the doorway. "I can't replace Lady, but Silver hasn't been himself since we put her down." He glanced sideways at me and with a wry smile added, "And no, this isn't my way of saying I'm getting remarried."

I smiled. I might've wondered, except around here, people were used to speaking their mind, just like in New York.

"How's Miss Essie?"

"Sweet as ever. She wants me to sing with the choir."

"She wants to see you happy again. It's what we all want." He stepped in front of me, gazed at the pasture with his hands on his hips. "Even Olivia."

"Olivia would rather I be happy far, far away from here."

"Believe it or not, Faith, people don't hate you for leaving."

"No. Just for coming back no better than I started."

He turned toward me, his hands still on his hips. "Okay, stop it. Stop this poor-me thing and understand that you are loved. You're here now. Might as well be part of this place again." He glanced away, stared at the window over the barn. "I'm not going to tell you what to do. Stay here. Go back. But you can't find your way unless you take a step." As he walked past me, he patted me on the shoulder with those big hands.

"I can't go back because I have nowhere to go back to, Daddy. And I can't stay here because . . ." I tried not to cry, but around Dad it was hard. He made me feel comfortable enough to.

He turned and wrapped me in his arms. "Don't you say that. You can stay here as long as you want." He stroked my hair. "You hear me?"

"He lied to me."

Dad listened, didn't pressure me to say what I wasn't ready for. But with my head on his chest, staring out at the pasture, I knew I could.

"And because of it, I have nothing left. Not even him."

"Why don't you tell me about him?"

The question surprised me, and I lifted my head to look at him.

"What? He's still your husband, isn't he?"

"Yeah."

"I'd like to know about him."

"'Someone to Watch Over Me' was our song."

"That's a good song."

"I know that was your song with Mom, and I know you're all alone, and it was my song with Luke and now I'm all alone . . ." I buried my face in his shirt. "I miss her so much, Daddy."

"We're just a big mess, aren't we?"

I nodded and laughed through my tears. I stood there for a moment and wiped them, saying nothing else. But then I wanted to say more. "He's very kind. He once bought a painting for me that he hated. Admittedly, it was pretty hideous. Hard to describe. Big and yellow. But he knew I liked it, so we hung it in our living room and he had to look at it every day but didn't care." I sniffled. "Not many people realize what he gave up for us. . . ."

"It's a sacrifice, and it should be. But nobody ever tells you it's a risk, too. Because it can be ripped away from you."

I shuffled uncomfortably under his vulnerability.

"There is always hope," he said.

"What about for you?"

"Even for me."

I closed my eyes and heard Lee's words, that it was going

to be okay. I clung to Dad but had to let their words slip away. I couldn't believe them. Perhaps there was a new hope I could find, but any other hope was crushed by bitter reality.

"Maybe a new horse would be good, Daddy."

28

LUKE

I DROVE TOWARD the Upper East Side, with my hands wrapped around the steering wheel of my Jaguar XJ like I was wringing its neck. My bloodless knuckles refused to relax their grip.

The idea that I was going to see him churned my stomach, so I thought of other things, but my mind tossed them aside as meaningless. And my mind was right. There was really only one thing that meant anything to me, and she'd fled. I wasn't totally sure where she'd gone but suspected it was back to North Carolina. We'd talked often about going there to see her family, but we were both busy . . . except I never bought into the idea that busyness was what was keeping her away.

Besides, we'd built a nice life together, and it seemed the less distracted we were from that, the better. We were insulated, and that's how we remained strong for so long. Or so I thought.

The thing with Faith was that she just didn't seem to belong in the scene we were both so familiar with. She was there, and she fit, believe me, but it never fit her, if you know what I mean. There was a richness to her that could never be paid out in gold or silver. And there was no amount of money that could buy that kind of heart.

She challenged me to be a better man and to live in the present, which I always had such a hard time with. She taught me about living in the moment.

She might not ever understand it. But I would do anything for her. Even this.

I easily found a parking space a few houses down from Jake's brownstone. I took my time getting to the sidewalk. Days ago I would've envied this lifestyle. The nannies walking the children. Dog walkers pulling at eager leashes. A quiet, tree-lined street that spoke to wealth and status. Faith and I had talked about moving to the Upper East Side, but I never wanted to be like Jake. Except sometimes I did.

I stepped onto the sidewalk and strolled, enjoying for a moment the fresh air. It was the little things, things that I took for granted before, that I would never take for granted again. I stood there for ten minutes watching one bird in one tree. It flew away. But I could not. So I walked.

I'm not certain how long I stood in front of Jake's heavy

red door, staring at the paint, admiring the old-world knocker engraved with the Carraday family emblem. Then I stared at my last name, tracing each line with my eyes, remembering the dignity that it held. Dad had started, as he tells the story, with $304 in the bank. He'd built an empire for himself. It had cost him a lot of things, but never his dignity and never his good name. And maybe that was what I was trying to save. That, and my marriage. Mostly my marriage. Except it seemed an impossibility at this point.

And that was what led me there, because there was something about Jake. *Impossible* didn't resonate with him. It was a word that never got in his way, just annoyed him. Sometimes he seemed like Superman to me. Not that he didn't seem like the devil, too. But more Superman.

I stood there for a moment longer, figuring by now neighbors were starting to notice a man just standing in front of the door, and then knocked, harder than I meant to.

The door swung open. Candace stood there in a floral wrap dress and heels that didn't seem to indicate at all that it was Sunday. Faith and I lived in sweats and slides on the weekends. She touched her pearls as shock and recognition passed over her face. "Luke . . ."

"Hi, Candace." I smiled. I always liked my sister-in-law. She was pleasant, proper, and always polite. It was like Jake had stepped into a machine and created the perfect match for himself. She was even tall, like him. "Is Jake home?"

"Yes. He's back watching the Yankees game. You know

where to find him." She stepped to the side and, after a second of me not moving, said, "Come on in."

"Thanks." I stepped inside. It had been a while. Candace had changed the decor. Upscale. Traditional. Hints of hip. I guess it wasn't all that changed. Different colors and patterns but same feel.

"Can I get you anything? Tea? Coffee? You know Jake—the fridge is stocked with anything you might want."

"I'm good. But thanks."

She touched my arm, and it felt a little strange because I sort of regarded myself as having leprosy these days and figured everyone else did too. I flinched, but it didn't deter her. Her eyes were warm. "Luke, it's good to see you."

"You, too. Thanks, Candace."

It was probably the shot in the arm I needed to head to the back and find Jake. I could hear the game on. The crack of the bat. The cheering crowd. With the surround sound he had set up, it sort of felt like I might be walking into the stadium.

He didn't hear me come in.

"Hey."

He turned, regarded me for a moment, but didn't look stunned. "Yankees are down."

"Can't win 'em all."

"Clearly you are not a real Yankees fan." He gestured with his glass for me to move into his line of sight and take a seat. "You want anything?"

"I'm good."

"At least sit down. You're making me nervous standing there like that."

There was a lot of seating to choose from. Leather lounge chairs. Wingbacks. Three different couches. The floor.

I chose a leather chair with an ottoman but couldn't kick my feet up. Nothing about this felt relaxing.

Jake finally seemed to sense the tension with which I carried myself. He set down his drink and leaned forward. "What is it?"

"Criminal deposition is next Monday." It was hard to say. All of it. "With the SEC."

Jake muted the TV. "You bringing Yates with you?"

"Yeah. He's telling me to take the Fifth."

"Nobody's taking the Fifth. You tell him to make a deal before you ever walk in there." Jake sighed loudly, looked jittery. "Candace, get me the phone! I'll tell him."

"I could go to jail."

The clacking of Candace's heels against the hardwood floors was the only sound. And maybe the thumping of my heart.

Then Jake laughed. A short, staccato laugh that broke the tension but not the reality. He looked hard at me. "You're not going to jail."

I stood, though not sure my legs could hold me up. "The deposition is the last step before the grand jury!"

"Calm down."

"I am going to get indicted over this!"

Candace walked in, gave Jake the phone, walked out. Jake set the phone on the table. "Sit down."

"I can't sit down. I can't—"

"Stop freaking out of your mind and sit down. Seriously, sit."

I sat. My body trembled at the thought of what was before me. And the flash of panic that I saw cross my brother's expression.

"Are you asking for my help?" Jake stared hard at me.

I couldn't look at him. "Yes."

"Okay. You talk with Dad about this?"

"What do you think?"

"Don't you think you should?"

"Picture that conversation."

"He's not Zeus, you know." Jake sighed. "All right. Fine. I'll get him to the deposition."

"Thanks. I should go."

Jake stood with me. "How's Faith?"

"Gone."

His expression said he wasn't surprised. "Probably better that way, right?"

This time I sighed. There was no way to answer that to Jake's satisfaction. I walked to the front door, let myself out, and stood looking at that tree again. I was so desperate to get Faith back, I realized, that asking Jake for help didn't even sting. It gave me some hope. But as I walked to my car, I fought the temptation to believe I was completely alone.

The family I had run from since I got my legs underneath me might be the only thing that saved my own family.

I stood under that tree and wondered if I should pray. But the sky looked too expansive. And the need seemed too heavy. And the broken man I knew I was could not fathom why God would take a single request from me.

29

OLIVIA

I WAS FINGERING through some music when I heard her voice. There she was, inching forward like a frightened mouse. Choir members, all of whom were over seventy, swarmed to her in greeting. I glanced at Dad.

"Pretty amazing she's here," I said. "And you too, you old geezer."

Dad laughed. "Are you kidding me? I'm practically the youngest one here."

"Ain't that the truth." I watched Faith hug and smile. "Well, we certainly can use her. We need a good, strong voice." I patted Dad on the shoulder. "Just please remember not to belt it out. When Essie Mae says belt it out, it means everyone but you."

"I've been practicing all week." Dad beamed, and I gave him a side hug. I'd never met anyone who had such a terrible voice, with such a terribly strong urge to use it loudly.

As if she parted her own Red Sea, Faith walked through the small crowd and toward the church stage. "Hi, Olivia."

"Hi there. Welcome." I smiled as best I could, especially in front of Daddy. The last thing he needed was to hear us squabble.

"Dad encouraged me to take a step, so this is it," she said, her arms swinging nervously by her sides.

"Super. This choir can always use an extra voice, but it's nice when it's an extraspecial voice like yours."

"Thanks. That means a lot coming from you."

"I'm no music expert. Just a faithful parishioner." Didn't mean for that to sting so much, but I guess it did. She looked down, and I was kind of sorry for it. Wasn't implying anything, though it's not my fault it's the truth. "Well, we best be getting lined up here. Essie Mae never accounts for the fifteen minutes she allows everyone to visit and catch up, which always baffled me because there's plenty of time catching up at the grocery store. Heck, we all live within a square mile of one another. What is there really to catch up about?" I glanced at her. "Except you." A wink helped that go down. I patted her on the shoulder. "Come on, you can stand next to me. I don't want Dad by me. Last time he joined the choir, my right eardrum never recovered."

Faith followed me up the carpeted steps. "You've always been so funny." I could hear the smile in her voice, and I had to admit, it was kind of nice. Way better than that mopey, poor-me business we'd been seeing since she arrived.

We stood next to each other and watched the other choir members file in, trying not to trip each other with their canes and walkers. Dad ended up on the end and looked a little disappointed he wasn't next to us, and Faith and I pretended to be disappointed too, waving at him. Unfortunately, landing on the other side of me was Betsy Cook, whose breath could cook a side of beef. Why I bothered with this silly choir I didn't know.

Well, I kind of did know. Nobody in the family knew this, but I always had a dream of singing. I never had that "wow" type of voice like Momma and Faith, but I held my own, and actually it had a nice tonal quality to it. But unlike Faith, I was fulfilled just serving the church with my voice. Didn't need all that fancy education and the bright lights and such. Unless you've sung in a Christmas cantata, you just don't know what you're missing.

But to each his own. Faith always needed more. She always had the more gaudy Halloween costume. And the fancier prom dress.

Essie Mae began our warm-up, and Faith cut her eyes sideways to me. "Ouch," she whispered. "This is how they sound all the time?"

"Only on the good days," I said, cracking a smile. It kind of felt like old times.

Essie Mae announced our song list for Sunday, including "How Great Thou Art."

"Oh, boy," I said, leaning forward to glance at Dad. "That one's his favorite."

"Yeah . . . he's not going to be able to contain himself."

It was four words into the first stanza that we proved ourselves right. Concern was visible on Essie Mae's face by the time "I hear the rolling thunder" boomed loud enough to nearly rattle the stained glass.

But even Dad's big voice didn't seem to outperform Faith's. It's like it floated above everything else in the room, like it was the instrument by which all other instruments were tuned. Every voice found its footing beneath hers, and the harmony was so marvelous, I actually got a little choked up myself. We hadn't sounded that good in years.

Essie Mae was having the time of her life, her hands running up and down those keys like she'd never suffered a day of arthritis. I looked down the rows and the old women were swaying and shifting and a few were raising their hands. This must have been what one of those old-time revivals felt like.

Faith had closed her eyes, but I had a feeling she wasn't missing a thing. This was her element. We all knew it. She knew it. And in my opinion, this was where she was supposed to be. Right here at home. I didn't say it at the time, but I always knew Faith wasn't ready for the world that was waiting for her out there. She couldn't be. All she'd ever known was this place. It was all any of us had ever known.

Essie Mae was tearing it up on that piano. "Uh-huh . . . yep . . . that's it, darlings. Belt it!"

Our voices might've shook the walls of the church. I wondered if they could hear us across the road at Bernie's store.

Essie Mae was fanning herself when we finished. "Ohhhh, that was like cool water on a hot, steamy evening. . . ." She tapped her pencil on the piano. "Everyone, indulge me for a minute, will ya? I just want to try something. It's been oh so long since we've sung this. Many of you will remember it."

As soon as I heard the first note, I knew it. I never thought it had a place in church, but Essie Mae always liked all those worldly songs. I growled under my breath, trying to avoid Faith's wide, panicked eyes.

"Calm down," I said. "It'll be fine."

It was a song, for crying out loud. I glanced at Dad, who had the same panic-stricken look on his face. Oh, brother. I faced Faith. "You know how much Essie Mae loved hearing you sing this. You and Momma. She's an old lady. She could be dead in twenty-eight minutes. Just see what you can do, you know what I mean?"

"It was their song," Faith whispered. I hated when she whispered. That meant she was about to cry. She looked at me. Sure enough, gigantic tears were welling in her eyes. "And mine and Luke's."

I took a deep breath. "Okay. Well, do the best you can."

She nodded. I didn't know what else to say. Faith started singing and the hairs on the back of my neck stood straight up. She sounded just like Momma. I closed my eyes. It took me straight back to a time in my life when I thought nothing could ever go wrong.

I remember sneaking into the living room late one night. I had every intention of going to the kitchen to steal a cookie or three but was stopped in my tracks watching Momma and Daddy dance to this song. Momma giggled. Daddy twirled her like he knew what he was doing. But it was the moment when she laid her head on his shoulder and sang to him that caused me to drop to my knees and watch with great intensity.

It was true love and I knew it. She sang like an angel and it was one of those times that is etched not just into your mind, but into your soul too.

Hearing Faith sing was like I was right there in the living room, hidden by a table and a doorframe. There was something about Momma that you just couldn't put your finger on. She was magic and hope and warmth and goodness all wrapped into one. When she walked into a room, all eyes were on her, but her kindness radiated as brightly as her persona.

I was pretty young when I realized you either have it or you don't, and there's nothing you can do to get what Momma had. I stopped wishing for it when I got married and had kids, because by then I knew that I didn't have it and never would. I had other things to deal with . . . Daddy and his grief, newborn babies, bills to pay, life to live.

Besides, it had already been handed out.

Suddenly the song stopped, like all the words had crashed into a brick wall.

I opened my eyes to see Faith carefully pushing through the elderly people and down the front of the platform. "I'm sorry," she said as she rushed past Essie Mae.

Everyone started murmuring. I looked at Dad, who was making his way down. I scooted past everyone and followed him.

Essie Mae was getting up from the piano, her poor face filled with regret. "Calvin, I'm sorry," she said.

Dad put a gentle arm on her shoulder. "It's okay. She's just not ready for that."

"Her momma used to sing it just like that. It was like seeing a ghost."

I watched Daddy's expression flicker like a slight breeze passing over a flame. Grief. Sorrow. All the things that I'd worked so hard to dig him out of. He turned like he was going to chase Faith out the door.

"Dad, she's okay. Let's give her a moment." I had to put it that way, for Dad's sake. But what I really wanted to say was that I was afraid she was going to sink and bring us and the whole community down with her. Because what I knew to be true was that she was revered in this county. Like the heartbeat to its dim life. I patted Dad on the arm. "She'll be okay. You know, just needs to get some of this stuff out."

Dad nodded, gazing toward the door. "I guess you're right."

"You okay?"

"Sure," he said with a smile, except I knew he wasn't.

"Maybe the two of you can talk later?"

"Yes, that's best," Dad said.

"Okay." I gave him a hug and turned to Essie Mae. "Should we get on with it, then?"

30

FAITH

I STOOD UNDER A TREE, letting the cold breeze blow the tears off my cheeks and hating myself. Loathing myself. Why couldn't I just sing that stupid song? Why did every little thing cause me to emotionally collapse?

I knew Essie Mae didn't mean anything by it. It was practically the community's theme song. Everyone loved when Momma sang it. Everyone loved when we'd sing it together. For all of them, it held good memories.

And I wished, for the life of me, that it held only good ones for me, too. But with all those memories came the burden of my reality. And reality was something I was having such a hard time facing.

"Hey."

I looked up, putting my hand on my chest. I thought I was alone.

"I'd ask if you are okay, but I can see that you aren't." Lee's gym shorts and the basketball under his arm told me where he was headed.

Tears fell though I willed them not to. "I'm sorry," I said, facing the wind again. "Just having a . . . moment. We have to stop meeting like this." I tried a grin that crashed and burned into a grimace.

He leaned against the tree, crossed his arms. "You know, when I was in New York, I was engaged."

"You were? I hadn't heard."

"Her name was Isabel. We had this amazing relationship. Best of friends. She was studying to become a thoracic surgeon. We spent all our time together."

"Sounds lovely," I said with a gentle smile.

"It was. It was perfect. Or so I thought. But turned out not perfect enough for her. Six weeks before our wedding, she dumped me. Had somebody better lined up."

"Oh . . . wow. Sorry, Lee. That's terrible."

"So I ran from here as soon as I got a chance and then ran back when I could. There were many reasons I chose to come home, but not all of them are noble or pure. We're all runners from something. You know?" He nudged me. "It's just that some of us prefer marathons."

I laughed. "Yeah. I think I'm Ironman material."

"I was admiring your muscular calves." He blushed just

as I did. "Um . . . that didn't come out quite like I meant it. Not that you don't have awesome calves. I was just making a . . . I'm drowning here, aren't I?"

I nodded, stifling my laugh. "Yeah. Sinking like concrete."

"That's my MO."

"You do it well."

"Thanks." He looked at me for a moment. "So, you going to be okay?"

"Yeah. I just needed some air."

The wind blew through the silence between us.

He cleared his throat. "Look, Faith, I don't know how to say this. But I know it needs to be said between us. And maybe it will help you in some way. I don't know how. But maybe it will."

I looked into his eyes. They were intense with care. He took a deep breath. "If you ever want to talk about that night, we can talk. Anytime. Anyplace. Okay?"

"Yeah. Sure. Thanks." I tried to smile, but no matter what, under no circumstances would I ever talk to him about it.

I sighed. That was my family talking, as usual. Now I just wanted to run. Again. Into that field. It beckoned me. There was something freeing about the way the wind tangled the hair and stung the eyes.

I was saved from my indecision by Dad.

"Faith?" He was walking toward us, his face a mess of concerned lines. "What are you doing? You okay?"

"I'm fine, Dad."

"Lee."

"Mr. Barnett."

"Just got a call from Hardy. His truck is in the ditch again. Gotta go help pull him out. I'm going to take Liv's truck over there. Can you give her a ride back to her house?"

"Sure." I noticed her, standing on the church steps, watching. "No problem at all."

Dad cut his eyes to Lee, who took the hint. "Um, I should get going. Desperately need a shower and some hamstring ointment. Sucks getting old. Talk to you two later."

Dad's eyes were back on me. "Are you okay?"

"I am, I promise. It just took me by surprise. I'm sorry to have embarrassed you by running out like that."

"Nonsense. Not worried about that at all. Essie Mae feels terrible."

"She shouldn't. It's nobody's fault."

"Thought we'd go out for barbecue tonight."

"Sounds good."

"The heart doctor says it's a no go, but it doesn't hurt now and again. Everything I read says you shouldn't deprive yourself."

I smiled. "I read depriving yourself can lead to early death."

"We must be reading the same articles." He grinned, then patted me on the arm. "Okeydoke, see you this evening."

I walked to Olivia, who was buttoning up her coat. "Giving me a lift home?"

"Of course." I smiled tentatively at her, and she smiled back. We got into my car.

"Fancy," she said.

I sighed. "Fancy got us nowhere. In fact, I think it got us to where we are now."

I expected her to ask more about that, but instead she said, "Tell me about your life in New York."

It surprised me. I glanced at her. "What do you want to know?"

"Everything."

I laughed. "Everything?"

"You get to go to fancy parties?"

I nodded. "All the time. Too many of them. After a while, they lose their luster."

"Just indulge me."

"Okay. Well, the way it works is that somebody throws a benefit party and people pay money to attend it and arrive in such expensive outfits they could feed an African village. There's food, but more importantly alcohol. Open-bar benefits are the most popular. There's music, and if you let it be, it can be fun. I won't lie. I've had my share of fun."

"You never really liked parties. Not even in high school."

"I know. I still don't. I have this friend, Maria, and she's always dragging me to them. But I met Luke at one."

"Tell me about him."

"Charming. That's the first word I'd use. And fearless. Funny. He could always make me laugh."

"Where'd y'all live?"

"Our apartment overlooked Central Park. It was nice. Not too big, but big enough. I loved art, so we had a lot of original oil paintings from new artists. The biggest one I ever bought was bright yellow. Kind of blobbish. Not sure why it appealed to me, but Luke bought it for me anyway."

"What made you leave Juilliard?"

I gazed out at hazy sunshine spread over the cornfields. I wasn't sure I really wanted to answer that question. Everybody, I guess, assumed it was some big event. The truth was, it was nothing more than self-doubt built upon insecurity, chiseling away at my resolve until one day I couldn't do it anymore. I decided to change the subject.

"Have you ever talked to Lee?"

"Sure. See him every Sunday."

"But *talked* to him."

"I don't know. Not really, I guess. I mean, I don't make a point of it, if that's what you mean. He sure seems interested in talking with you, though."

"Don't even go there."

"Just a sisterly observation."

"He was in New York, like me. Same time I was, too."

"Heard his fiancée dumped him."

"Anyway, just wondering if you ever talked to him. About that night."

Olivia stared forward, expressionless. "Why would I?"

"I don't know. Just thought that you might."

"No."

"Me either."

"No point to it."

"You're right."

We drove in silence for a little while.

"You know, nobody ever asked me."

"Asked you what?"

"If I had that same dream. Same as yours."

"What dream is that?" I asked, looking at her.

"Singing."

I felt the tension in the car. I wasn't sure what to do with it.

"I just always wondered why nobody asked me. Why nobody had that same expectation of me. I mean, I know I could've never made it. I'm not nearly as good as you and Momma."

"Liv—"

"No, no, it's true," she said, holding her hand up at me. "I get it. I mean, yeah, here in Columbus County at the country church, I'm all that and a bag of chips, but I recognize that's as far as I'm going to shine. I don't think anybody ever knew that when I was younger, I dreamed of singing at the Grand Ole Opry."

"Really?"

"Yeah." Her smile turned to a grin. "I used to sing by myself out in the barn, when nobody was around, pretending to be up on that big stage, in front of hundreds of people. But you know, I couldn't even get the guts up to sing in front of anybody, so I bet I would've chickened out in front of a real crowd."

"You have a lovely voice. You always have."

"Guess so. But I didn't have 'it.'"

"It?"

"Maybe people with 'it' don't know they have it. It's hard to define."

"Liv, you never gave yourself enough credit. You still don't."

She stared out the front of the car. "I'm happy here. You know? I really am. Got Hardy and the girls. Got a nice house and some land. Got Daddy. Church. I'm happy."

"I'm glad," I said, putting my hand out to her arm. "I really am."

"I want you to be happy too."

I gripped the steering wheel. "I'll get there." Just not today.

A bit of silence passed between us, but it was easy silence, the kind we used to enjoy when we were younger. But then, with a hissy undertone that sliced through the quietness, Olivia said, "I don't want you to talk to Lee. Let bygones be bygones, Faith. That's how we do it around here. No reason to go bringin' up the past." She glanced at me and nodded that I should agree.

I nodded back, but I was lying.

31

CATHERINE

"What's your name?" I whispered. But before he could answer, the pain crashed over me again and I screamed. *God, the anguish. Must You torture me? Must it be this way?*

I felt him wipe a tear. When I opened my eyes, tears were running down his own face. I wanted to wipe them. But I couldn't move. My eyes drifted to his arms. Muscles bulged from beneath his short-sleeved shirt. Blue veins protruded from his temple. His neck. But the panic that had seized his expression for the last however many minutes wasn't there. That kind of frightened me. It was the one thing I could count on every time I opened my eyes. Where did it go? What did it mean that it wasn't there?

I couldn't get out what I wanted to ask and wondered why my body wasn't letting me stay unconscious. Why I wasn't going into shock. And then I realized the pain had vanished again.

I was alone with my thoughts, dizzy with panic and regret and hope and despair. It just seemed that I wasn't going to pull out of this, no matter how much I willed it or wanted it.

And now I wasn't sure I did. I loved my girls so much. I loved Cal more than life itself. But it was time I faced my God.

I saw myself crumpled in a ball at His feet, ashamed that I couldn't look at Him. I'd made mistakes in my life. Plenty of them. Spread out over a lifetime, maybe they didn't add up to much, but brought before my eyes, they caused me to hide my face. I couldn't bear to look at them.

I felt filthy. Naked. Raw. My mistakes heaped in front of me as evidence, too much to lift or move. There was a stench to them, like rotten garbage.

I wanted to vomit. I wanted to run. But as quickly as the terror had cloaked me, more images of my life breezed into the darkness. I lifted my chin as they lit up the darkness like fireworks. And in all the sweetness that floated above me, I saw a hand. I couldn't see it with my eyes, but I could with my heart. I saw Him through it all, like a transparent light glowing behind a thin fabric. He was quiet but not timid. Kind but fierce. His goodness hovered over my entire life, and I did not see a moment when He was not there.

Even the times when I thought I was totally alone.

I saw the day I decided to give up my dream of singing. I sat on a golden hill, the grass dead from a long winter. My knees were pulled to my chest and my arms wrapped around them. The sky looked like a torch, with the sun's dying light glowing from behind a storm cloud. Distantly, I heard the thunder. I remember listening for God's voice.

The flashes of lightning, hollow and ghostly inside the clouds, brought me my answer.

I had an entire community urging me to go, to pursue my dream, to put Columbus County on the map. I had people coming to tell me about all the times that one of my songs changed their lives, in one way or another. I even had a music manager from Nashville tell me he'd sign me as soon as I made it out that way.

All the voices. All the promises. All the opportunity.

And then there was my heart.

32

FAITH

Church had been a constant since I was a kid, and there was hardly ever an excuse that got us out of it. Not even the stomach flu, if you hadn't thrown up in the last six hours. As much as we hated it sometimes, I grew to appreciate it more when I became a teenager. I understood the richness of tradition and how it bonded our family together.

But if I was honest, I never thought much beyond the Sunday dinner prayers or the candlelit singing of "Silent Night." I didn't seem to have the faith that my parents had or for which I was named. Maybe I felt I was in it by proxy.

When I met Luke, we talked about how we were raised. Both Christian, and that was a relief. But it was never a part of our daily lives. We even eloped, and that was the part I regretted most—that it was more legal and less spiritual.

It wasn't that I dismissed God. I said my prayers, but not often and not consistently and most certainly with less enthusiasm than I gave to most everything else I did in my life.

Not until I was driving to North Carolina, in the quietness of the car, did my soul do more than just glance upward. It stared, hard, into the still, silent vastness where we all hope God dwells.

When I was little, I asked my dad why God didn't speak to me. He asked me how I knew whether or not He was speaking. I told him that I couldn't hear Him. Dad smiled and said that was because I was listening with my ears. Then he put his hand over my heart and said that I had to listen in there.

"Why? That seems awfully hard to hear inside your own body," I said.

He replied, "Just the opposite. It's quiet in there, so He can speak and be heard. Outside, there's a bunch of noise." I remember thinking how smart that was of God, except what I didn't realize was how much I wanted to listen to all that noise.

I looked at Dad as we drove to church together now, in his truck. His temples were so gray. Creases sliced into the sides of his face. He was whistling a hymn, but I didn't recognize which one. He looked happy. But after Mom died, I'd known that Dad was struggling, and I had noticed that I hadn't seen him pray at all. I asked him why, if he was mad at God.

It was a bold question because Daddy had always been a private man, and he didn't speak much about things that concerned the heart. But I remember him looking at me with eyes that had squinted against a thousand suns and saying, "Sometimes there are no words to pray, but that doesn't mean that God doesn't know what you're saying."

Driving back from New York, God and I had an entire conversation and I never spoke a word. But more was said and heard in that car ride than maybe in my whole life.

I missed Luke. So much. I missed the phone calls during the day. The little silly presents he'd bring sometimes when he worked late. I missed the way he always looked like I took his breath away when I wanted to show him a new blouse or dress. I didn't want to miss him, but I did, so I let that stay in my heart where God could find it, safe and sound.

"Dad?"

"Yes?"

"Can I ask you something? Personal?"

Dad's eye twitched, but that was nothing new. If you weren't talking about NASCAR, football, hunting, or the almanac, it usually made him uncomfortable. "Sure."

"Did you ever forgive Mom? For dying?"

Dad's eyes cut sideways. "What kind of question is that?"

"Because I don't know if I ever did."

"It wasn't your mother's fault."

"I know. But I was still mad at her."

Dad's shoulders slumped a bit and he softened. "I know what you mean." His fingers tapped against the steering wheel and we didn't say much more, except to comment on the nice weather and the farmer selling pumpkins from the back of his truck.

Dad parked the truck and we got out. Eddie and Sherry Beltram waved at Dad, and I sat for a moment and watched him converse with his two good friends. There was a genuine warmth there. Good-hearted laughing. I wondered if I had that at all in New York. Did I have one true friend there?

Maria? She liked me, I knew. But I wondered: if I declared I'd never go to a party again, would she give me the time of day?

I shut the door of the truck and glanced to the far corner of the parking lot, where I saw Lee sitting in his truck, slamming back a cup of coffee. I glanced at Dad, who was still with the Beltrams, so I decided to go catch up with Lee. He was getting out, balancing a Bible and the coffee while tying his necktie.

I laughed as I watched. "You're in a hurry to get to church," I said as I approached. I took his coffee to help him out. "Must've been quite a night. Hope you remember her name."

The remark seemed to take him by surprise, and instantly I realized that while that joke might've flown with any number of people in my circle of friends, it probably wasn't appropriate here in a church parking lot in Columbus County. With a guy who once had a fiancée. Ugh.

I was about to apologize when Lee said, "Actually I remember both their names."

My eyebrows rose. Maybe I was wrong. "No kidding."

"First was Agnes. Eighty-nine. Heart attack."

I bit my fingernail. Yeah . . . I was definitely wrong. "Oh, um, sorry."

"Next was Bella. Six. Car wreck." I immediately noticed his bloodshot eyes, punctuated with dark circles. "Didn't make it."

"I don't know what to say."

"Walk with me?" For all the times he'd been courteous to me, he now seemed withdrawn.

"Sure."

We walked across the parking lot together, our conversation empty of all the chatter we'd become accustomed to. Instead, he told me about the family that survived: a brother who was eleven and both parents. I could hardly hold back tears as we entered the sanctuary.

"I best let you get to your post," he said without a smile.

"Sure. Thanks. Very sorry for your night."

"It happens. It's what I do."

I took a deep breath and hurried to get my robe on in the choir room, then joined the rest of them in the vestibule.

"Cutting it kind of close, aren't you?" Olivia asked.

I adjusted the collar. "Dad drives like time doesn't exist."

"True enough."

I watched Lee, hunched over in the pew, his hands against

his forehead, praying, I knew, for that family. I felt sick to my stomach.

"Heard it was a family next county over," Olivia said.

I hadn't realized she was watching me. "A six-year-old girl died."

Olivia nodded. And then the organ started and we sang the opening hymn, "How Great Thou Art." I could hear Daddy and Olivia, and it was weird, but there was something to our voices being one. A chord of three. A cord of three. I looked at Hardy, who sang with spirited gusto. And the little ones, Victoria and Nell, standing there singing with no hymnbook. They knew it by heart.

Soon we were dismissed to our seats. Daddy and I sat on the end, Olivia and the girls in the middle with Hardy. We were all sitting together and it felt good. I knew Lee was behind me. I wanted to turn and check on him, see if he was all right, but instead I stayed quiet and listened to the pastor, who was already well into his sermon by the time I really tuned in.

". . . The point of the prodigal was not that he had run away. The truth is, we all run at one point or another."

I felt my cheeks flush. Was Pastor Jim looking straight at me when he said that?

"In fact, the prodigal story isn't about the prodigal at all, but about our Father, waiting with His arms open wide, with the past forgotten."

I couldn't help but look at Daddy. That's exactly what he did for me, whether he knew it or not. If I had to imagine it,

Dad probably felt like a failure. His grief had been so deep and dark after Momma died that there was no room in him to help us through ours. But what I realized as I listened to Pastor Jim was that all along, there had been a hand there, on my shoulder. On his too. On all of ours. It was the hand that Momma talked about when I was very young. She said that God would hold my hand when I felt lonely. Or afraid. Or confused. But she reminded me that His hand would be there in the good times too. She said that it was how she knew she was supposed to stay in Columbus County and how she knew she was supposed to marry Daddy and make her home here.

"Someday," she said, "you will hear your heart and listen and follow your dream. You will need His hand to help you."

"Where was your dream?" I asked her.

"My dream happened to be right here at home."

I tuned back in to Pastor Jim. Boy, was my mind wandering these days. I was going to have to work harder at listening to more than 30 percent of the sermon.

"We're all prodigals," Pastor Jim was saying, making a large gesture out toward the congregation.

But then my mind slipped back to the past, and I thought about Luke. It struck me that maybe that was all we had in common anymore . . . that we were both prodigals. Should I have run? Should I have given him a second chance? I'd barely let him try to explain before I took off. But what was there to explain? What else was there to say? He'd lied to me and possibly committed a crime.

Time had again passed. I missed some witty story or joke from Pastor Jim. The roar of laughter snapped me back to attention.

"So . . . how do we treat the prodigals who return to us?"

I gulped, maybe audibly, and fought the urge to look at Olivia. But at the same time, I had to ask the question, what would I do if Luke tried to return to me?

Before I knew it, time had flown once again and I was following Dad out of the church and down the steps. A hand touched my arm.

"Faith," Pastor Jim said, "thank you so much for singing in the choir. You have the voice of an angel."

"And you apparently have the voice of a prophet," I said with a gentle smile.

He laughed. "It's easier to be a prophet in a small town."

"I guess so. Well, I enjoyed the sermon." I was pretty sure I heard most of what God intended.

"Thanks. And welcome home."

I sensed Pastor Jim was about to remark further, but Dad must have too, because out of nowhere his arm wrapped around my shoulder and his hand shot out toward the pastor. He pumped the handshake like Jim was a water well. "Thanks, Pastor. Always enjoy your sermons."

As we walked to the truck, I saw Lee. He was headed toward his truck. Usually he did quite a bit of mingling.

"Dad, give me a minute, will you?" I hurried to catch up with him. "Lee, wait."

He turned, surprised. "Sorry, I didn't see you. I'm in my own little world."

"Look, I feel . . . stupid. I am so sorry about this morning. Stupid joke."

"No worries. Just a bad day. It happens."

"Anyway, you're welcome to join us for Sunday dinner if you'd like."

"Oh, um, thanks, but—"

"I'm sure you're going home. Getting some sleep."

"Next shift starts in . . . oh, great, two hours." He reached for his door handle.

I touched his arm. "Lee, who do you talk with about this stuff?"

"Other than God?"

"Um, yeah."

Lee shrugged. "I don't."

"Try me. Sometime. If you'd like." Even as I said it, I knew I shouldn't have. But the air was filled with the tingle of dancing in the gray areas of life.

"Faith, sweetie, loadin' up over here." Dad. Bringing me back to reality.

Lee stared at me, and we had a moment. Just a glance. But we seemed to understand each other.

"It's going to be okay. You know that, right?"

"If you do." He smiled, gave a quick, distant wave to Dad, then got in his truck.

Back by Dad's side, I was greeted by my nieces.

"If heaven had music," Nell said, "I think it would sound like your voice."

"Aww, sweetie, that is so kind. Thank you." I bent down to give her a hug.

Victoria tugged on my shirt. "You wanna wrestle later?"

I laughed as I knelt down further. "I'm not sure my muscles are strong enough for you."

"She is pretty weak," Olivia chimed in with a smile that did nothing to cover up the insult.

I ignored her. "Vic, maybe you could show me some of your moves later."

She followed a high five with a knuckle bump and then a ruffle to my hair. "Awesome."

"All right, let's get back to the house," Dad said.

"Calvin, you wanna pull a couple of trout from the river after dinner?"

"Not today, Hardy. Feeling a nap coming on."

"Since when does my daddy pass up fishing?" Olivia asked, sliding her arm around his waist. "Still coming for dinner, though, right?"

"It's Sunday, isn't it, darlin'?"

"Can I bring something?" I offered though immediately regretted my intrusion into their moment. Olivia took everything wrong, so I figured she'd take that wrong too. She hesitated, looked at Dad.

Then, "Okay. That'd be nice. Why don't you bring dessert?"

"Okay."

"Something easy, you know. Don't go to any trouble."

"It won't be as fancy as what you make." I grinned. "We might all have to settle for Rice Krispies treats."

Hardy said, "I love Rice Krispies—" Olivia's expression cut him straight off. "As a cereal. A little milk. How they crackle and all that. Too bad they don't, um, crackle when they're in, uh, treat form."

Man, Olivia had a knack for causing people to turn instantly awkward. Situations too. Pretty much anything.

"Okay then," Dad said, genuinely confused by Hardy and the Rice Krispies conversation. "We'll see you later."

I climbed into the truck with Dad and he gave me one of those looks that any girl knows, if she knows her father at all.

I felt like I was eight as I asked, "What?"

"Nothing."

"Come on. What is it?"

"You're making dessert. I didn't even know you could cook."

I laughed and laid my head against the window, gazing at the interminable sea of corn that lined the sliver of black tar road leading us home. "I want to do it for her."

"Who?"

"Olivia."

"You have nothing to prove here."

"I know. I do. I promise I know that now," I said, almost convinced of it myself. "But for Olivia, that's what you do. That's home. And family. And love. It's all wrapped up in cake."

Dad's face lit up. "So you're doing cake?"

"No. Sorry. Can't even make the boxed kind. But," I said, "I did learn to make chocolate chip cookies from scratch from my sister-in-law."

"Hmm."

"Hmm? Too good for chocolate chip cookies?"

"Hmm, I didn't know you had a sister-in-law."

His expression broke my heart. I shook my head, didn't look at him. "I'm sorry, Dad."

"What's her name?"

"Candace."

"Candace. From New York?"

"*All* New York. Nice, but very proper. Very social. Has a hard time dressing down."

"You looked very nice today, by the way."

"Thanks."

"So that means Luke has a brother or a sister?"

"Brother. But . . . they're not close. They used to be. But they had a falling-out."

"Maybe they'll reconcile."

"Doubtful. There's too much history. Bad blood."

"When you got your blood running in each other's veins, there's not enough history in the world to keep you from one another." He rolled up his window an inch or two, though he was driving so slowly there was hardly a breeze anyway. "You ever gonna call him?"

"Luke knows where I am, has my number. If he wants to find me, he can."

"That's fine as long as you're okay with the idea that he might not."

I couldn't even fathom it, to tell you the truth.

"Luke and I are great at the fairy tale. It's the real-life part that we have trouble with." For whatever reason, that teared me up. But I was kind of a basket case anyway. I knew what I knew. That his possible indictment wasn't the first time we'd lost our grip on reality. If it hadn't been this, it probably would've been something else.

"Don't worry. That's the truth for just about everybody."

I glanced at him. "I have a hard time believing that about you and Mom."

"Well, she died, didn't she?"

I nodded, taken aback by Dad's bluntness. The man was a master at beating around the bush and then planting a whole new one. "Yeah. She died." I balled my fist up, put it against the window, and propped my cheek there. "I should've brought him here. I'm sorry."

"You never have to be sorry with me, baby. I just want you to be proud of who you are."

"I'm proud of you." When Dad squirmed, I let him off the hook. "Anyway, I just wanted to do that for Olivia. Make something for dinner."

"Then that's the right reason to do it," he said. "And no, I have nothing against chocolate chip cookies as long as they're not made with fake sugar or applesauce or something horrible like that."

"I'll give you one right out of the oven," I said.

Dad grinned all the way home. He looked tired, so I let him rest and took a stroll out to the stables. Silver's ears twitched as I brushed him. And before I knew it, I'd saddled him up and was riding west, unaffected by the brisk fall breeze.

Dad had told me he was thinking of entering Silver into the fair next month. Thought the two of us could work to get him ready, bring him to the fair together. I wanted to resist this in a way, falling back into the old times, the way things were. Because even though I wasn't there, a huge part of my heart was still planted in New York. And there was so much I had to come to terms with. Eventually Luke and I were going to have to talk, at the very least to resign ourselves to the idea of divorce. Eventually I was going to have to return to New York.

But eventually was as far away as I wanted it to be. So I lost myself in this country. Among the corn and the emerald tracks of soybeans. Below a sky so thick with blueness that the clouds looked like the white sands of the Caribbean.

This once was my storybook land. Fields of wildflowers. Deer leaping and bounding over oceans of green, waving grass. I lay over Silver, my cheek nestled against his mane, my fingers combing over his muscular body.

I wanted to stay here. Right here. This was perfect peace. Here I swam in the waters of tranquility.

But it ended with the distant wail of sirens that grew louder with every slow breath. I heard the same sirens the day my mother died. And had heard them in my head for years afterward.

They weren't in my head today. An ambulance raced past me, pulling with it the grass and the dust.

And my heart.

33

OLIVIA

"Daddy! Daddy, hold on! God, please . . . Wake up—"

Hardy knelt beside me. The girls stood nearby, huddling next to one another. Crying. "Girls, can you wait outside for the ambulance and tell them where to go when they get here?"

Nell nodded, guiding her sister out.

"He's still breathing," Hardy said.

"Hang on. Help is coming," I whispered to Daddy, my lips near his ear. Outside, the sirens were getting closer and closer.

Even as I held Daddy, I wondered where in the world Faith was. Her car was out front. Had she taken that old horse for a ride? She had no business riding him around. He could barely stand up.

Voices. And then the EMTs were hurrying through the front door. I stood and stepped back, allowing them in. "Please, please help him."

Hardy rushed to my side and put his strong arm around me. I leaned into his chest and he covered my cheek with his hand. "This can't be happening."

"It's going to be okay," he said. "It's going to be okay."

"Dad?" Faith's shrill voice came from the back of the house. Hurried footsteps; then she appeared in the living room. Tears. I hated her tears. "What happened?" she asked nobody in particular.

I stomped over to her. "What have you done?"

"Me?"

"I would've never left him! Never! That's why I came over, because everybody that knows Daddy at all knows he never passes up a chance to fish. He didn't look right. Didn't you notice that? Or were you too busy talking to Lee about all your drama?"

It should've felt awful coming out, but it didn't. I could finally breathe, for the first time since I found Daddy unconscious on the floor.

He'd hit his head, and it was bleeding down the side of his face. Faith stared at him as the EMTs worked at getting him on the gurney. She held a hand to her mouth. It was shaking. I glanced at Hardy, who looked like he regretted witnessing everything that I'd just said.

"We need to get him to the hospital," the dark-haired EMT said. He turned to Faith, who stood closest to him. "I need a list of any medications he's on."

Faith shook her head, looked at me. I stepped forward. "I've already got that in my purse. I also have his doctor's phone number."

They wheeled him outside. Dad wasn't moving at all.

"I'll ride in the ambulance," I told Hardy as I followed, grabbing my purse on the way out. "Can you get the girls to Rebecca's house?" My voice cracked and quivered.

"He's going to be okay," Hardy said, helping me into the ambulance.

Faith was coming out of the house, still crying. She stood and stared at me, wordless, motionless.

I took in a deep breath. Steadied myself. "Get to the hospital as fast as you can. Go ahead and grab his medications. They're on his sink in the bathroom."

"Okay." She nodded frantically. "What else?"

"Grab his billfold. It'll be on the kitchen counter. Has his insurance card."

"Okay."

"Faith," I said, and her searching eyes stayed still, looked deeply into mine. "It's going to be okay."

The doors shut and I sat on the small bench across from Daddy as the EMT took his vital signs.

"How long to get there?"

"Fifteen minutes," the EMT said. "He's stable. That's a good sign."

"Daddy, I'm here. Right here," I said, taking his hand. But I couldn't say anything more without getting choked up, so I sat there like a pathetic lump on a log, staring out the back of the ambulance, wondering if they could drive faster.

I never said this to anyone, but I always wondered about Momma, being by herself in the ambulance. I wondered if she was scared. I wondered why nobody at the scene thought to ride with her.

I sat there, holding Daddy's hand but picturing Momma. I squeezed my eyes shut because I didn't want to think about it anymore.

I still carried my favorite photo of her in my purse. She was standing in the fields, holding her sun hat, in a bright-yellow dress. So bright it almost hurt your eyes to look at it. That's how I wanted to remember her.

Faith, she'd always been the one to wonder more about the accident. But I didn't want to know. It wasn't how Momma wanted us to remember her. I didn't want to remember Daddy like this either. He was such a tall, strong man. But strapped to the gurney, he looked weak and helpless.

After Momma's funeral, Daddy hardly spoke, for weeks it seemed like. I knew he needed to grieve, but Faith needed more from him. I could tell that even then she was starting to pull away from him, from this family. Chasing dreams on greener grass. Guess she found that green grass is overrated.

"He's coming to," the EMT said.

I knelt down in the cramped space. "Daddy? Can you hear me?"

He mumbled something. I stroked the white bandage on the top of his head. "You took quite a fall. You may be looking at some stitches."

"I'm sorry . . ."

"Don't say that. This isn't your fault."

"Where's Faith?"

I tried to smile. "She's coming. She wasn't there when you fell."

"Sir, do you remember how you fell?" the EMT asked.

"No. I don't remember anything."

"He wasn't feeling well," I inserted, "after church. Wanted to lie down."

"Take a nap," Dad countered. "Not unusual on a Sunday."

"Except when he turns down an opportunity to fish."

"I was just tired," Dad said, looking away.

"Have you been tired a lot lately?" the EMT asked.

I looked at Dad. He hesitated, and that hesitation said it all.

"A little."

"It's just been a tough week or so. Some family things. Probably drained him."

The EMT took new vital signs and I watched as the hospital came into view. They pulled into the small circular drive and the rear doors opened. I hopped out, but when I looked back, he was convulsing.

"Daddy? What's happening?"

"Seizure," the EMT said, gently shoving me to the side as he backed the gurney out of the ambulance. Dad's whole body was shaking and I only saw the whites of his eyes. His hands were bent inward toward his stomach.

They wheeled him through the sliding-glass doors and I ran after them. A large metal door opened but a nurse stopped me. "We'll update you as soon as we can."

"But I'm his daughter."

The nurse left and I stood there alone, my purse hanging off my arm. My breath kept catching in my throat. I backed away from the door, looked toward the waiting room. Babies' hot-tempered screams rattled my nerves. Coughing. Sneezing. A swarm of unhappy sick people.

This was where we stood when Momma came.

I rushed outside, gulping air, crying out, clinging to my own arms because there was nothing else to cling to. A haze of cigarette smoke lingered by the door. I hurried past it and to the small mound of grass on the other side of the ambulance.

I collapsed, but my knees never hit the ground. Instead, I was caught up by two strong arms, underneath my own. When I opened my eyes, there she was, her face close to mine, her eyes shining with tears.

"Faith . . ."

She stood me up and embraced me. "Come here."

34

FAITH

"Come on," I said, grabbing Olivia's hand.

"But—"

"Come on!" I dragged her through the doors and into the waiting area. The nurse was busy taking the temperature of an uncooperative toddler. "Let's go," I whispered.

I punched the large button that opened the metal door and went through, walking at a brisk pace. Behind me, I heard Olivia following, whispering questions I ignored and comments I didn't even want to hear.

Once in, the doctors and nurses all seemed too busy or complacent to notice us. I walked from one ER room to the next, looking for Daddy.

Then I heard Lee's voice. "What have we got?"

"Found unconscious by his daughter. Had a seizure upon arrival."

Another voice, this time a male's: "Blood pressure and pulse are through the roof."

"What are the—?" Lee's words were cut short by something.

Olivia and I stood at the opening of the room, where a crowd of people flocked around Daddy. I could see Lee clearly through a parting of heads. His expression said it all. He recognized the patient.

"Do you know him?" a nurse asked.

Then I heard Dad's voice and it brought a crashing wave of relief. "Yeah, he knows me. He probably wishes he didn't."

A few chuckled. Lee smiled, but I saw concern in the deep wrinkles of his forehead.

"Daddy!" Olivia rushed in. A nurse grabbed her, but Lee okayed it with a gesture. He found me standing on the sidelines. He didn't smile, but his eyes were intense with defiance and resolve.

"Okay, let's get to work," Lee said. "Alice, get the CT guys ready upstairs. We need a look in there ASAP."

"Daddy, we're here for you. Faith's here too." Olivia hovered over him.

"Calvin, we're going to take great care of you," Lee said, his voice scrubbed of emotion. Professionalism was kicking in, and that's where I needed him to be.

"We're ready for him upstairs," Alice said.

"All right, let's get him up there," Lee said. I stepped aside as they rolled him out. Lee glanced at me, but not long enough for me to read his expression.

In mere seconds, Olivia and I were left alone. Two chairs sat against the wall of the small room and we dropped into them simultaneously. For a long time we didn't say anything, just listened to the noises around us. I wondered where Lee was. I wondered what Olivia was thinking.

But we just sat. I was dizzy with emotion and worry. We were offered water by the man who came to mop the floor. I guess we both looked pathetic and parched. We declined.

Then Olivia moved her purse from her shoulder to her lap. "I'm sorry," she said. "I didn't mean those things back at the house. I was just scared."

"It's okay if you did mean them. It's true. I haven't been around. I didn't see the signs."

Olivia held a tear against her eye. "It's just that Daddy doesn't ever stop. He's slowing down, sure. But . . ." She tore at the tissue she'd fished from her purse. "That day, Faith, I knew."

"What are you talking about?"

"I felt something was wrong. The day of Momma's accident. I couldn't voice it. I didn't know what it was. But something didn't feel right inside of me." Tears streamed down her face so fast there was no use trying to catch them with her tissue. "And for the rest of my life, I've been listening for that to come back. I've been afraid that it would. I tried to prepare myself because I didn't want to ever be caught off guard again. And so I've spent most of my life listening to my gut, and maybe that's why I've missed so much of my life."

I pulled her close and she laid her head on my shoulder, sobbing into my sleeve. "Shhhh, it's okay. It's okay . . ."

"Daddy can't die. He just can't."

I squeezed her shoulder, but I couldn't stop thinking about Lee's eyes. I'd seen fear there. I didn't know why. But I knew we soon would.

"You know," I said softly, "Momma always said love was risky. But it's worth it."

"But what if you have to say good-bye?"

I thought of Dad. I thought of Luke. I thought of the day I left this place. The good-byes seemed endless. The thought of saying good-bye permanently to Luke felt like death itself.

"I guess I never said bye to Momma," Olivia said, sitting up. She pulled out a picture from her purse. I couldn't see it as she held it to her chest. "I took care of Daddy and I married Hardy and I had the girls and life just went on."

"That's how Momma would've wanted it, Olivia. She wanted us to go live a full life."

"My heart aches every day for her."

"Mine too."

Olivia withdrew the picture from her chest and showed it to me. "You remember this?"

I took it from her and looked it over. Of course I remembered it. Dad had taken the picture. Mom was wearing her favorite yellow sundress and white lacy sandals. She looked gorgeous.

"That's it," I breathed, the thought slamming me right through my heart.

"What?" Olivia asked.

I looked at Olivia, crying myself now, shaking my head at how I could've missed it. "That awful painting I bought when Luke and I were . . . It was big and . . . yellow." I stared at the picture. "That's what drew me to it. This photograph. Mom wearing her yellow dress. I didn't know it at the time, but that's why I fell in love with it. It made me feel closer to her."

"Every year that passes, she feels farther away from me," Olivia said. "Sometimes I can't hear her voice anymore. Or remember how she smelled."

"I know."

"And I promised myself I would never forget her."

"You're not forgetting her, Liv," I said, putting my hand on her shoulder. "I see her when I watch you with Nell and Vic. You're an amazing mother, the way Momma was amazing. You have this grace. This sixth-sense kind of way about you. You just know what to do. You make it seem easy and effortless. You take care of your family the way Momma took care of us. That's how you are keeping her memory alive."

"And you sing just like her."

"So she's in us. Every day, right?"

Olivia nodded. She sat up a little. "I don't know much about Luke, Sis. But I bet he's worth fighting for."

Her remark took me by surprise. "Why?"

"Because he's deep in your heart."

"He lied to me. A big lie. Lies."

"I know. But I've found the very best things in life are worth the hardest fights. You know Nell caused me thirty-six hours of labor? Sweating like a pig. My back aching. She just wouldn't come easy. And Vic, well, she was perfect on the birthing side of things. Then she learned to talk and things went south. Stubborn. Moody. Opinionated. Guess she's got a lot of our dad in her."

I laughed. "They're so adorable. Both of them."

"Do you believe God brought you and Luke together?"

I thought for a moment, taking deep breaths and trying to clear my mind so I could really answer that question. "I think I do. I thought it was hopeless that I could ever find someone like that. He was real, Liv. Unconventional. Courageous. Never swayed by popular opinion. He loved his family but loved me more and made a tremendous sacrifice by marrying me. He still kind of pays for it to this day."

"He left a comfortable, easy world so he could be with you. Maybe that's your anchor."

"Anchor?"

"The thing by which everything else is attached. You gotta start somewhere and work your way back. So start there."

The sound of footsteps caused us to look up. Lee rounded the corner into the room, carrying X-rays and a heaviness with him. He turned on the screen and secured the X-rays so we could see them. He took a moment, looking at both of us, letting his doctor's veil down a bit. His gentle smile was perhaps meant to calm us, but I could do nothing but wait, holding my breath and my sister's hand.

Olivia looked stoic. Her back was straight as a board. "How's he doing? What's going on?"

"We're getting him a room upstairs for observation. I'd like to keep him overnight."

"For?" I asked.

"Okay," Lee said, rubbing his hands together. "At this point, the test results indicate he has a high-grade astrocytoma."

Olivia and I just stared at him.

"It's a form of malignant brain tumor."

I felt Olivia's hand go limp in mine. Lee stayed on the other side of the room, gazed at the X-rays, then at us. "Here's the deal. I'm almost certain that's what I'm seeing on the CT scan. See? Here. And at a different angle, here. Now, I'm just an ER doctor, so we're going to need to verify this with a neurosurgeon, but . . ." He sighed, looking at each of us. "It's pretty textbook."

I wasn't sure what shock was, but all I knew was that I didn't feel like I was in my own body.

Lee pointed to the CT scan again. "You can see here in the discolored area the tumor, and the jagged, uneven edges of the mass are classic—"

"I've heard enough. I get it," I said.

But Olivia pulled her hand out of mine. "I want to hear it. Tell me everything."

I stood, walked to the door, but couldn't get myself to

go out. Lee's voice faded in and out of the thick dread that silenced nearly everything else around me.

"The edging is the telltale indicator of malignancy . . . I'd like to refer him to a neuro-oncologist in Wilmington . . . Michael Whalen . . . he specializes in brain cancers . . . we can get Calvin in tomorrow. . . ."

If I stood there any longer, I was going to vomit.

Outside, I was cold. Or numb. I wasn't sure. My fingers were clutched into fists and my fists were balled in my armpits. I stood there in the wind and didn't cry. Just stood there.

Below the darkening sky, I felt laid bare by God. Filleted by His hand. My soul screamed to be let from its cage, but there was no way out. It was forced to stay and see and hear and experience the worst life had to offer. The agony was inescapable. Even as I tried to run from it, I could only stand and let it consume me.

I'm not sure how much time passed. I didn't even remember the bench on which I found myself sitting now.

Then a hand.

I looked up and was surprised to see Lee. He was in his scrubs, rings of sweat around his armpits and his neck. "Hi. May I?"

I scooted over.

"I'm very sorry about your dad," he said.

"Thanks."

"They've made tremendous advances in cancer treatment over the—"

"Save it," I sighed. "I don't want to hear the pep talk."

"It's not a pep talk. It's the truth."

"The truth." I let that word hang in the air for a moment. Then I said, "You know, Lee, I wonder if things had been different, if . . . you know."

"Yeah. I know."

"I mean, we seem to be kindred spirits. There's an easiness here. But there's that thing between us. That heavy, horrible thing."

Lee looked down, stared at his Reeboks.

"We're good at ignoring things."

"Maybe."

"But how do we get past that thing?"

Lee leaned back, looking up at the sky as he rested his elbows on the top of the bench. "Why do we need to?"

"Maybe I need to. For me."

"Maybe you do." He said it knowingly.

I also leaned back, tried to rest my tense muscles, tried to breathe. There was no going back if it started. Once I asked for the truth, I was going to get it. And I knew from experience that truth could be as painful as lies. But what I'd learned was that the truth never caged you.

As darkness settled, so did my soul. I looked at Lee. "Okay."

He stared at me. "You're sure?"

No. I wasn't sure. But as Momma said, love is risky. And maybe, just maybe, this was an act of love.

35

CATHERINE

NOTHING BUT A PURE AND FIERCE TRUST in God can put a mother's fears to rest. I'd spend evenings knitting a scarf while I needled my way through the angst I felt for Olivia. She was awkward and self-conscious. Always had been, since the day she managed to catch her reflection in a mirror. She had a hard time making friends but was loyal to the ones she had. She got her hard edge from Cal and her quick wit from me. I knew she could bulldog her way through life, but I wanted her to glide and fly, too. I don't think she ever saw herself anywhere else but Columbus County. But then again, neither did I. If she ever wanted to go, I hoped that she would.

Then there was Faith, who got everything good about me, if there was anything at all. Her voice, younger and fresher, transcended mine every time we sang together, and I loved every second of it. But she peered into the world with wide, frightened eyes. I wanted more gusto from her. I wanted her to take the bull by the horns, to demand life cough up all it had for her.

The pain was coming and going, but it was distant pain as if my body were miles long and the pain came from the end of the road. It was tolerable and thin if I didn't choose to notice it.

Slowly I unwound all the vines that wrapped so tightly around me and anchored me to the girls and Cal. My deep love for them, the kind of love that caused my life to have meaning on this earth, had to stay behind. But as my fingers loosened in their fatigue, there was a gift of peace, an assurance that the God who was taking me away would stay present for the ones I had to leave behind. I felt myself rest beneath my fate. Resign myself to the will of the Father, understanding that the pain in their future would eventually lead them to this same door, but that along the way, all the delights of life would be the hinges on which the door hung.

I said good-bye in my heart and expected grief, but instead there was hope and light and well-being. Perfect well-being. I would be unable to give them one final message. All that would be left standing were the minutes that I lived on this earth and the hope that I lived them in such a way that I didn't need to say more.

I knew suddenly that it was no longer the young man in the ambulance whose hand I held. And like a wave exploding against a rocky ledge, I felt alive, so much so that I wondered how long I might've been dead. Pure pleasure that did not exist at all on earth shot through me, except it seemed to have been there all along.

And then, there He was.

36

OLIVIA

In the tiny hospital room, I kept sipping coffee, little sips, little sips, even though it was barely warm. I was ingesting coffee, maybe thinking it was hope instead. I craved anything that would relieve me from what I faced.

Since the day Daddy turned forty-seven, I had done everything in my power to keep him safe and healthy. I took him to all his doctors' appointments. Made sure he took his heart pills. Didn't let him eat cake except on Sundays. There was nothing I'd left undone.

But I didn't see this coming.

My gut didn't tell me anything.

Maybe if I hadn't been so caught up in the whirlwind that was my sister, I would've noticed something earlier.

I wanted to stare at him, take in his lovely face. I always thought Daddy had such a kind face. His eyes were pinched and sharp, but he had this wide grin that crinkled all the skin on either side. His broad nose never let me forget he was stronger than me.

I didn't bother going to hunt Faith down. She had to do what she had to do. If she couldn't face this, for once I didn't blame her. I made certain I would no longer be surprised to see her hightailing it away from anything that hurt. But I also made certain that I'd be here if she came hightailing it back.

"Daddy," I said, setting down my coffee while picking my optimism back up, "we're going to get through this." *We* wasn't quite as defined as I'd have liked, but in our part of the country, *we* was always used, even if you were standing there by yourself. *We'll see you later.* It was the way community was acknowledged.

Daddy was fast asleep, his chest rising while the air blew hollowly through his crookedly open mouth.

"We'll get you the best care, the best doctors. I just read in *People* magazine where this lady got her whole body cut in half, and then they took the tumor out and put her back together, mostly. So we can do this. Okay? We can do this."

I was back to sipping coffee and pretty soon all that was left was the Styrofoam, so I ended up chewing that all to bits. My fingernails were next, but then Daddy woke up.

He groaned and looked around, disoriented. I scooted

next to him and took his hand. "You're in a hospital room, Daddy."

"Why?"

"You collapsed at the house."

"I just needed a nap, that's all."

"And had a seizure."

Dad's grogginess lifted like a sundress on a windy day. "Seizure, you say?"

I nodded. "Scared us to death."

"My head hurts," he said, blinking at the ceiling. "I remember Lee."

"Yeah. Lee took good care of you."

Dad turned his head, looking at me with a seriousness that his playful side rarely let emerge. "So lay it down for me."

He knew. I could tell he knew. Must've been who I got my gut reactions from. "It's not good," I said, willing myself not to cry. The tears stung but they didn't get all bulby.

"Didn't figure."

"It's a malignant brain tumor at the base of the skull. Some big fancy name that only a doctor can pronounce. Lee's already got an appointment for you tomorrow afternoon at the oncologist. A doctor that specializes in this sort of thing."

"Big guys with ugly dispositions?"

I cracked a smile, but just as I did, those stupid tears slid down my face. "It's not going to be easy, I'll tell you that. But we'll get through this just like we get through everything else."

"Where's Faith?"

How did I know that question was coming? I glanced to the door. Every time I heard footsteps, I thought it might be her.

"I don't know."

Dad looked at me with a sad smile. "She'll come back."

"She always does."

"But you're here," he said, and he squeezed my hand. "Thank you, Liv. You've always taken good care of me." His eyes watered. "Even when I was unlovable."

"Daddy, stop that talk. You've never been unlovable."

"I never wanted to be a burden on you girls," he said, looking away. "I'd hoped to live to the ripe old age of eighty and drop dead of a heart attack in the middle of the field. No thanks to you, my blood pressure is perfect."

I laughed. He laughed too and gave me one of those Daddy winks that could quiet storms.

"You're no burden," I told him. "You never will be."

He nodded but was already falling back asleep. Except he held my hand tightly and didn't let go.

37

FAITH

LEE SUGGESTED we go inside to the cafeteria on the first floor of the hospital. It wasn't crowded, but a number of people sat around at the tables, some eating, some watching the TV. Lee got a small salad and a cup of soup. I decided on a Coke and nothing else. We sat across from one another and I let Lee eat for a minute. I needed to gather myself and decide exactly what I wanted to know. I wasn't even sure how to ask the questions. Whether I should. Whether I would regret it or it would set me free.

Lee was quiet as he ate, not looking up at me but lost in his own thoughts. Then he said, "I had been on the job for two months."

I braced myself. It was coming, whether I wanted it or not.

I thought carefully about my first question. "How long did it take you to get there, once you got the call?"

"Thirteen minutes. Back then there was no permanent ambulance service for that side of the county because of how unpopulated it was."

I nodded. Thirteen minutes. I let a few quiet moments pass.

"What did you see when you drove up?"

"Two pickups. One was on its side in the ditch. The other was in the middle of the road, very crumpled. That was hers."

"Was she still in there?"

"Yes."

"Was she awake?"

"No. Not when we arrived. But witnesses said that she'd opened her eyes twice."

"Where was the man that was killed?"

"He'd been ejected from his truck, along with all his beer cans. He was found twenty-five yards from the intersection. He'd died instantly."

I took a breath. And another. I looked at Lee, and I knew he wouldn't go on without me. I had to steer the boat.

"How did you get her out of the car?"

"She was pinned very tightly between the steering column and her seat. The fire truck was coming, but there were three men who stopped and one had a chain saw, so he cut through the front part of the truck and made some other cuts and we managed to pull off the top of it."

"Was she awake then?"

"The noise from the chain saw woke her up. But she didn't know where she was."

I had to pause. I took a sip of my drink, hardly able to pull the straw to my lips because my fingers were shaking so badly. I decided to focus, to bring to mind the things that I'd always wanted to know, the things that up until now only my imagination had been able to fill in.

"How long did it take you to get her out?"

"I'm not certain. Maybe ten minutes. A lot of people were helping."

"Once you freed her, you put her on the stretcher?"

"Yes."

"And she was, um . . ." My voice cracked, for the first time. "Injured badly."

"She was."

"Did she know how badly?"

"She couldn't see her injuries."

"Was she in pain?"

"I could tell she was in pain. I don't know how much. Her body had to have been in some shock."

I steadied my hands on my kneecaps. "What were her injuries?"

Lee paused for a moment. For the first time he looked hesitant. "The steering wheel had crushed her and caused a large gash through her stomach. My first priority was to stop the bleeding and . . . to just stop the bleeding."

"And what?" I stared intently at him.

Lee nodded and put his hands on the table. I saw flashes of memory cross his eyes. "And then we loaded her into the ambulance."

"Was she awake?"

"Sometimes."

"Did she talk?"

"No. Her, um . . . her jaw was crushed on the left side, so she couldn't open her mouth."

"So she didn't say anything at all?"

"She couldn't. But she would open her eyes sometimes and look at me, and it was like she was talking with her eyes. I kept myself very close to her so she could see my face."

"You talked to her?"

"I did. I kept talking to her—I told her to think about her family. To fight for her family. But she would lose consciousness a lot. She was unconscious for most of the ride."

"Most, but not all."

"Not all." He smiled a little at some thought. "I held her hand."

"You did?"

"Yes."

"Why?"

"I had one hand on her stomach, holding pressure. And it just seemed . . . like she needed someone to hold her hand.

To tell you the truth, I think it was more that she was holding mine."

I took another steadying breath. "I know . . . I know this is an impossible question, Lee, but I want to ask it."

"Okay."

"Do you think she was scared? Did she look scared?"

Lee took a long moment to think. He seemed to scan all of his memories, examining them like a doctor would. Then he took me in and didn't hide the fact that he was searching my face. For permission? For a reason? I didn't know. I just sat there and waited.

"She was confused. Disoriented. I could see it in her eyes. But a lot seemed to be going on inside." He touched his chest. "Here. I don't know if she was scared. She didn't look scared. When she would open her eyes, I'd talk to her and tell her to stay with me, and she looked like she was trying to do that, but then she'd fade back."

"Did you think she would make it?"

"She was gravely injured. I was surprised she was alive, but some people have a lot of fight in them. I could tell that was true about her. Even as badly injured as she was, I sensed feistiness."

I couldn't help but smile. "You sensed correctly." I looked down at the table. "You know, I always feared I would talk to you and this would be how it would end up."

"How?"

"I guess I wanted her to say something, you know? Say her good-byes. Wish us a good life. Tell us that she loved us. Something." I looked away. The tears finally drained. "Over the years, I sometimes imagined Momma's last words being, 'The music is how you live, not what you sing.'" I laughed and blotted my eyes. "I know that's so ridiculous. I just wanted to be with her in that moment."

Lee reached across the table and took my hand. "Are you kidding me? You and Olivia and Calvin . . . you were what she was fighting for. I know she was fighting, Faith. I could see her trying to hold on. And maybe she gave you her final words in the way she lived her life."

I wiped my eyes again, trying to take a deep breath. "She died before you got to the hospital, didn't she?"

Lee nodded. "She did. It was the last minute of the ride." He let go of my hand but kept his eyes on me. "But you should know that I am nearly positive even if she'd made it to the hospital, they couldn't have saved her life. Being an ER doctor now, I know that sometimes there are injuries you can't recover from."

"That's what I feel like," I said, crying all over again. "That all of this . . . Momma, Luke, Daddy . . . I'll never be able to recover."

"You're hanging in there just fine. Life hurts. But running parallel with all of its burdens and griefs are blessings and delight."

I stared at Lee, trying to figure out how he could reach so deep, understand me more than I understood myself. Maybe Momma had spoken to me. Maybe that's what her whole life was about, to tell me that one thing, to make me realize truth in the only language I knew how to speak well.

I noticed Lee still had half his meal left. "I should let you eat," I said. "And I should get back to Daddy."

I stood and Lee did too.

"Thank you, Lee. Thanks for telling me all this. Thank you for being there for her."

"There's one more thing," he said, stepping to the side of the table so there was nothing between us.

I held my breath. I wasn't sure I could take one more thing.

"Back in New York, there's a hospital in Midtown called Memorial Sloan-Kettering. That's going to be his best shot. They're the best at what he needs. You should take him there."

"Okay."

"And he needs to get in as soon as possible." He rubbed my arm, squeezed my elbow, and started to step back. But I stepped forward and kissed him on the cheek. Shock ran through me even before I was able to pull away. I stumbled back a bit and he caught me, I guess afraid I would fall. And maybe I would've. Maybe I already had.

"I'm sorry," I said.

Lee didn't say anything. I suppose there was not much more to say. I exited the cafeteria and hurried to the front desk, where they told me Dad was in room 565.

I got on the elevator, trying not to pay attention to the scent of cafeteria food wafting up the shafts, mixing with sterile and unsterile smells. The elevator opened on the fifth floor, and my feet felt heavy coming out.

A large window stretched between two long hallways, each with signs indicating which room numbers were where. I was supposed to go right, but instead I just stood there, looking out the window that gave me a spectacular view of my part of the country.

I took out my cell phone. I wanted to call Luke. I couldn't do this without him. I couldn't face life without him. Lee was stable, good, decent, present. But Luke had my heart. He had since the night he took me out of that stupid party and onto the rooftop patio.

Everything in me was screaming that I couldn't handle this, that I needed to run. But it was like telling an animal at the zoo to run for its freedom, even though it was locked in a cage.

I stood there wishing I could feel the warmth of the sun, but being chilled instead by the predicament in which I found myself. Here I stood, but unable to go in and face what terrified me the most. I couldn't even make a step sideways, toward my father, who was in his greatest time of need . . . again.

Did he know yet what was in store for him? I couldn't imagine myself saying the words to him.

Then I felt a hand on my shoulder.

Olivia.

"Are you okay?" she asked.

I searched her eyes. There didn't seem to be any sarcasm

in the question. I wanted to say yes because I knew that was the answer she was hoping for. She was so strong, so resolute with everything. Life needed to be tackled, one problem at a time, and she tackled everything that came her way. And sometimes mine, too.

I stood there with my back against the window, with nowhere to run and nothing to say. I'd failed her. Again. And I had nothing to give as a peace offering. It was just me. Pathetic me.

She reached toward me, and honestly, I thought it was to slap my face. But instead she touched my cheek, said, "Come here," and then pulled me into an embrace. It was almost like she speared me and left a hole because I suddenly started gushing sobs that I couldn't control. Emotions poured out of me that hadn't seen the light of day in years.

"I'm sorry," I said with my head on her shoulder. "I'm sorry I can't be strong."

"You are strong."

"I'm not."

"You're no Joan of Arc, but you're strong. You just don't know it yet." She lifted my head and brushed my tear-soaked hair away from my face. "I love you."

"Why?"

She smiled. "Because you're my sister." She stepped back but kept ahold of my shoulders. "Now. I have to run home, get my girls and Hardy situated, and pick up some of Daddy's nighttime things. The doctors are going to release him in the morning and get him scheduled with that neurosurgeon as soon as possible. Can you stay with him?"

I nodded.

"He already knows what he's facing."

"You told him?"

"Yes."

"I'm sorry you had to do that alone."

"Whatever you were doing, Faith, I know that it's what you needed to."

I tried to wipe my eyes.

I watched her walk to the elevator, and then I turned down the hallway toward Dad's room. My legs felt steadier. A certain resolve set in. Dad was going to be okay. We were going to be okay. I knew it.

38

LUKE

I MUST'VE CALLED a dozen friends, a half-dozen acquaintances, and at least a couple of enemies, seeking refuge, counsel, help. Not a single returned phone call. In fact, my phone hadn't rung all week. Jake wasn't even calling. Tonight I realized I'd been sitting in my favorite leather chair for three hours. Consumed by miserable thoughts, time hardly seemed to pass.

I spent a considerable amount of that time wondering what prison was like. Wondering how many years I'd be there. Wondering how easy it was to kill yourself once you got there.

Twisted up with those sunny images were thoughts of

Faith. What was she doing? Where did she go? Would she ever come back or even speak to me again? This was by far the worst moment of my life, the point lower than the lowest, and I was facing it without her. She was the one person I knew who could get me through it, who would help me believe I'd get through it.

I took another sip of bourbon, the only friend keeping me from losing my mind at the moment, and stared at that horrible yellow painting that hung six feet tall over our mantel. With her gone, it now just seemed like a gigantic squirt of mustard.

I set my glass down and walked over to it. With one hefty lift, I got it off the nail and onto the ground. I turned it around and leaned it against the fireplace. There. I wouldn't have to endure that any longer. It was the simple things that kept me from leaping out the window.

I wasn't sure what I was going to have to endure, and that was what made this torture. But most of all, I wasn't sure if I'd ever see Faith again. And that made it unbearable.

I picked up the picture of Faith's mom, Catherine, and stared hard into the woman's eyes. "Tell me what to do," I said, squeezing the frame. "Just tell me what to do! I'll do it! I'll do anything to get her back!" The frame fell from my hands and crashed onto the wood floor. The glass cracked right down the middle, and the metal frame bent at one corner. I kicked it clear across the room, and it hit the leg of the dining room table.

But the ceiling might as well have crashed in because a

weight so heavy I couldn't stand beneath it crumpled me to my knees, and I sobbed into my balled fists. "God! God!" I shouted, not caring who heard. Hoping, maybe, somebody would. "God, please help me! Help me!" I screamed, the sound muffled by my fists against my mouth.

I fell to my side, nearly in a fetal position, then rolled to my back and stared at the ceiling, which was intact and staring back at me. Except, for the first time, I saw past it. Upward, over me, to something higher. I lay out of breath, willing myself to pray, but it seemed I didn't need to. I settled down inwardly. I became vulnerable, sprawled out on my wood floor like I needed a chalk outline and body bag. I kind of felt half-dead. But I realized I wasn't dead. I was surrendered.

I could not control my life anymore. It was completely out of my hands. So I surrendered to a God I hardly knew but sensed I could trust. Or at least I tried.

I was definitely going to have to surrender to somebody, and in less than twenty-four hours, it would probably be the Feds.

39

OLIVIA

MORNING ARRIVED like a NASCAR crash. I'd jolted awake to the fear I'd forgotten something important. I used to have those kinds of fears when Nell was just born. I'd startle awake to the thought that I'd left her at the mall. Or in the bathtub. My irrational mind seemed to have no limit in those early years.

I sat up in bed, breathing heavily, realizing suddenly that Hardy wasn't there. And the sun seemed especially bright, like it did the morning after a long night when everyone has the stomach flu.

Dad had bickered with me until the nurse finally slipped him something through his IV and he passed out to the everlasting gratefulness of everyone involved. I always knew Daddy would be a bad patient. I just didn't realize he'd be unbearable. I think if they could've checked him out at 3 a.m., they would've. He complained about the toilet being too tiny and the nurses not being pretty and it just got worse from there.

My feet hit the ground. I could smell something cooking. In the kitchen, I found Hardy serving up bacon and scrambled eggs.

"Hi, honey."

"What's going on?" I asked.

"Just got the girls up and ready. Figured you needed some rest. I took off work today. I can do their lessons."

Bacon hung out of Vic's mouth. "Grandpa going to be okay?"

I glanced at Hardy. I hadn't yet prepared what I was going to tell the girls. Hardy deflected it back to me the way a husband and wife can have an entire conversation through their eyes.

I looked at them, their big eyes, their expectant faces. What could I say? How could I spin this? A couple of years ago, I'd managed to talk them through the divorce of our friends Jeff and Shelly without them ever knowing what was going on. I'd explain away everything, until they were living apart, we were seeing them separately, and the girls never noticed a thing.

But that was then. They were smarter now. Older. Wiser than me sometimes. Nell's expression told me that she knew something was serious. Vic looked like she was following her sister's lead.

"All right, girls," I said, leaning on the counter and giving them my full attention. "I'll be straight with you."

"But she's leaning over," Vic whispered to Nell.

Nell replied, "Shooting straight, Vic. That means being honest."

"Oh."

"Girls, Grandpa has a tumor in his brain. A tumor is a kind of cancer, and cancer is something that is growing inside your body that shouldn't be."

"Like how Daddy's tummy keeps growing?" Vic asked, pitching a thumb to Hardy.

That made me smile and Hardy chuckle.

"Except cancer is more like a disease. Something that your body is trying to fight off because it's not good for you at all."

Nell's eyes narrowed. "Is this bad, Momma?"

I nodded, slowly, steadily. "It is bad, Nell."

"Is Grandpa going to die?" Vic asked.

"Well, you know what Grandpa always says. Everyone is going to die sometime."

"Grandpa always says that when he doesn't want to answer a question," Nell said.

I felt myself squirming under my own words. "Girls, I can't answer that question. This is serious, but we're going to find Grandpa the best doctors. The very best." I touched each girl's arm. "No matter what, it's going to be okay. Now, I have to go get Grandpa from the hospital."

"That's a good sign," Nell said to Vic. "They don't let you away from the hospital if you're getting ready to croak."

"Good point," I said. I looked down, realized I had slept in my clothes. Oh, well. I grabbed my purse as I realized how late it was. "I gotta get to the hospital. Dad's going to have a cow."

Hardy walked me out to the car. "He do okay the rest of the night?"

"Seizure-wise, yes. Otherwise, no. He's going to be a real bear on this, Hardy."

"If anyone can handle this, it's you."

I teared up. "I'm not sure."

He pulled me into one of those giant Hardy hugs. "You can do this."

"What if we lose him?"

He patted my back and opened the car door for me. I drove away in silence. My stomach turned with each awful thought that managed its way into my exhausted mind. I'd imagined what life would be like without Daddy, but I never gave it serious thought. He was strong and loved life.

It seemed like only seconds until I was at the hospital, going up the elevator, walking to his room.

To my surprise, he was up, dressed, his bed was made and he was sitting in the chair with his arms crossed. When he saw me, he stood. "What took you so long?"

"Sorry," I said. "I had to take care of some things with the girls."

"Yeah, well, every second I stay here, there is a better chance they're going to kill me." He gestured toward the call button. "Nurse said you gotta sign something to release me. See what I mean? Release me? It's a prison here. I'm surprised they didn't handcuff me to the bed."

"Me, too," I said, raising an eyebrow at him. I hit the call button and the nurse said she'd be right in. And she was, like she'd been hovering in the hallway. She handed me a sheet, marked three Xs to sign, and started to walk out.

"Shouldn't we take him out in a wheelchair?" I asked.

She glanced at him. "Take him out on a gurney, for all I care."

I turned to Dad. "Making friends, I see."

"She was the worst of 'em. I'm calling the hospital to complain."

"Okay, we'll look into that later. For now I guess you're going to have to walk yourself out of here."

"Fine by me." He swept past me, but I noticed he limped a little and was moving slower. His stride was so long, I usually had trouble keeping pace with him when he was in a hurry, but not today.

We drove in silence. He looked lost in deep thought. I wasn't sure what to say, whether to bring it all up or not.

Then he said to me, "What do you think of that Lee character?"

"That Lee character? You mean Lee Reynolds? The doctor?"

"That's the one."

"The one you've known for years?"

"Or so I thought."

"Dad, he was great to you last night. He got you stable, delivered the medical information himself instead of passing us off to some doctor we didn't know."

"Hm." He looked out the window again, silent.

I kept my eyes ahead and my hands on the steering wheel. "So we're getting you into an oncologist—"

"Don't even think about taking me back to your place. I want to go home."

I knew there was no point in arguing. At least Faith would be there. Wasn't sure if I was comforted by that or not. Did she have any idea what taking care of him would entail?

Did I?

I got him home, but neither of us tried to help him in. He looked tired, though. And suddenly older than his age. He flopped down into his favorite chair.

"You hungry, Dad?" I asked.

"Ate that hospital food and I think it permanently killed my appetite."

I had to agree. My appetite was gone, but it wasn't the hospital food. I grabbed Faith by the arm and led her into the kitchen, where we could get some privacy. I took out the medications the nurse had given me the night before.

"I've written this all down. It's all the medication he has

to take. I've included on this list the other medications he was on before. He can take all but one of those, and I've marked that one." I handed Faith the list. She scanned it three or four times. It was pretty straightforward, so I wasn't sure what the holdup was. "He'll try to get out of taking the cholesterol medication. Don't believe anything he says. The doctor still wants him on it."

"Okay."

"Now, he has an appointment at three with that oncologist, so make sure he gets some rest. I'll be over to pick him up. He's going to gripe about this, but don't let that intimidate you. He can kind of be a big baby."

Faith smiled. "Okay."

"If he has another seizure, call the ambulance first and then me."

I saw Faith lose her breath, right there in front of me.

"911."

"Yes. Got it. Thanks."

"I'll be back over this evening, after I finish with the girls' school. I'll bring dinner, so don't worry about that. I suspect he'll be sleeping most of the time."

Faith looked at me. "Why do you do all this?"

"Do what?"

"Take care of everyone all the time."

"They need me, of course. Why else?"

"I wish I was like you."

I snorted, accidentally. But I snort when unexpected

things fly up my nose, like a gnat or a bizarre statement. "Why would you even say that? You're kidding, right?"

"Liv, your heart is so big. There's room for Daddy and Hardy and the girls, the church and . . ."

"You."

Tears welled in her eyes. "And me. I could never do what you do. Be who you are."

"And you couldn't pay me a hundred fertile chickens to get up on stage and do the things you do. At least at my age and hip size."

"Did."

I paused. Man, this was one broken girl. A broken marriage. A broken dream. Now a broken daddy. "I want to show you something."

I walked to the living room. As expected, Dad was out cold and snoring, which I was never happier to hear. I started looking through the bookshelves and underneath in the cabinets. "I know it's here somewhere . . ."

"What?"

"Shush now. Stop talking. I'm trying to think." I opened the far left cabinet. Bingo. "Found it." I pulled it out. It was heavier than I remembered.

"What is it?"

"Come here." I patted the couch and she sat next to me. I opened the scrapbook and laid it in her lap. "I made this a long time ago. I was cleaning out the attic last year and thought Daddy might want it, so I brought it over here."

I watched her look at the pictures as though they were

someone else's. Each time she opened a new page, her fingers would touch another picture.

"It's yours," I said.

"You did this?"

"Yep." I watched as she took in all the dance recitals, musicals, concerts, award ceremonies. "I started it when you were in high school. I figured somebody needed to track all your steps since you were going to be a big star and everything."

"My Juilliard acceptance letter . . . I can't believe you kept all this."

"Faith, we're sisters, and that means we're there for each other and we hold each other up when we need to. But it also means we speak the truth to one another, and the truth is that you can't live your life running from Momma."

"I know." She put a hand to her quivering chin.

"Momma had her turn. Now it's your turn. Momma chose her life and now you get to choose yours." I got up. "You look into that New York hospital Lee mentioned?"

"No, I'm sorry. Not yet."

"Probably best. There's no reason to make him travel all that way. We've got good docs here. Call me to let me know how he's doing. I'll see you in a little while." I walked out, past Daddy, who was still slumbering in his chair, and to my truck.

As I drove home, something struck me. Hard. In the face of everything I thought to be completely right.

I blinked past all my reservations. Because I had many.

And part of me thought I might be sacrificing one to save the other. Was it worth the gamble? Would I even be able to do it?

I knew that girl. I knew what she was capable of, even if she had no clue. But what was I capable of? I could push her, but could I step back and let go?

No. Too much was at stake.

But then again, I had never really liked that word *no.*

40

LUKE

I SLIPPED ON MY SUIT JACKET and drew my tie up tight against the collar. All conservative colors. I pulled my sleeves down and looked into the mirror. Stared down the man who got me into this mess. He looked tired. Defeated. Even vague, like a skyline in fog.

I turned and went to the kitchen, deciding I better get something into my stomach. It was going to be a long day. The longest day. I hadn't eaten much lately and my cinched belt was proving it. As I got the toaster going, I found myself longing for hash-brown casserole, Faith's signature dish from the South. She wasn't the best cook, and most of the time we ate out because neither of us had time to do much else, but every once in a while she'd cook something of her mom's. And it was always spectacular. She said before she died, she'd learn to make chicken-fried steak with white pepper gravy. I joked that if she learned to make it, we might both die early. But happy.

I checked my watch as I slathered some butter onto the toast. Toast. Nothing to toast to now.

I stood and chewed my food at the counter, barely tasting it but instead drifting to my other world, the world that no longer existed. I just couldn't let it go. It was all I wanted, and nothing that I could have anymore.

I stared at the couch that I'd quietly sat on when Faith marched out the front door with suitcase in tow, struggling with its weight, its awkwardness. I sat watching her, where I would ordinarily take the baggage and carry it myself. Half of me hoped it would be too much to even get to the car by herself, and she'd give up on it and come back. The other half refused to help her walk out on me. So I just sat. Watched her go. Didn't get up off the couch for another three hours.

Move on. These words had started drifting through my subconscious last night and had come to the forefront of my mind this morning as I got ready. I wanted to grieve, but something told me I'd grieved enough. I had to pick myself up off the floor.

Except I knew no amount of resolve would fix anything. Undo anything. Create a miracle.

I could stomach only half a piece of toast. I threw the rest in the garbage and knew it was time to go downstairs. I picked up my briefcase, took one long, deep breath to try to keep my insides from shaking, and went out the door.

Downstairs, the sleek black limo idled on the street. It looked like an expensive pair of Ray-Bans soaking up the morning sunshine.

Ward stepped out. "Good morning, Mr. Carraday."

"Hi, Ward." He opened the door for me and I slid into the dark, odorously clean interior of the limo.

Jake and Dad sat across from me, both overdressed as usual. Dad was glancing through some papers, but he looked up as I entered. "Luke. Holding up?"

"Guess so."

"How are you holding up?" Jake asked with more intention.

"Terrific," I said, and the edge in my voice explained the ridiculous answer.

"Okay," Jake said, "I know this is going to be a tough day. I get that. But you have to keep your head high, okay? You have to stay steady."

I looked at Jake and maybe for the first time in a long time, I understood him. What I'd tried to run from was the very thing that was keeping me steady right now, at this very moment. I had two of the strongest men I knew holding me up. Maybe that's what they'd been doing since I was born.

Dad nodded, peering just a little over his reading glasses, then went back to whatever it was he was reading. Jake was still talking while his thumbs flew over his BlackBerry. I sat there and watched the two of them, thinking about the hundreds of contacts I had through my work. The numerous acquaintances that had stayed steady in my life for years. Even the friendships that had been built around late nights at bars and parties and pool tables. I must have known a thousand people, but only two . . . *two* . . . were by my side now.

My stomach turned as I felt the limo pull to the side of the street. Outside, a crowd of photographers and journalists huddled together like they were inside a bunker or something. Shouting. Flashes. A roar of words I couldn't even understand.

Dad set the folder down beside him, slid the glasses off his nose, and tucked them in his pocket. "Remember, no matter what happens, we stick together. Understand?"

I nodded. Dad had said that hundreds of times to me as a kid. On an African safari. On a fishing expedition in Alaska. In a crowded room at a Christmas benefit.

"Dad . . . ," I said. I felt like a kid. Small and vulnerable. Unsure. "What's this going to do to your company?"

Dad had what I liked to call the Clint Eastwood squint. It popped up when he was trying to read a menu and had forgotten his glasses. I'd also seen it when one of his employees was babbling nonsense to him. He was never aware of how intense it made him look. And it was staring me down right now. "It's time to go" was all he said.

Though I was closest to the door, I couldn't manage to even open it. Soon Ward stood there. I could see his hand against the door.

Then it opened. The shouts assaulted us like bursts of

sand in the face, blown by dynamic wind. I blinked rapidly, trying to keep my calm, but one shaky leg out of the car and I knew this was going to be difficult. Within seconds, a hand was on my shoulder, and soon I felt a body close to mine. Jake.

I glanced back to make sure Dad followed. He slowly got out of the limo, seemingly unfazed by his age or the audience. He patted his pockets, presumably to make sure he had his glasses and his phone, then smiled mildly at everyone and dismissed questions with a flick of his wrist.

Soon the three of us were walking side by side, pushing against the mob. Ward helped. And so did two police officers. But it was like treading through mud. We were shoved. I lost my balance, but Jake caught me under the arm. "Keep moving," he whispered.

I kept my eyes focused on the top of the stairs of the federal courthouse. One step at a time.

Out of all the voices shouting at us, one filled the air, like the ocean noise of a seashell right at my ear.

"Austin! Aren't you worried that defending your son is going to bring down your company?"

My heart sank, even though it was my worry too. I kept walking, but I felt Dad's hand release my arm.

"What did you say?" Dad's voice growled like a menacing dog whose hair was standing straight up on its back.

"Keep walking," Jake said, but I couldn't.

Dad's eyes were fierce as he turned to face the reporter, his neck literally stuck out, his finger pointed directly at the man who asked the question. "This is my *son*!" His arm shot out and he was pointing at me now. All eyes shifted from Dad to me. I felt myself stand a little taller. "*My* son! No stock is worth losing him." His hand was around my arm again. "Come on, Luke. Let's go."

We walked toward the imposing white stone columns of justice above us. And Dad's hand never left my arm again.

41

FAITH

I'D SAT FOR THREE HOURS watching Dad sleep, studying how often his chest would rise and fall. It was good that he was sleeping peacefully, but it was unnerving too. I was afraid if I took my eyes off him, even for a minute, he might stop breathing. Or go into a seizure. So I watched until I couldn't watch any longer, and then I called Lee.

"I was planning on stopping by anyway," he'd said over the phone.

And he did. Just as Dad was waking up, Lee pulled into our long driveway and parked his truck next to my car.

"Lee's here," I said, going to the door.

Dad rubbed his eyes. "Why?"

"To check on you."

"Oh, brother," Dad groaned. "That's why I wanted to leave the hospital, so I wouldn't have to endure any more of that."

"Don't act like a brat, Dad," I said in my stern voice. "It's just a precaution."

Dad mumbled something I couldn't hear as I opened the screen door for Lee. "Hi," I said warmly. "Thank you so much for coming."

"How's he feeling?" he asked from the entryway.

"Grumpy."

"I'll take grumpy." With his doctor's bag, Lee made his way to the living room.

"Dad, Lee's here," I announced.

Dad mumbled something again, his eyes focused on an ESPN show.

"Hey, Calvin. How are you feeling?"

Dad's gentle eyes had the capacity to turn sharp when he wanted them to, and let's just say they were as sharp as Olivia's tongue. "Well, Lee, I've got a tumor growing in my brain, so I'm feeling about as good as you'd expect."

Lee glanced at me for support. I urged him on.

He cleared his throat. "I'm going to check your vitals, okay?"

"It's not my vitals that have a tumor, now is it?"

"Daddy, please. Lee is here to help."

"Fine," Dad sighed. "Do what you must. But hurry up about it."

"I just want to get a good look in your eyes," Lee said,

pulling out a small light from his bag. He sat down in front of Dad, on the ottoman that Dad usually used for his feet.

"You're blocking the game," Dad said. Whined, really.

"I just want to look . . . Can you look here in my light? . . . Right here in my light . . ." Lee put his flashlight down. "Calvin, I can't get a good look when you watch the TV."

"Come on, Daddy. Help him out."

Dad huffed and stared right into the light. As Lee checked him, Dad said, "Doctors don't usually make house calls, do they?"

"Not usually," Lee said, studying his eyes.

"And you're not a cancer specialist. You're an ER doctor."

Lee glanced above the light. "Yep."

"So who exactly are you calling on?" Dad asked.

Lee sort of froze. So did I. Then I rushed to Lee's aid. "Dad, he's just coming by to help us out."

"Hm. You done?" he asked Lee.

"Close enough. You look pretty good, Calvin."

"Great. Then leave me be."

Horrified at the way Dad was acting, I escorted Lee to the door. I lightly touched his arm. "I am so sorry. I'm not sure what has gotten into him."

"It's okay," Lee said. He opened the door and walked out. I followed him.

"Is it the tumor making him act like this?"

Lee laughed as he threw his bag through the window of his truck. He turned to face me, leaning against the door. "No. He's just trying to protect you."

"Protect me? From what?"

"Me." Lee studied the ground. So did I. I think we were staring at the same spot.

"That's . . . that's silly."

"No. It's not." He looked up at me. Stood upright and took a step closer. My heart was pounding out of my chest. "Dads know these things about their daughters. They have a sense of when they're vulnerable."

At the word *vulnerable*, I shivered. I felt myself wanting to be held. Like he was a magnet, I stepped closer to him. I closed my eyes, willing myself not to think about him touching my face, stroking my hair. Then I opened my eyes, which had filled with tears, and found Lee's.

"I'm sorry," I whispered. "I shouldn't have—"

"Shh. It's okay. You didn't . . . I was the one who . . ." He took a deep breath and pulled something out of his pocket. He handed me a small business card.

"What's this?"

"It's the name of the doctor you need to get in to see in New York. Dr. Joseph Sinclair, at Sloan-Kettering. He's the best in the world at these types of cancers at the base of the brain."

I stared at the card. Blinked at the address.

Lee continued, "I've made some calls to my professors back at Columbia to see if I can get him in, but I haven't heard back, and truthfully, that route is a long shot."

"Okay, well, thanks for trying. Hopefully this doctor here can—"

"Faith. Listen to me. He won't have a shot without Sinclair. It's stage IV. It's on his brain stem. Sinclair is your only hope."

Lee's words hit my heart hard, a sucker punch straight into my soul. "But . . . how do I . . . ?"

"Your in-laws, Faith. They're pretty connected in those circles."

"My *in-laws*?"

"They're probably your only shot at getting in. You should call Luke."

"Lee, I haven't talked with him in . . ." It felt like forever.

"I would take your dad now, to New York, and stay there until they can get him in to see Sinclair."

"But . . ."

"If you don't, your dad will likely die. He doesn't have much time." Lee opened his car door. "I won't stop trying to make phone calls either. Hopefully something will work."

I backed up as he started his truck. "Okay, thanks."

"Go to New York. Call Luke."

He drove off. I stood there in the dust of his truck, choking on my new reality.

42

OLIVIA

HARDY WATCHED ME walk from room to room, from chair to sofa, from front door to back. He sat at the kitchen table, observing restlessly. Finally he threw down his hat. "Olivia, what? What is this? You've been scurrying round here like a scared squirrel, saying 'She can't handle it' over and over again. Who can't handle what?"

Admittedly, my legs were tired and so was my finger, for the number of times I'd twirled and untwirled my hair. I sat at the table with him. "Faith."

"Faith can't handle your dad being sick?"

"Don't know about that one yet," I said, thumping my

fingers against the table. "But I was thinking about having Faith take Daddy to the doctor's appointment this afternoon with that oncologist."

Hardy looked genuinely confused. "But why?"

"I know, I know," I said, irritated that he wasn't following my train of thought, even though I wasn't really even giving him a track. "But see, Faith doesn't believe in herself, Hardy. She's lost her marriage and her dream and her sense of—what do you call it?—self-worth."

Hardy was nodding. Sort of blankly.

"She's just this tiny scared mouse. She even nibbles like a mouse. You watch her eat and it's like she thinks the corn on the cob is going to jump right off that plate and beat her to a bloody pulp." I sighed as I looked at Hardy's poor, confused face. "She's a smart girl. She can handle taking Daddy to the doctor."

Hardy studied his calloused hands. "But can you?"

"What's that supposed to mean?" I barked, even though I knew exactly what it was supposed to mean. And it wasn't even supposed to be an insult, but everybody knew I was easily insulted. Even me. I let myself calm down a little. "I know. That's why I've been pacing this floor like you the day Nell was born."

"I think you're right," Hardy said. "I think she can handle it. And I think it'd be good for you, too. To let go a little."

Hardy, I knew, was a wise man. He let me talk a lot and rant and rave and do what I do, but when the time came to speak the absolute truth, Hardy was there.

"Maybe I should send a tape recorder with her. We got one around here?"

"Nope. Wouldn't be a good idea if we did."

"Right." I put my elbows on the table, folded my hands, rested my chin there. "Okay, so our cover is going to be the kids have the stomach flu."

"Fine."

"Anything less and she won't believe I can't go."

"Sure."

"And I can't go. I have to let her do it."

"Yep."

"Nell! Vic! Get in here!"

The girls scurried in from their bedroom. I felt both of their heads. "Burning up, the two of you."

Vic felt her own head. Nell piped in, "You can't feel your own fever." She looked at me. "But I don't feel sick."

"You look pale. You feel pale?"

Vic felt her skin again. "A little. What's *pale*?"

"It's when all the color drains from your face," Nell said. "Like the time you asked Mom what fornication was in front of the preacher."

"*Okaaay* . . . let's forget that for now and get you two some chicken noodle soup. I have to go check on Grandpa."

"I want to go!" Nell declared, which of course I predicted.

"Not with a fever, honey."

"I don't even feel sick."

"By night's end, you two will be puking your guts out."

"Cool," Vic whispered.

"I got the soup," Hardy said, raising an eyebrow at me. What? He knew by now my child-rearing tactics were unconventional. But I didn't want this coming back to bite me. Faith had to believe this was her journey. Destiny. Fate. She was into all that stuff, but it had to be authentic.

My cover would be that I was starting to feel nauseous too, blah blah blah. I wasn't going to have to fake the paleness. I was sure that at the moment I had to tell her she was on her own, the color really was going to drain from my face.

I grabbed my purse and walked outside. Funny, I did feel nauseous, too. Could I really let the fate of my beloved father rest in the hands of my totally screwed-up sister?

I guess this was what the pastor was referring to all those times he talked about a higher calling. The higher road. Here it was. And it hurt like heck.

43

LUKE

The day Faith left, I was sitting on our couch, slouched and uncomfortable in my own clothes. I could hear the hangers clanging against one another as she pulled clothes off them. Her shoes clicked against the wood floors of the bedroom. But there was no other sound.

I sat there fuming. My bitterness was combustible. *For better or worse. For better or worse.* It kept going through my mind, the day we married, how she looked me right in the eye and told me she'd stick by me. For better or worse. And now she wanted to walk out on me? Fine. Fine! Do it.

I didn't know if she wanted me to try to stop her or not. But if she did, my pride kept me from saying anything.

And she was gone. Just like that.

"Luke, snap out of it!" I looked up to find Jake snapping his fingers in front of my face.

"Sorry."

"You have to focus, okay? You've got to hold it together in there."

"I know. I just have a lot on my mind."

"Push it all aside. Right now, right in that room, that's all that matters."

Dad stepped up. He had his game face on. Stoic. Bigger than life. Powerful. Behind him was the family attorney, Cecil Yates. "It's all going to be all right. I've always looked out for you. Always will."

"So you're clear on what you're supposed to say?" Jake asked.

"He's clear," Dad said, putting a heavy hand on my shoulder. "Right, Son?"

"Yes. I'm ready."

Jake looked the most self-assured, like he didn't doubt his plan for a second. Suddenly the heavy door in front of us opened. One of the prosecutors for the SEC stood there with his hand on the door, looking pleasant and professional. "Gentlemen, come on in." Like it was a typical business meeting.

Dad went first, followed by Jake. I was stepping forward when my cell phone rang.

And it was Faith's ringtone.

Jake turned, stared at me as I pulled out my phone. "Put it away," he growled.

I looked at the caller ID to verify. It was her. Now? *Now?* My thumb hovered over the green button.

Jake threw his hands up and gave the prosecutor a mild glance. "Luke, it can wait. I promise. Whatever it is. Whoever it is." We locked eyes, and he knew in an instant *who* it was.

"You have to get this in order," he said. "Let's go."

He was right, of course. What would I say to her at this very moment, anyway? I hit Mute and slid the phone back in my pocket.

But my heart broke. She finally called, and I was up to my eyebrows in this mess. I couldn't even take her call. I sat down between Dad and Jake, across from three prosecutors, two men and one woman. All three of their faces were sober and stern. I put my hands under the table.

A man with a bald head, whom I recognized as Wright, opened a folder and began to speak about a plea deal. I heard about every fifth word, as my mind just kept flashing to Faith, over and over. My cell phone had vibrated in my pocket, indicating she'd left me a message. My heart tingled with anticipation. Was she calling to tell me she wanted a divorce? Or to tell me she wanted to come home?

Finally I focused on the prosecutor, who was mostly spouting off legal mumbo jumbo. He was just finishing up formally offering me the plea deal. He looked up, smiled pleasantly, and waited.

"No," I said. Small word, but I'd had to practice the response a lot this morning.

"No?" he asked, glancing at his female colleague.

"No."

"You're saying no to a plea."

"That's correct," I said, taking a deep breath. It reminded me of the scene in one of the Indiana Jones movies, where he had to take the first step and believe the bridge was there even though he couldn't see it. Dad and Jake told me this was what I had to do, but it felt like I was stepping off a ledge.

The smirk on the prosecutor's face said I was about to take a free fall.

"I didn't commit a crime." I said it firmly, like Jake told me to.

The prosecutor looked at Yates. "I hope you're not giving him this advice."

"You guys aren't exactly leaving him many options, are you?"

The prosecutor's nostrils flared. "We're giving him a great option. Cooperate and he'll get a plea. No time, probation, lose his broker's license for five years."

Dad leaned forward, put his hands on the table, and folded them together. "Full immunity and he tells you everything you want to know."

"With all due respect, Mr. Carraday, this is one of the greatest cases of criminal fraud in American history. No one gets immunity on this one. Not even your son."

Then something happened in that room. Nothing palpable. But the entire mood shifted. Yates looked at Dad. Dad looked at Jake. Jake looked at the prosecutor. And there was an unbearable silence that I thought might resemble what happens right before the guillotine drops.

"If you wouldn't mind," Jake said in that authoritative voice he tried often on me, "we'd like to speak with you in private." Except he was saying this to the prosecutor.

Awkward silence, except for the squeaky noise being made by my chair rocking back and forth.

"Okay . . ." The prosecutor sounded as baffled as I felt.

The agent who'd cuffed me back at Union Square stood, but Jake nodded toward him. "You, too, Agent Wright." Wright sat back down. Then Jake looked at me. "I'll see you outside."

"I should . . . ?"

"Wait outside." Jake's voice was calm, controlled.

"Sure." I smiled like I knew the drill, but I honestly had no idea what was going on. I walked out and stood in the hallway. Then I pulled out my phone and dialed my voice mail.

Her voice sounded as pure as a waterfall. *"Luke, it's me. I need your help."*

44

FAITH

". . . AND I TOOK the thermometer out, and it read 102, and no kidding, she puked right there on the floor in front of me. Then Nell comes running in and says she's just puked in the toilet. I heard this stuff was going around, but man, it just hit us out of the blue."

"Liv, I'm so sorry."

"It happens." She was blinking rapidly and looking a little pale.

"You don't look so good yourself."

"Yeah . . . I do feel a little queasy. Listen, Faith, I think you better take Dad to his appointment with the oncologist this afternoon."

"Um . . . about that . . ."

"Now, hear me out," Olivia said, popping off the couch and starting to pace like she did when she had something important to say. Or think about. "You're perfectly capable of this, Faith. You're a smart girl. You don't believe in yourself nearly enough. You don't give yourself credit. You hear me? You've fallen on hard times. Everybody does. But part of picking yourself up includes doing things you don't think you can do." She stopped, waggled a finger at me. "And I know you don't think you can do this, but you can. I wouldn't put Dad's life—his whole life—in your hands if I didn't think you could handle it."

I stood and took Olivia by the shoulder. "I think you should sit down. You really don't look well."

"I don't feel that great."

"You're really pale."

"Anyway, I don't want to hear a word about it, okay?" Olivia said, turning to me as we sat on the couch. "That's just the way it's going to be."

I took a deep breath. A really deep breath. I kind of felt like the blood was draining out of my face too. By Olivia's expression, I knew I was right.

"Good grief, Sister, you look like you're about to pass out. I'm asking you to take him to the doctor, not the morgue."

"Liv, please. Just . . . just hold on, okay? I need to tell you something."

"What?"

"I need you to hear me. To really listen."

"I'm listening."

"I'm not taking Daddy to the oncologist."

"Of course you're not." She sighed loudly. "All right, fine. I'll do it. I just thought you might want the chance to prove to yourself and everybody else that—"

"I'm taking him to New York."

I didn't think she could get any paler, but I was wrong.

"What'd you say?"

"I'm taking Dad to New York. To Sloan-Kettering. There is a neurosurgeon, Dr. Sinclair, who is the best in the world at removing these kinds of tumors."

Olivia was blinking rapidly again, apparently trying to process the information.

"Lee is the one that told me we need to get him there. So that's what we're going to do. It's his best shot. Our best shot." I put a hand on her knee. But she jerked it away.

"When is his appointment?"

I paused. This wasn't going to go over well. "He doesn't have an appointment."

"What do you mean?"

"We're trying to get him one. Lee has tried to work through his Columbia acquaintances to get him in but hasn't had any luck. So I've asked . . ." I'd known this wouldn't come out easy. But it didn't come out at all.

Olivia stared at me, then motioned for me to continue. "Yeah? Asked who?"

"Luke."

"Luke?"

"Lee said I should try to use the Carraday family to get Dad in. It's still a long shot, but they've got a lot of connections. I know his dad donated money to the hospital. I remember going to a benefit . . ." My words trailed off as I watched Olivia growing tense.

"So that's your plan? Just skip this appointment, hope Luke comes through for you?"

"I've got to give it a shot, Liv."

"What if he doesn't get in?"

"I'm going to have faith that he will. That's why we're leaving this evening. I'm driving Dad to New York. We're going to stay in a hotel there until we get in."

Olivia shot to her feet. "Are you crazy?"

"I'm not crazy—"

"That's your plan? Luke coming through for you? Dad in a hotel, on a wing and a prayer?" She turned, walked around the coffee table, stood at the far end of the room like I had the plague or something. "Dad will never go along with this."

"He already has."

Tears welled in her eyes—big, plump . . . the kind that burst out of you so fast you don't even realize you're crying until you feel them drip down your cheeks. "Why would you depend on Luke? His family?"

"Because they're good people, at the end of the day. They never liked me much, but they're good people."

"Dad can't travel, Faith. He's frail. Have you noticed? What is that?" She gestured toward the living room, where Dad slept. "His fourth nap of the day?"

"He's—"

"Dad doesn't travel well. Don't you know that? He hasn't left home in years. He hates big cities, and you're taking him to the biggest city!"

"To try to save his life!"

"His life? Or yours? Isn't this just a scheme to get back to Luke? Using Daddy and his illness?"

"How dare you," I said, standing. "I would never do that."

"Are you sure?" The color was back in her cheeks. Bright red. "Because habits are hard to break."

"What habits?"

"Selfish habits."

We both tried catching our breaths. Our chests heaved up and down.

Then she put her hands on her hips. "If this isn't about Luke, then maybe it's about Lee."

"What is that supposed to mean?"

"I see how you two are. Chummy. Laughing. Enjoying each other's company."

I looked down. I couldn't deny those accusations. A part of me—a big part of me—was tempted by Lee. Finally I looked at her. "It was Lee's idea to go to New York. It was his idea for me to call Luke. There's nothing going on between us."

Suddenly Dad was in the doorway, bleary eyed, his shirt crumpled from the recliner. "What's going on in here?"

Olivia's whole demeanor changed as she turned to Dad.

It was gentle and sweet, and her large brown eyes stared at him like she was a little girl. "You're going to New York?"

"I am," Dad said.

"You didn't even ask me."

"It's my tumor."

"But . . . you've always asked me for my opinion." The pain in her voice was nearly unbearable. I was starting to see where she was coming from. This was a blind side hit for her. And Dad never blindsided her.

"Faith was here. She told me the plan. I thought it was good."

"You hate hotel rooms," Olivia said, wiping a stray tear.

"And big cities. But that's where all the specialists are. Now, I'm hungry. Figure we better eat a good, well-priced meal before we take off. You and Hardy want to join us?"

Olivia just shook her head.

"They have the stomach flu," I told Dad. He walked toward his bedroom. I looked back at Liv. "I'm sorry. I didn't mean to cut you out of this."

"Really." She walked toward the door. Took her purse and swung it over her shoulder.

"Liv, please. I'm just doing what I think is best for Daddy."

"You two have a good trip. Let me know if I can be of any help."

The door slammed shut, and I was afraid our relationship had too.

45

LUKE

I COULD HEAR them talking inside, but only muffled voices, buffered by the heavy wooden doors that had shut behind me. Nearby, I'd found a wall to lean against. My legs were wobbly, mostly because I didn't know why I had been dismissed from the room. But my heart felt stronger. Just hearing Faith's voice stirred a hope in me that I'd lost the day she walked out.

I listened to her voice mail five times, to make sure I was hearing her correctly and also just to listen to her. Calvin was sick, but I could hear it in her voice . . . she was dying inside. I'd never met her father, but Faith always spoke fondly of him. I remember thinking that if we ever had kids, I wanted them to feel about me the way she felt about him.

A certain guilt followed me whenever she talked about Calvin. I'd taken her away from something or kept her from returning. She didn't want to return to North Carolina, but I should have urged her to reconsider.

But for a while, we were complete, just the two of us. Our happiness was wrapped up in one another. What else did we need?

We needed the fairy tale not to end.

I looked up the phone number and dialed it, keeping my eye on the conference room door.

"Dr. Sinclair's office."

"This is Luke Carraday, calling for Dr. Sinclair."

"I'm sorry . . . what was the name?"

"Carraday. Luke Carraday." I cleared my throat; my own name was sticking there. "It's a rather urgent matter. Dr. Sinclair and I are members of the—"

"He's not available."

"I see." Sweat started soaking through my shirt. "Do you know when he might be in? Like I mentioned, it's very urgent and I would appreciate it if—"

"I'll let him know you called."

"Tell him I really need—"

The line went dead. And so did my resolve. Finally Faith was reaching out to me, and I couldn't help her. My name was like a curse now. I shoved the phone into my pocket and then tore my fingers through my hair. I had to find a way.

Suddenly the doors to the conference room opened. Jake walked out first, then Dad. I stood up straight, trying to ignore how damp my body was. Jake walked toward me, smiling. "Come on. Let's get out of here before they change their minds." He took a piece of paper out of his pocket and handed it to me.

"What is this?"

"Your immunity deal."

I walked with both of them. Dad had his hand on my shoulder. "Are you serious?"

Jake put his arm around me too. "Yeah."

I clutched the piece of paper. We walked swiftly like we might be running from something. Soon we were inside the limo. I was breathing hard, but I wasn't sure if it was the walk or the news.

I stared at the paper, then at Dad and Jake. "How'd you do it?"

"Details later. For now, work. But tomorrow we celebrate."

I nodded. Even grinned. I folded the paper and tucked it right next to my phone. It was freedom, but I wasn't free because I still had to help Faith and get her back in my life. And no immunity deal was going to accomplish that. It was on my shoulders.

46

OLIVIA

I THINK I really did make my kids sick. A mom can do that. When she's off kilter, everything else is too. I'd made Nell cry, twice, by being snappy. Now both kids were sitting in front of the TV, wrapped in blankets, sniffling.

"I'll get their lessons done."

"I just wish you'd talk to me about it," Hardy said, bringing the books and notepaper to the table. "Why won't you tell me what happened over there?"

I couldn't. I could barely keep myself from crying. I needed to focus on something else. I could cry later, when the family was in bed and I was up at 2 a.m., unable to sleep.

Hardy stopped me as I headed back to the kitchen. "What happened?"

I glanced at the girls. They were enthralled with the TV, which I never let them watch during the day. "I knew this would happen . . . ," I whispered.

"What? That she couldn't take him? We can take him."

"She is taking him. That's the point. She's taking him away from me."

Hardy pulled me into the hallway, out of the girls' line of sight. "Your dad loves you, Olivia. How can you doubt that?"

"Yeah, he loves me. But he loves her more. And I knew the day she returned, she'd get all the attention. She'd get his heart. I mean, are you kidding me? New York? She's convinced him to go to New York? I can't convince Dad to go to Whiteville. He says it's too big and crowded."

"He's going to New York?"

"Some fancy surgeon at some big hospital. She called Luke for help, to get him in. They're going to drive to New York, hoping Luke can come through."

Hardy took a deep breath, rubbed my shoulders. "Well, maybe this is what your dad needs. It's a serious tumor."

I nodded. "I guess I'm feeling left out," I said with a sad smile. There was only one person I could be this vulnerable with, and he'd known me since I was eighteen years old.

He pulled me close. Stroked my hair.

"I'm being a big baby about this, aren't I?"

"Olivia, you care about people. You care deeply for your dad. That is no crime."

Outside, we both heard the sound of a car driving up. I peeked out the window.

"Ugh! No!" I turned to Hardy. "It's Faith's car. I thought they'd be off to New York by now." I stood on my tippy toes and put my face close to Hardy's. "Please tell me I don't look like I've been crying. Am I splotchy? I always get splotchy."

"You look just fine."

I opened the front door but was surprised to see it was Dad walking up the porch. Faith stayed in the car. I could only see her shoulder.

I waited for him. Kept my hand on the door, don't know why. Dad looked pensive. I'm sure I looked peeved. I tried not to, but I'm just one of those people who can't hide their emotions very well.

"Olivia, I want to talk to you."

I flashed back to when I was fifteen and I'd snuck out of the house.

"Yes?" I tried to hold my ground.

"I know you're upset. And I'm sorry about that."

I nodded, mostly surprised because Dad wasn't one to talk about emotions. Ever.

"You know how I hate big cities. And New York . . . well, I'm not sure I'll survive the traffic there."

I smiled. "Yeah."

"But I want you to see the big picture."

"The big picture."

"The biggest picture you can see."

I wasn't sure I was following.

"Dad," I said, "what if you have a seizure along the way?"

"Lee gave me some medicine that should help that. And he told Faith what to do if it happens."

I gestured toward the car. "You're leaving now? This late?"

"Faith's driving. She'll be fine."

"Dad, I have to say, I don't think this is a good idea."

"I know." And then he reached out and hugged me. "Liv, you've been the best daughter a man could hope for."

Tears gushed down my cheeks so fast they fell off my face for lack of room.

"There, there," Dad said. "I wasn't trying to upset you."

"I'm sorry. I don't know where this is coming from." Each word came out breathy.

"I couldn't have made it without you," Dad said. That's all he said. And maybe that's all I needed to hear. He stepped back. "I have to get on the road."

I nodded.

"Take care of that sweet family of yours. Hope they get better," he said with a wink that told me he hadn't bought my story. Maybe he knew what I had planned. Maybe he was letting Faith sprout her wings and fly.

But to New York?

As Dad walked back to the car, Faith ducked so I could see part of her face. She gave me a quick wave. I gave her a quicker wave back.

And then they left.

I wiped my eyes and prayed that whoever this Dr. Sinclair was, he'd be a miracle worker.

47

FAITH

DAD SLEPT FOR most of the journey, woke up around 7 a.m., and was ready to eat. I knew he'd pick the greasiest truck stop we could find, and sure enough, right off the interstate in Philadelphia, we found Tubby's and it looked the part.

"I bet they serve chicken-fried steak for breakfast!" Dad said, rubbing his hands together as we got out of the car.

"Glad to see your appetite's back." I opened the door for him. "Don't make me return to New York to find you a heart surgeon."

"Come on," Dad growled. "A little gravy never hurt anyone. My grandparents had biscuits and gravy every single day of their lives."

I didn't argue, but I was starting to see what Olivia had to put up with.

Inside, the air was so thick with grease that the floor actually felt a little sticky. Despite the fact that three waitresses were wiping down tables, I still didn't hesitate to pull out antibacterial wipes from my purse.

Dad watched me as I wiped the tabletop. "Not a bad idea," he said. "The closer we get to New York, the bigger the germs are."

"Funny," I said as I rubbed antibacterial gel onto my hands. "So how are you feeling?"

"Hungry."

"Dad."

"What? Isn't that a good sign?"

The waitress came, took our drink orders, and then Dad said, "You know, I miss your mom's cooking. Still to this day, I miss it." I tried not to look startled, but Dad wasn't good at this kind of talk. "It was so hard after she was gone. I tried to cook for you girls. That didn't work out too well, if you remember."

"I remember a roast with black smoke rising from it."

"And that was still edible. The other times were even more disastrous."

"You did fine, Dad."

"But I miss her cooking. The way she oversalted the vegetables. Undercooked the eggs. The way the icing on her cakes was so . . . there's not even a word . . ."

"Perfect?"

"That'll do."

The waitress returned with drinks, then took our order. Dad had the chicken-fried steak. I had the vegetable omelet.

"I talked to Lee. About the accident."

Dad sat there, didn't say anything.

"It was just something I had to do."

"Fine."

"I guess I was hoping she said her good-byes to us, said something—anything."

"Her injuries . . . she wouldn't have been able to speak."

"I know. You still miss her as much? I do."

"Yes. As much as the first day."

We talked about some of our favorite memories. It was how someone deceased should be remembered. But I couldn't help but wonder what my memories of Luke would be. He wasn't deceased. And he wasn't dead to me. So how was I supposed to remember him?

It was like Dad read my mind. "You heard from Luke? About that doctor?"

"I got a text from him. Said he's still working on it." It was the first time I'd heard from him since I left, and that's all it said: I'm working on it. Of course, all I was calling about was my sick dad. Maybe that's how we'd be: just two people communicating on the most basic level possible.

Once we were back on the road, Dad fell asleep again. It was so obvious now, how tired he was. It broke my heart to see such a strong man falling victim to this illness. I prayed hard, the rest of the way. Prayed for my daddy. Prayed for things to be okay. Prayed Luke would find this doctor and we'd get in, and I wouldn't look stupid for driving us all the way out to New York on "a wing and a prayer."

It's just that something, other than Lee's recommendation, told me to go. I couldn't identify it. But there was an urgency there, and just like before when I left, I was following my heart, praying it wouldn't lead me astray.

But this time I wasn't running from something. I was running to something. Hope. Answers. Healing.

"It's going to be all right, Dad," I whispered. "Everything is going to be fine."

I turned on my GPS and listened for directions to the hotel Dad insisted we stay in, a Holiday Inn Express in Midtown, one that I hoped wouldn't stand a chance against my wipes. But as I turned in, my heart sank. This was going to save us money, but probably not my sanity. I drove into the half-circle drive and kept the car running as I went inside to check us in. Dad stayed asleep, which bothered me because he was a light sleeper in the car.

Inside a tired-looking woman with a sagging chignon and a "Becky" name tag tried her best at a bright smile. "Welcome. How can I help you?"

I gave her my credit card and prayed Luke hadn't suddenly decided to cancel it. I kept telling myself Luke would come through, Luke would come through. But my heart tugged a different direction, reminding me there was only one who promised never to leave me or forsake me. So as

Becky ran my card, gathered the room keys, printed papers for me to sign, I prayed for help. For everything.

I glanced outside to see if Dad was okay. Becky was in slow motion as she walked four feet to the printer, then back to the desk. With bloodshot eyes she willed into merriment, she explained our room location, that a complimentary breakfast was served, and that elevator two was broken.

Back in the car, Dad grumbled as I shut my door and drove to the rear of the hotel. He woke up as I parked.

"We're here."

"That was some kind of nap." He grinned at me. "I might stay up all night."

"Good for you."

"Did they say if they have SportsCenter?"

"I forgot to ask. Come on, let's get our bags up there."

Dad insisted on carrying the luggage, but it wasn't a pretty sight. Soon enough, though, we were in the room. Thankfully there was ESPN. Dad viewed our modest accommodations like we'd landed a five-star. He kicked his shoes off and fell on top of the bed with his hands crossed behind his head. "This is nice!"

"It's just temporary until we can get a little apartment or something more long term. They have breakfast here, you know, and I'll pick up some food so you have something in the room if you want. You want something to eat?"

Dad had something in his hand, a brightly colored pamphlet that he'd grabbed off the nightstand. "I want to go to a show."

I pulled the heavy curtains shut, hoping to block out some of the noise. "Sorry it's so loud, Dad. But everything is loud in New York."

"*West Side Story*."

I turned. Was he serious? I'd been waiting on the punch line.

He held up the pamphlet. "Your momma told me she was going to play Maria on Broadway. It was her favorite. Her dream."

I smiled. I knew the story. "And she told you this on your first date."

"That's right!" He slapped the pamphlet with the back of his fingers. "I want to see if anybody can do it better."

"*West Side Story* it is."

"We have to have some fun while we're here, right? Why come to New York and not see the city? The sights?"

I raised an eyebrow. "Dad . . . you hate big cities."

He turned up the volume on the TV. "Maybe people change."

48

LUKE

WHEN JAKE SAID we'd celebrate, I knew he hadn't counted on Dad wanting to come along. We were both surprised when Dad said we'd be going to Malone's for a long lunch the next day. A big deal because Dad didn't stop work for lunch unless it was business. It was Dad's favorite off-the-map place to take guests and people he wanted to impress. It was fun going with him . . . brought us back to when we were little kids. The smell of cigars and expensive liquor. Laughter that roared throughout the boys' club. It was at the top of a high-rise, and Jake and I would press our hands and faces against the glass, just like we were asked not to, and peer into the city. The streets seemed alive with furious light. The sky looked closer, heavier. We'd bring marbles or dominos to play. Those seemed better than our electronic toys. Inevitably, one of Dad's friends would find us at a table and want to join in. We felt like giants. We didn't realize that's exactly what Dad was raising us to be.

Through a four-course lunch and three rounds of drinks, yesterday's events weren't mentioned at all. I still did not understand what happened and tried to ask Jake about it, but he said we'd talk later. "Enjoy this!" he said, toasting the air. "You're free, little brother!"

It felt good. Even my cell phone was lighting up from time to time, a friend here and there who dared to talk to me again. But I was only concerned with two calls: Dr. Sinclair and Faith. Faith had texted to tell me she was in town but didn't bother letting me know where they were staying. Nothing from Dr. Sinclair's office.

Jake had sensed my concern, but it wasn't the time to talk about it. We toasted, poured, talked about the glory days, and shared dreams for our future. It was nice to see Dad's face light up with gusto. "These are my boys!" he kept repeating to every new acquaintance he saw at the lounge.

I was back at my apartment by afternoon and drifted to sleep wondering how in the world I was a free man. I didn't doubt it, but neither did I understand it. I slept fitfully, listening for the door to open and Faith to arrive. I knew it was only wishful thinking she'd come home, but I couldn't give up hope.

I woke up an hour later and lay in bed watching the ceiling, planning. I had to come through for Faith. It might be my only way to win her back.

I showered, put on slacks and a button-up, then headed to Sloan-Kettering. Not so long ago, one phone call, from my secretary no less, would've had this taken care of. But those days were over. I had my freedom, but my mistakes cost me dearly. I had my family back, save one. And she was the most important.

Dr. Sinclair's office was modest considering his reputation. The carpet was stained, the waiting room small, the magazines months old. A TV was mounted in the corner, its picture fuzzy and its screen *not* flat.

Sitting well below the fairly high Plexiglas window was a large woman in bright-blue scrubs. Her hair was slicked back in a tight ponytail with a blue streak in it and her makeup consisted only of bloodred lipstick. Without looking up, she slid the window open and continued typing as she asked, "Your name?"

"I wanted to see about getting my father-in-law in to see Dr. Sinclair."

"You got an appointment?"

"No. I wanted to come in person and—"

"Your name?" She grabbed a sticky pad and plucked the pencil from behind her ear.

"Luke." My last name wouldn't come out.

"Skywalker or what?"

"It's terribly urgent that I get my father-in-law in."

She eyeballed me. "Well, I'm Darth Vader, so unless you can unleash the Force or a last name, it ain't gonna happen."

"Carraday. Luke Carraday."

"Carraday . . ." She stood, looked me up and down, put her hands on her hips. "And which brother are you?"

"The one who runs." I kept my stare squared on hers.

"How'd those handcuffs feel?"

"Makes me appreciate my freedom even more. I was given immunity yesterday."

"Whoopty do." She sat back down. "That's what's wrong with this country. Money buys you out of your worst sins, doesn't it?"

"As a matter of fact, I didn't—"

"'Course you didn't." She slid the window shut.

"Wait! Please! If I could just talk to Dr. Sinclair, I could—"

"Explain this is a life-and-death situation?" Her voice was muffled through the glass. "You and hundreds—and I mean *hundreds*—of other people." She turned back to her computer. "Sorry. Money's not buying you in this time."

"I'm not asking . . . I just need to . . ." But the phone rang, she snatched it up, and I found myself backing out of the tiny room. I stood in the empty hallway. I'd failed Faith. Again.

My phone vibrated with a text. From Faith. Any luck?

49

FAITH

I AM UNCERTAIN how old I was. Small, maybe five or six. But I remember her distinctly. She wore a white eyelet dress and dusty flip-flops. She'd been mopping the floor the last I knew, and we'd been sent to our rooms to play quietly until she was done.

I'd snuck back, probably because I heard her singing. I peeked around the frame of the door, one half of my face showing, my cheek smooshed against the wood. She was twirling around the floor, the wet mop her dance partner, belting out a song I didn't recognize from church. Later I would know it . . . "I Feel Pretty" from *West Side Story*. That day, it was just a song, but it entranced me. She entranced me.

Her long, fluid limbs, her ballerina body, twirled and twisted, weightless like a tumbleweed. I wondered who she sang it to. But I remember realizing that my momma had dreams like me. I'd run in the pasture and dream I was somewhere far away. Daddy would let me ride Lady or Silver and I'd pretend to be a cowboy. There she was, far away, dreaming.

"Mommas have dreams too," I explained to Olivia when I told her what I'd witnessed.

"What in the world would a momma be dreaming about?" she asked.

I didn't know exactly then. But I knew it was something special because she never saw me standing there.

I glanced at Dad. He was comfortable in our budget seats, taking in the show, the music. He had that glow to his skin. It usually surfaced when he talked about good memories.

I remembered later, as a teenager, singing "I Feel Pretty" as Essie Mae played the piano and Momma stood nearby, beaming like light reflecting off the tin roof of the shed. As I sang it, I felt a sense of empowerment. The words bubbled up in me, refusing to stay put. I felt like Momma felt. I knew the power of music. And as I suspected, it had been with me as long as I could remember. It would be with me far along in my life too.

Early in my marriage to Luke, maybe six months into it or so, he found me in the kitchen, singing this same song. His cheek was pressed against the doorframe. He was grinning, almost laughing. I stopped midnote when I saw him.

"Why'd you stop?"

"You're standing there watching me!"

"Why don't you sing more? Your voice is beautiful."

"My mom loved that song. It's from *West Side Story*."

"I know. I've seen the show half a dozen times."

"I wish you could have met her," I said, walking into his embrace.

"I have. I see her every day."

That was how Luke was. He always knew how much I loved her. He held me when I cried and never asked me to get over it or move on. He just knew.

He twirled me back into the kitchen. "Don't stop singing!" But I was giggling too much to carry a note.

The song was ending. Dad and I both stared forward, but I slid my hand into his. A tear slid down his face and I couldn't bear it, so I just closed my eyes, held his hand, and prayed. It was in the middle of a Broadway musical, with lights and show tunes and tight applause, that I got down on my knees. Not physically, but in my heart. I surrendered because what else could I do? Trust what this life was giving me? Everything that gave me happiness was temporary, and all that was rooted deeper could be pulled up. I felt myself less attached to this world. My feet felt lighter and the sky looked closer. I realized I was nothing more than a vapor in the wind, no more than a blade of grass that withers under the sun. I could do nothing to save my mom. Or my dad. Or my marriage.

I was weak.

But I knew there was one who was strong. I knew nothing

was in my life that hadn't passed through His hand first. So for the first time in my life, I truly trusted the God that my momma told me would never leave me alone.

50

LUKE

I WAS NOT entirely sure if I was drinking out of the joy of immunity or the sorrow over Faith or the frustration over my inability to help her father. Nevertheless, I was drinking and thankful for it. My stomach had been hurting and my head pounding for over twenty-four hours, with a short reprieve when Dad took us out to the lounge.

I didn't really know why I was free. Or how. Didn't know if my name would ever mean anything good in this town again. Didn't know if Faith planned on talking to me beyond her father's need for help. Didn't know if I could do something as simple as get the attention of a doctor.

"Gotta feel good, huh, kiddo?" Jake said, punching me in the arm as we both slumped over our drinks at the bar.

My phone lit up. Another text from Faith. Anything to report?

"Told you it was taken care of," Jake said, squeezing my shoulder a little too hard. He slapped me on the back and grinned sloppily.

I nodded, but I was staring at my phone, wondering how to reply.

"Yesterday you were peeing the floor over the thought of going to prison. You get immunity and you're acting like you got the death penalty."

I glanced up. "Sorry."

"What's going on?"

There's something about brothers where the harder you try to hide something, the more they seem to know. As much as I tried not to press my lips together and look away and tighten the grip on my glass, I did all those things and then flagged down the bartender.

"Faith." It sounded so heavy coming off his tongue that it seemed to fall to the bar and make a *thud*.

I let the bartender refill my bourbon and Coke before I said, "She's back in town."

"Of course she is. You're off the hook."

"It's not like that."

But Jake was already seething. His nostrils flared with every breath. He stirred a drink that was already thoroughly stirred.

"Her dad's got brain cancer."

Jake dropped the stirrer back into his glass and looked at me.

"She asked me to get him into Sloan-Kettering. I called Sinclair, but . . . I'm not exactly a guy people want to do favors for, you know?"

"Oh my gosh! *Luke?*"

Jake and I turned at a voice that was both familiar and alarming. It's just instinct, but when *oh my gosh* is followed by my name in a tone that can shatter glass, I pretty much know there is trouble to come.

Maria. Dressed as desperate as ever. I was hoping for a polite handshake, but she went in for the big squeeze anyway. A long squeeze. I wasn't sure where to put my hands. With that kind of top, it all seemed inappropriate. I finally settled on her bare shoulders.

"How are things going?" she asked, her voice high and frenzied, as if life were the same as before. As if I could answer that question simply, like usual.

The awkward silence was filled by Jake. "Fantastic," he said, jumping in as though trying to save the mood before I could torpedo it. "Luke is officially a free man tonight!"

Oh, boy. Leave it to Jake to drunkenly double entendre the situation. Maria was wide-eyed, but it was hard to tell why.

"From jail, he means." I tried a definitive smile but ended it with a sheepish sip of my drink.

Jake's hand shot out from his side. Maria slid hers into his. "I'm Luke's brother, Jake."

"Jake, Maria. Maria, my brother, Jake."

As luck wouldn't have it, the barstool next to me opened up and Maria pounced on it like it was a free diamond bracelet. I leaned back, figuring the conversation was going to continue with or without me.

"So," she said, "this is a party night, huh, boys?"

"Without a doubt," Jake said. "Whatcha drinkin', Maria?"

"Alamo Splash."

"Good for you. I like a woman who can hold her tequila."

"Too bad Candace isn't here. Jake's wife. For you to meet."

But my words might as well have been mixed right into the drinks. They continued to chat as I took my phone out and texted Faith. Not yet.

I was pretty sure that I should've just said "never." Except that was too painful to even consider.

The next thing I knew, hours had passed and Jake and I were playing some stupid ESP trick on Maria, who was either dumb as a brick or playing along. Or both.

"No way!" she screeched as we pretended that I knew he was thinking of Napoleon Bonaparte. We'd had our fun with it over the years, using taps and snaps and all sorts of other subtle signals. It'd actually become quite a good little art form, appreciated only by those totally wasted out of their minds. "How did you do that?"

"I'm telling you, it's ESP. Brother-to-brother ESP."

They roared with laughter, but I felt a tug to leave. "Guys, I gotta go."

Jake eyed me and set down his drink. "He's gotta go. *I'm*

the one who's gotta go because I actually have a wife and kids at home."

"Ouch."

"It's a gift," he said with a mischievous grin and a slap on the arm.

Even with the slight, I still felt the urge to hug him. "Thank you."

And he knew I meant it. "We're family. Nothing's more important." He turned to Maria. "Maria, it was a pleasure. See you around."

We watched as he wove his way through the skinny bodies on the dance floor. Outside, I saw him duck into a cab, already back on his phone.

"I wish I was psychic," Maria said, her finger tracing the edge of her martini glass.

"Why's that?" "'Cause I would love to read your mind."

"No, you wouldn't."

"Seriously, I would. I mean, I used to talk with Faith about you all the time. How she could never figure out what you were thinking. I know I never could . . ." She moved her drink aside and fully faced me. "What's going on? Are you guys talking?"

"No."

"Is that your idea or hers?"

I ordered another drink.

51

FAITH

"My daddy actually likes show tunes." I smiled at him as we walked, my arm through his, along the thinning streets of Midtown. I watched him as he gazed up at the lights. He seemed to be enjoying himself.

"You know what? I do." He pointed down the street. "*But* I still want a pretzel and a beer." And he picked up the pace. I hadn't seen Dad walk that fast in a while. He took a wad of cash out of his pocket. "You look like you can help me with the pretzel," he said to the vendor. "What's it going to be around here? A hundred bucks?"

"Daddy . . . ," I said, swatting him. My phone sounded and I prayed it was Luke, except my stomach rolled a little bit at the thought of actually talking to him. Didn't matter. "It's Olivia," I told Dad.

"Tell her I'm dead—see what she does."

While Dad purchased his pretzel, I stepped away and answered. "Hello?"

"Hi, it's me."

"Hey."

"I wanted to say . . . I'm sorry. I'm sorry I doubted you. I know you're only trying to help him."

"It's okay," I said as I watched Dad put extra salt on his pretzel.

"Daddy sleeping?"

"No . . . just enjoying himself here."

"It sounds loud."

"We're fine. He's been tired but holding up okay." He didn't look tired as he stuffed his face with the pretzel. He looked full of life. And joy. "He wanted to see a show."

"A show? What kind of show?"

"*West Side Story*."

"The play?"

"Musical, yes."

"I think the brain tumor is showing itself in weird ways."

I laughed. "Maybe." Dad was chatting it up with a cab driver now.

"I have good news."

"You do?"

"Sloan-Kettering hospital just called the house. They can see Daddy. At noon tomorrow."

"What?"

"I know. I just went by the house to feed Silver and check on things and noticed his answering machine light was blinking."

My head was spinning with hope. How could that man over there be so sick? He looked perfectly fine. But inside, the urgency wouldn't go away.

"Looks like your Yankee boy came through after all."

I took in a deep breath and smiled. I knew he would. I knew it. "I'll call you tomorrow, okay?"

"Please. As soon as you know anything."

"I will. I promise."

I walked to Dad, who had already finished his pretzel. "I think I'll have another one of those."

"You're eating like you're dying," I said with a smirk.

"Exactly! How about a hot dog?"

"How about we get you some rest before you actually kill yourself with a heart attack."

"Come on . . . you take me to the big city and I don't get to have any fun?"

"You've had plenty of fun. The hospital called. Left a message. We have an appointment tomorrow."

Dad looked surprised. "What do you know."

"I know we need to get back to the hotel room."

"You're such a killjoy."

"I'll take that as a compliment."

"It's not."

I smiled and hailed a cab. "I know."

The short drive back was spent with Dad mostly lamenting that I wouldn't let him have a hot dog. Funny how you can be dying and can even lose sight of that. But once we got back to the hotel, he'd settled down a bit, and I could tell his strength was draining fast. He tugged at each shoe like it weighed more than his leg, and then he fell back onto the bed as if he'd just spent the day baling hay.

I walked over and adjusted the pillow for him. He folded his hands over his belly like he always did when he took a nap. "Let's get you ready for bed," I said, but he waved me off with a mumble, something about not needing pajamas. It broke my heart. He was too tired to change. Maybe the show was too much. "You've had a big night. Tomorrow's even bigger."

I sat down on the bed and stared at his face, sunken more than usual. Lines crisscrossed his cheeks like the fork marks on a peanut butter cookie. His breathing slowed and I found myself watching each breath, counting out the seconds between them.

Then Dad's eyes popped open and cut to me. "Stop it. You're acting like Olivia."

"Yes, well, Olivia's done a good job of keeping you alive and well, so maybe I need to be more like her."

Dad rolled his eyes.

"And since you were only faking being asleep, let's get another pill down you," I said as I held it out in my hand. I picked up the glass of water with my other. And punctuated it all with a bright smile.

"Oh, brother," he groaned. He sat up a little and took the pill, then lay back down. "That was a good thing he did."

"What?"

"Luke. Kind of thing a man does when he loves somebody."

"What's that supposed to mean? One phone call on our behalf and he's off the hook?"

But Dad only chuckled, then closed his eyes again.

"Not so fast. You can't say something like that and then fall asleep."

Dad opened one eye and looked at me.

"So he gets you into a fancy hospital and you want me to run over there and forgive him for lying to me?"

"No. But I do think you should talk to him."

"And say what, exactly?"

"That's between you and your husband."

"I can't leave you here."

Dad smiled. "Baby, I may have a brain tumor, but I ain't gonna die tonight."

And before I knew it, he was asleep. For real this time.

I went to the closet and found a blanket to cover Dad up with. At least he'd managed to take off his tie.

I knelt by his bed and put my hands on his arm. He didn't even move. Bowing my head, I cried out a prayer, mostly in my head. I don't know how long I prayed. I don't even know when I stopped. But I could not imagine losing this gentle man, not after how he loved me and took me back. He was everything a girl could hope for in a father.

"I know You can save him," I said, over and over and over, until I believed it. And then, all at once, I found myself praying for Luke.

52

OLIVIA

I HUNG UP the phone with Faith and fluffed my hair. It was a nervous habit I'd acquired before doing anything uncomfortable. And this counted for more than uncomfortable. I would've never believed I could do this. Would do this. But here I was, with my suitcase between my knees. I called Hardy, holding the cell phone close to my ear. It was hard to hear at the airport.

"You okay?" Hardy asked.

"I guess so."

"Having second thoughts?"

"I don't know."

"It's okay. You don't have to go."

"Why am I going?"

Hardy knew rhetorical when he heard it.

"I mean, don't I trust her? Don't I trust him? Of course I do. But I should be there. It should be the three of us together. Making the decisions about what kind of treatment Daddy's going to get. Right?"

"Can't go wrong with another opinion."

"If I didn't trust Faith, I would've stood in front of her car and made her run me down when she told me she was taking him to New York. But I did no such thing." I slumped. "I just can't lose him, Hardy. I can't. He's my daddy." My throat strained hard to keep my emotions all tidy. "What if the girls lost you? You're their daddy. You can't go. You can't leave them. And he can't leave me either. He just can't." I drew in an overly deep breath, the kind that makes you cough out the extra air. "So. I am going, just as an adviser. Just to make sure we're all hearing the same thing, because you know how doctors can talk, all gibberishly."

"You're there for support. That's what you told me. And you know they'd both appreciate support."

I sighed. "Hardy, we both know that I've never been able to support a thing in my life. I'm loud and bossy and I always take over because nobody can do nothin' right. I am fooling myself if I think I can."

Hardy went back to listening.

"I love my sister. As much as I hate to admit that she's affected my life like that, it's true. I don't want to run her off or upset her. I can't be having her estranged from us for another decade."

I imagined Hardy was on the front porch, looking out into the dark sky, chewing on a dead blade of grass that he must've plucked from beside our concrete porch steps. "Liv, you don't give yourself enough credit."

"I think, Hardy, that I give myself too much credit."

"Now just shush and listen. You know what is good and true and right, and you've always stood for those things. You've allowed your sister back in your life, even though it was hard and you were hurt. And now here you are, willing to travel all the way to hell, just to help two people that mean the world to ya."

"I'm going to get murdered in New York, aren't I?"

"Like I said, just don't make eye contact with anybody."

"I know this sounds kooky, but I kind of feel drawn there. I don't know if it's for selfish reasons or not, but there's not too much that'd make me go to a place like New York."

They called my flight to board over the loudspeaker. "Guess I better get on with it."

"You're sure you don't want to call, let 'em know you're coming?" Hardy asked.

"Don't want anybody derailing my plans. Besides, Faith's gonna think I don't trust her."

"Can't imagine why . . . since you don't trust her enough to tell her you're coming."

"I gotta do things the way I gotta do them."

"You always do," Hardy said. "That's what I love about you. You got all your directions?"

"Everything you printed off the computer, I guess. Directions to the hotel. To the doctor. All that."

"You're sure you shouldn't call?"

I looked straight toward the lovely young lady taking tickets. I was certain. Nobody liked surprises, I knew. But then again, sometimes you just gotta invite yourself to the party.

53

LUKE

I WASN'T SURE how many drinks I'd had. Enough to keep me glued to my seat talking to Trouble, yet not so many as to not see I was dancing in the dark with the devil. Maria exuded everything a man wanted in a woman . . . on the outside. She knew it, and she knew how to roll her shoulders in just the right way . . . how to play coy, protective, innocent . . . whatever mask she wanted.

And she always smelled good. And her hair, it liked to flop across her eye. She'd give it a gentle shove out of the way. It was glossy, like plastic. And that wasn't the only plastic she was using to her advantage, either.

"Look, I love Faith," she said, talking with her hands.

I followed her fingers, which seemed to keep pointing me in the exact direction I shouldn't be looking. "You know that. I miss her. But she just left, Luke. I mean, don't you think she owed it to you to talk it out?" Her eyelashes batted, waiting for an answer. Her mouth formed a tiny little O, pursed, waiting for an answer.

I leaned back, tearing myself out of her vortex. "I'm the one who lied to her."

"You were protecting her!"

I took a long look at Maria. Her face was lit up with the exclamation. But her eyes were saying something much different.

"I've really got to get going," I said. I pushed a fifty to the bartender.

"Oh, wow . . . me too," she said, quickly glancing at her watch. Not one to be left in an awkward position, Maria followed me out of the bar, one hand touching my arm as we made our way toward the door.

But it felt a little like slow motion, and I decided I better get a cab. I whistled as Maria stepped up beside me.

"Drop me off in Murray Hill?"

Ugh. I really hoped I hadn't said it out loud, but by the sour look suddenly emerging on Maria's face, I might've. "Sure," I sighed.

Inside the cab, it was relatively quiet. I stared out the window, and Maria stared at me, and that took the entire seven-minute cab ride. It pulled in front of an apartment building, trendy but older.

Maria's hand slid from my shoulder down to my forearm. "Thanks for the ride." She started to take money out of her purse, even though she knew good and well I'd never let her pay.

"I got it."

"You're sure?" Surprised eyes.

"Yeah."

"It was so great to see you."

"You, too."

"Good night, Luke . . . and, um, if you need to talk, call me. You know where I am." She said it like she was out of breath . . . or wanted to be.

"Thanks."

She opened the cab door, kicking her long, bare legs out first, then slowly standing. She shut the door and the driver waited for her to walk in front, even though the back would've been faster.

And we were off.

The cab was just pulling up my street when something shiny on the seat beside me caught my eye. When the next streetlamp's light passed through the window, I realized it was Maria's sequined purse.

"Oh . . . great." I sighed and pulled out my phone, working my way through my contacts to find her, wondering how evil her plotting was. Before I could think much further about it, her purse vibrated, then started in with some techno-dance song.

Part of me wanted to just leave the purse there, pretend

I didn't see it, but I knew that could open her up to all kinds of problems. And I couldn't pretend I hadn't been blessed by somebody's good graces myself. So I paid the cabbie and took the purse as begrudgingly as when Faith used to make me hold hers in public. I tucked it under my arm and looked up at the dark, fifth-story window of my home. The empty sidewalk seemed warmer than what I'd find when I opened the door to my apartment.

But I didn't have any other options.

Well, that wasn't completely true. I stared at the purse. I could just run it back to her . . . just . . . talk . . .

I took a breath—a gasp, really. It was getting to me. It was all getting to me. How could I even conceive of doing that to Faith? I hurried to my apartment, took the elevator, and let myself in. I closed the door, locked it, turned my back against it. Caught my breath. I'd leave the purse with the doorman tomorrow and hopefully never see Maria again.

I didn't want to think about Maria anyway. I wanted to think about how to face Faith. Or how to even get near her. Was it possible to feel like a bigger failure? I'd messed up everything between us and still couldn't even do a simple favor for her.

I plopped down in my usual chair these days, the one that I stared out into space from, and wondered how badly I'd damaged the family name. When I couldn't even summon a return phone call from a man I'd known since I was a teenager, things were looking pretty grim.

From my chair I could see the dimly twinkling lights of

the city. Before, I'd gaze at them and see all the possibilities the city had to offer. Now they just reminded me that my light had gone out.

I had to face the idea that my marriage was probably over. Even managing to get out of my predicament couldn't change the circumstances in which I found myself. I rose and walked to the window, gazing out at skyscrapers that many men had jumped from. Before, I couldn't conceive of what would drive a man to fall to his own death. Then I wondered what might stop a man who had nothing left. Now I had . . . hope.

I decided to write Faith a letter. I figured she wouldn't take a phone call from me. Besides, there was a lot I needed to say and it couldn't be said in the middle of a heated argument, which I guessed ours would turn into.

It took me a while to find stationery. I guess we just don't write letters much these days. I found some in the top of the closet, a boxed set my dad had given me when I'd decided to leave his company and go out on my "new venture." I hadn't appreciated it back then like I should have. It was a gesture from Dad that I didn't see because of my own blind ambitions.

Sitting at a desk we'd had imported from Spain, I stared at the blank sheet of paper. It kind of reminded me of a fresh start. Lots of possibilities. If only life were that simple.

Dear Faith, I wrote in my best penmanship. I'd always had nice handwriting, to the point that I had to scratch it up a bit in high school to keep the taunts away. *I am sorry. More than you'll ever know.*

How could I express in words what I was feeling, what I would give to have her back? I'd give all of this up. Every cent of what I had left, anyway. But I was afraid to say it, afraid she'd think I thought it was about the money I'd lost, and it wasn't. Maybe it used to be, but walking through the fire can scorch off a lot of excess.

After a few more moments of staring at ten words, I dropped the pen to the desk and returned to my chair, where I turned on the TV only to find myself standing on the courthouse stairs, my face distorted by the wide-screen TV effect. Behind me, towering though he wasn't much taller, was my father, Austin Stanford Carraday. Had he aged? How had I not noticed him hunching more? Squinting more? They cut to a closer picture of us, and I noticed his eyes shimmering with emotion I hadn't caught before. And his hand was on my shoulder, too. I suspected it had been there all along, but I chose not to feel it. I didn't unmute the TV. I didn't really want to know what they were saying anyway. I just watched the two of us, and my mind drifted to the time when he was strong enough to pick me up and toss me into the sky, as if I weighed nothing. I thought he hung the moon. There stood the man I thought took everything from me, but the truth was he'd already given me the world.

There was a knock at the door suddenly, jolting me from the quiet habitat of regret I'd created for myself.

God, please! That same feeling of relief, freedom, pure joy that I felt at the courthouse shot me straight out of my chair. I stumbled into an end table and knocked over a vase rushing toward the door. I am not sure why I thought she wouldn't give me two seconds to open the door, but just in case, I killed myself getting there. Lunging for the knob, I yanked it open, startling the woman on the other side.

Maria.

"I am *such* an idiot," she said, rolling her eyes and shrugging her shoulders while managing to look not the least bit regretful.

"Your purse."

"Bingo."

I waved her in and walked to the kitchen counter to retrieve it.

"I always loved this place, Luke."

"It'll probably be up for sale soon. Wanna buy it?"

"In a second. Just need some money."

I held the purse out to her, stretching my arm a little further so I didn't have to step closer.

"Thanks." But she set it right down on the arm of the couch. She gazed about, like it was a starry night or something. "It still feels like a home."

"I haven't changed anything."

"Still have that silly old painting, don't you?"

We both stared at it for a moment, resting awkwardly against the fireplace.

Then, "Luke, do you remember the night you met Faith and me?"

"Sure."

"I wanted you to talk to me, but you chose her."

She stepped closer. Caught my eye. Lowered her tone to a whisper. "Here's your second chance."

There's a lot that goes through the mind of a guy when he's being tempted. Through the fog of her perfume, I wondered if I could actually be alone. If Faith and I never got back together, could I do it? Would I want to? Would I be too much of a train wreck for anyone else to love?

I looked at Maria. She had this intensity about her, a wild-animal-stare kind of intensity. You weren't sure if you were interesting or about to be eaten.

But all I could see was Faith. That's all I wanted to see. At that moment, when I pretty much wished Maria would just eat me alive, I knew there would never be anyone but Faith.

I put my hand between us. "It's time for you to go home."

And it was just as I said it that a key rattled in the front door. Before I could really identify the sound and believe it was what I was hearing, the door swung open and there stood Faith, staring at the most awkward and regretful moment of my life.

"Faith?" I gasped, and the gasp wasn't for the fact that I was engaged in something I shouldn't be, but because I was so surprised to see her. I think I elbowed Maria out of the way as I walked to the door.

She said nothing. She didn't have to. Her face told the whole story . . . at least the story she thought she was seeing. Before I could reach her, she closed the door. I ran out to the hallway, but she'd taken the stairs. I followed after her, down the concrete, echoing stairwell, calling her name.

I didn't catch up to her until we got to the street.

"Faith, wait! Please!" I said as we reached the sidewalk.

Finally she turned. In the four years we'd been married, I'd never seen that expression on her face, and it shocked me. Disdain. But in her eyes, there was a sorrow that I could barely look at. And that sorrow made me realize she hadn't shut me out yet. I reached for her arm, then thought better of it.

"Let's not have this moment," she said, breathing harder than she should've been. I knew adrenaline was shooting through her, that fight-or-flight mechanism kicking in like her life was at stake. I knew it was. *Our* lives.

"There is nothing there!" My voice was shrill, panicked, my fists clenched as I gestured toward the apartment. "Go ask her. I swear, nothing is happening. Nothing happened."

She stood perfectly still, her nostrils flaring, her voice growling and low. "I am not asking her anything. Ever."

That had been a mistake. Of course I shouldn't have told her that. But there was a desperation inside me that seized any sense of self-control, any sense of self-respect. I was not far from dropping to my knees. She turned suddenly, walked with an assuredness that told me she had no intention of turning back.

"I wasn't with her! I'm not with her!"

I chased after her, grabbed her arm this time. Faith swung around, yanking it back. She took a few steps, gazing into my eyes like she was hoping to find some humanity there. "Thank you," she said quietly, "for helping my father."

Her fingers rose, hailing a cab.

"Wait . . . what?"

"Thanks for getting him in."

"But . . . Faith, I didn't . . ."

The cab arrived and she opened the door, giving me a long look. "Then never mind. Good-bye, Luke."

She disappeared and the cab sped off as if it knew she was fleeing.

"I'm sorry . . ."

I whipped around. Maria stood there with her purse tucked under her arm, shaking her head like she'd just witnessed a car wreck.

"No, you're not." I stormed past her.

She reached for me. "Luke, I—"

"Get away from me. Leave. Now."

54

OLIVIA

I EXPECTED TO BE OVERWHELMED the moment I stepped off the plane. The plane ride alone was an experiment in the steadiness of my nerves. But the airport was easy to navigate, and the cab even easier to find.

Before I knew it, a polite young man named Ahab was welcoming me to the city. "I can tell, your first time, no?"

"Yes."

"Welcome to the greatest city on earth!" Ahab said cheerily.

"Well, you haven't been to Columbus County, North Carolina, but . . ." I gazed through the windshield of the car at the wattage. A lot of wattage. All the buildings twinkled against the dark sky. "I think you're probably right. We don't have skyscrapers."

"Or Broadway," he said with a side grin.

"Nothing wrong with open fields and fresh air," I said, but not boldly enough to withstand Ahab's obvious love for this city. "This is pretty spectacular." I handed him the address to the hotel Faith said they were staying in.

"Here for business or pleasure?"

"Neither." Now Ahab was getting a little too chatty.

"Whatever the case, I hope you enjoy your stay."

"Ahab, you're nice enough. Well worth the tip I know you're expecting."

"What can I say? I like to meet new people."

"I'm more the kind to keep to myself, but I guess I am in New York. Not a good place to come if you can't tolerate people."

"What is your name?"

"Olivia."

"Well, Ms. Olivia, I think you'll find our town friendly enough to your liking."

I sat back, gazed out the window, and let the city take me in. I tried to imagine what Faith's life was like here. Rich socialite. Hard to grasp. But I had to admit, I might like it for a season. Wouldn't give up the farm, the girls, Hardy, for anything, but I could play here for a little while.

The traffic alone was a shock. But the horns and the hums of the cars fell into a rhythmic sync, like all the instruments of an orchestra tuning themselves at the same time.

The cab was quiet except for Ahab humming something softly.

"Ahab, thank you for your kind welcome to the city."

"You're most welcome, Ms. Olivia."

"I'm here because my daddy has cancer, and we're seeing a specialist."

"Oh, I am so sorry to hear that. I will say a prayer for him," Ahab said, and I believed that he would.

In an hour's time, Ahab was pulling to the front of the Holiday Inn. He hopped out and hurriedly opened the door for me. I handed him cash, told him to keep the change, and waited for him to get my suitcase.

My first and only friend in New York City. Ahab. I thanked God for the kind man he sent to drive me here. Now I had to find the room.

I was just pulling up the handle of my suitcase when another cab arrived. I got out of the way and was still trying to figure out why my handle was stuck when I heard, "Olivia?"

I looked up to find Faith walking toward me. "Faith!" I was relieved but caught off guard. As was she. Her eyes were wide. She wasn't smiling. "I can explain," I said hastily. "It's not that I don't trust you, Faith. You have to know that. I just wanted to be here, with you both, and hear what the doc—"

Her arms shot out; she grabbed me by the shoulders, pulled me into a tight hug, and whispered, "I'm so glad you're here."

Then she burst into tears.

I got her calmed down and we walked down the street to an IHOP. I had something that said "fruit" and "whole wheat" but tasted like dessert. Faith only had coffee. She looked even thinner now that I hadn't seen her in a couple of days. Her eyes were bloodshot and I knew she'd been crying.

"I caught him with Maria . . . my best friend."

I lost my appetite right along with her. I set my fork down. "Tonight?"

She nodded. "Dad urged me to go over, try to make some peace. He said any guy that would go to the trouble to help his father-in-law, like Luke did, was worth at least a conversation." A tear dribbled down her cheek. The waitress was refilling her cup and noticed, but I gave the gal a move-it-along look. "I walked right into our home and there he was in the living room with her."

"Naked?" I gasped loudly. Too loudly. An elderly couple turned. I guess *naked* shouted in the middle of a pancake joint is weird even in New York.

"Shhh!" Faith said. "No, not naked."

"Kissing?"

"No."

"Hands not where they belong?"

"No, no. They were just standing there. But you should've seen the look on Luke's face. Guilt, Liv. Total and complete guilt."

"What'd he say?"

"That it was nothing, of course." Faith sniffled. "All these years, I knew Maria had a thing for Luke. I never fully trusted her, and I hated it because I thought I was just being paranoid." She looked up at me as she blotted her eyes. "You know, I always measured everyone against you."

"What do you mean?"

"When I'd meet somebody. A potential friend. I always judged them in regard to how they treated me. I guess all those years I was in New York, I was looking for a sister."

A lump stung my throat—a big, juicy one that got me all teared up. "Faith, I should've never . . . let so much time pass. I'm sorry."

"I'm the one that ran."

"But I know I made it hard to come home." I took my spoon, scooped some whipped cream off my pancakes, and offered it to her. "Pure whipped sugar?"

"Yes." She smiled and put the whole thing in her mouth. "Gwood."

"I know."

"I kind of want to rub it all over my face."

"Weird by even New York standards."

We laughed. But her smile didn't last too long.

"I miss Momma."

"I know you do, sweetheart."

"It's like our life was this beautiful story and her character just disappeared right in the middle of it. Just gone."

"Faith, the thing that lets me get up each morning without my heart falling into a million tiny pieces is that I know we will see her again. Momma had made her peace with God long before the accident. She gave everything over to Him, including how long she was supposed to be on this earth."

"It haunts me," Faith said, staring into her coffee. "That it can all be gone instantly."

"Not gone. Just temporarily removed. God promises that one day all of our tears will be wiped away. Until then, we dig our way through this mess with our hands."

"I have to confess something."

"What is it?"

"I believe Luke."

"Believe him?"

"About Maria. I could see it in his eyes."

"Why didn't you tell him?"

"Because that would mean I'd have to forgive him for lying to me. For destroying all we had."

"Sometimes 'all we had' is not close to 'all that could be.' Sometimes you have to lose the thing you think is perfect to see the better thing on the other side."

"You think we can be saved?"

"I think it's no mistake you're back in New York."

"We never fit into his family either. They never accepted I really did love him." She stirred her coffee like she'd just poured something in it.

"I'm never going to fit back into my jeans if I eat this by myself. Come on, help me out," I said, handing her a fork. She didn't even hesitate. I wondered when she'd eaten last.

We finished pretty fast and walked back to the hotel. "Let me get a room," I said as we approached the front desk.

"Don't be silly. Two king-size beds in there. Come on, there's plenty of room."

"Dad's going to freak out when he sees me."

"He's asleep. And as much as he complains about you mothering him, I promise that he couldn't live without you." She put her arm around me. "Neither can I."

There's not too much that can make this old farm girl cry more than once in the same month, but that theory was being tested pretty severely.

We got to the room. Dad didn't even rustle as we entered. "Get in your jammies. We'll find a late-night movie," Faith said, and I swear I was transported to the age of ten.

The last thing I remembered was giggling.

55

LUKE

I FELL ASLEEP at ten after five, and my alarm rang at six, blaring out that it was time to wake up and also that my life was as promising as a call from a debt collector. If it was possible to die of a hangover from life, I was in danger. I managed to sit up, get my feet on the floor, and trudge to the bathroom, where I had the unpleasant task of looking at myself.

"No wonder she left you," I groaned, my eyes swollen half-shut and the left side of my face as red as a blood orange. Except I knew it wasn't because I looked hideous. Faith was good, and good people love the heart, so I knew I had to dig deeper.

Sure, last night was a misunderstanding, but I had to take responsibility for it. I should've never let Maria into the apartment. I should've never had drinks with her. I should've never . . . the list was endless, wasn't it?

I'd tried to call Faith, over and over like a crazy person. I'd texted her. But I was only met with silence. And in the face of silence, I realized that I could only control so much in my life. I couldn't control her or what she thought of me. For many years, I'd controlled my universe, with quite a bit of ease if I was honest. It was what the Carradays did. We controlled. We were in control. We never lost control.

Right now all I knew for sure was that I had a giant mortgage to pay and a reputation to restore. And my father had offered me a way to do both. So I pulled on my favorite suit, a brown Louis Vuitton with a blue paisley tie. I brushed my teeth and combed my hair and tied my shoes. I took this for granted for so long . . . the act of going to work. The act of getting out of bed with something to look forward to. I'd fallen into a lot of things, including the grind.

As I drove to my new job, I wondered how Dad could even take me back. I'd brought shame to the family name, brought disgrace to my marriage, and to top it all off, had to have my brother and dad bail me out of my own mess, literally. I was the cautionary tale with the twist ending.

Except I hoped this wasn't the end. I couldn't give up on Faith. I had to keep fighting until there wasn't anything left in me. The problem was that I didn't have a game plan. I was at a loss as to what to do next.

At Carraday headquarters, I was surprised to find my parking spot still painted with *Reserved* along with a brown metal sign displaying my name. Surely this hadn't been there the whole time, since I left?

I took the elevator up to the seventieth floor. Observed the new TVs that had been installed in the elevator, tuned to CNBC, the stock market ticker tape rolling brightly across the bottom. The doors swished open and I stepped out gingerly, like the floor might fall out from underneath me . . . or the room might start to boo. I was hoping I could make it to Dad's office without being noticed.

Then I heard a pop. That'd be just like me, to get shot in my own dad's office by a disgruntled employee. I realized that I had indeed not been shot but greeted by Mona, who stood at her desk and clapped for me. My face flushed so badly that I was certain I was about to spontaneously combust. I was just about to give the cutoff sign to Mona when several other of Dad's inner circle employees stood and clapped.

"What are you clapping for?" I think I actually said it out loud. If I did, nobody heard me. I tried a gentle, amiable wave, but that didn't seem to calm it down. All I could do was walk forward, smile pleasantly, hope there wasn't a cake.

Finally it died down and I got to Dad's office. I rounded the corner and stepped in. He was at his desk. He rose with a wide, open smile and hurried to . . . hug me? Like bear-hug me. The kind that embarrasses you in front of the elementary school. I patted him on the back.

Then two hefty arms grabbed me from behind and I was

lifted off the ground. I didn't even have to turn around. I knew it was Jake.

"Wow," I said, out of breath from shock, among other things. "Thanks . . . I don't know why everyone is clapping."

"They're glad you're back!" Dad said. "So am I. Welcome home, Son."

More clapping. I thanked everyone, stepping out of Dad's office to give them a grateful smile. Closing Dad's door, I put my briefcase down and sat in one of his chairs. In fact, it was the same chair I'd sat in to tell Dad I wanted my money and I was leaving him.

"Dad . . ."

"I know—we have a lot to talk about. I've scheduled in an hour and a half to—"

"I can't . . . Don't give me a job, Dad."

"Of course I'm going to give you a job."

"I thought better of it—" Jake grinned—"but he wouldn't hear of it. He wants you back. So do I."

"That was a chapter. A painful chapter, sure. But it's over now. Time to start a new one," Dad said.

A rush of relief squeezed around me like another bear hug. I resisted a good tear-up by rubbing my hands together and switching subjects. "How did you get me that immunity deal?"

Dad had his reading glasses on now and he peered at me. "Don't ask questions like that, Son."

I looked at Jake, who I knew couldn't resist the inquiry. "We cut a deal with the SEC the minute you left our company and started with Michov."

"What?"

Dad dropped his glasses to his desk and looked resigned to explain. "We knew they were after Michov, and so we offered a few of our most trusted clients to pose as investors in exchange for your immunity. As long as you never invested anyone else's funds, the deal was in place."

I am certain my jaw dropped. I looked at Jake. "That's why you cut me off at the gallery that night."

Jake nodded. "That whale wasn't on the protected list."

Dad looked unsure that I was processing what they wanted me to understand . . . that even when I wandered off to do my own thing, they were watching over me. "We protected you, Son, because we love you."

I sat there, wondering how much control I ever really had in the world. But how much did I want? "You never really let me leave, did you?"

"I let you go where you wanted to go, but nothing passed to you that didn't first pass through me."

And I knew it to be true because even at my lowest moment, I always felt my dad's hand on my shoulder.

"Dad?"

"Yes?"

"Thank you."

Jake, who was leaning against the wall, walked forward, uncrossing his arms. "Okay, we better get this guy back to work before he turns into some sort of sad sack."

I nodded.

Dad said, "Jake, give us a minute, will you?"

Jake left and Dad stood, put his hands in his pockets, the way he did when he was about to dole out wise advice to me as a kid. "Where do you and Faith stand?"

"She won't take my calls. I've tried everything. I think she's done with me. I'll probably get served any day now."

To my surprise, Dad looked disappointed. Upset, even. "I'm sorry to hear that."

"You are?"

"I am. You and Faith are more alike than you realize. But she's got a good heart. I hope she finds forgiveness for you, Luke." Dad returned to his desk. "Your office is set up. Time to focus."

"Okay."

I walked out, turned right, and went to find my office. I assumed it was the far back one, near the utility closet. The one nobody wanted. The one I deserved. I walked past the corner office with its bright sky view and its spacious bookshelves. I glimpsed the name on the door. *Luke Carraday*.

How could this be? I nearly ruined the family name and I got a corner office? I reached up to touch the nameplate, to make sure it was real, when my phone rang.

It was Faith's number. I quickly answered. "Faith?"

56

FAITH

THERE ARE TIMES you just don't want to open your eyes. I'd been in a deep sleep, the kind that makes you feel like you've sunk into your mattress and it is protecting you from the outside world. And there is a moment between wakefulness and sleep that seems like perfect peace, like the way heaven must feel all the time.

My body felt weightless and my mind felt clear. My heart didn't ache.

Stay here.

I wondered if this was how Mom felt right before she died. If this was what beckoned her on to eternity, I would've gone too.

But it was quickly rattled away by a snore and then a snort from Olivia, who turned over and mumbled something about cake batter in her sleep.

I opened my eyes, stared at the ceiling, and all the heartache rushed back. My reality had returned. But I had my sister and my dad. There wasn't much more I could ask for.

I turned to look at him, but to my surprise, the bed was empty. Even made.

"What time is it?" Olivia asked, her voice groggy and two octaves lower.

I looked at the clock for the first time. "Good grief. It's nine!"

"I haven't slept till nine since before the girls were born," Olivia said as I rolled over to face her. "Did the beauty sleep do me any good?"

I laughed. "You don't need beauty sleep, my dear."

"Tell that to this old face." She rubbed her eyes. "They have continental breakfast here?"

"Until nine," I sighed. "But you didn't come all the way to New York for oatmeal and toast, did you? You need a bagel! Maybe we can talk Dad into it. He's been pretty gung ho on the local food."

"Where is Dad?" Olivia asked, rising up on one elbow.

I pointed to the bathroom door, which was closed. "Getting ready, I guess."

"I wondered if he even noticed I was here," Olivia said. "I can't believe he didn't wake up with all that chattering we did last night."

"We have until noon to get to the hospital. Time for a little sightseeing anyway," I said.

"You feel up to it?"

"Sure. I still love this city. It's not home, but it's interesting."

"Get our mind off of why we're here."

"Yeah." And I had to remind myself of the real reason we were here, and it wasn't to feed into some fantasy notion that Luke and I were meant to be together, against all odds. I had to find my own way to say good-bye to it all, but I wasn't sure how to do that. Right now, though, I had to focus on Dad.

"What's he doing in there?" Olivia asked. "I have to pee. The man doesn't have a lot of hair to comb."

I laughed. "Dad, hurry it up in there! You've got two girls that have to go potty!"

"Remember the time he didn't believe that you had to go and you went all over the tractor seat?"

"Oh yeah. He never made that mistake again. And I never made the mistake of drinking the whole pitcher of lemonade."

"You loved your lemonade!"

"Yes, I did." I sat up in bed. "Dad? You okay in there?"

No answer. We glanced nervously at each other and Olivia flung her legs to the side of the bed and got out. "He's going deaf, you know." She knocked on the door. "Daddy? You okay?"

We listened. Olivia's eyes grew wide as she glanced back at me.

"Dad?" She quickly opened the door.

I jumped out of bed, but Olivia walked out of the bathroom before I got there. "He's not there."

"He's not there?"

We both looked at the made bed. "Dad went out without us?" Olivia gasped. "In New York City?"

"Okay, let's calm down. At least we know he's okay. Let's just call his cell phone."

"Dad doesn't have a cell phone, Faith. He just got an answering machine four years ago."

"Wait . . . look—a note," I said, pointing to the table beside his bed.

Olivia rushed over like it might hop away. She snatched it up. "'Be back soon.'"

"'Be back soon'?"

"I'm going to kill him. He knows better than this."

"Where would he be going? To look around the city? Without us?"

"Maybe he wants to gorge on local cuisine."

I nodded. "That's highly likely, actually."

"So . . . what do we do?"

I smiled. "Let's enjoy ourselves."

57

LUKE

The last time I'd been to Battery Park was when I'd brought Faith there after we'd first met. As a lifelong New Yorker, I had fun taking her to the various hot spots and a few off-the-map ones too. Though she'd lived here for years, she'd mostly kept to the places that she was familiar with. She'd not ventured much south of Juilliard, so we spent many weekends touring Manhattan and other parts of New York.

From where I stood, I could see the exact tree we'd sat under, just three weeks into our relationship, where we'd had a five-hour conversation that seemed like thirty minutes.

I took a deep breath, trying to shake the image, wondering if every memory would have her attached in some way for the rest of my life. I scanned the crowd, looking for a red jacket.

There, near the ferry and tour boat docks. My hands shook, so I stuck them in my pockets and walked forward.

The man had a presence, I'd give him that. Even with his back turned.

"Calvin?"

He turned, his face pleasant, stoic. His eyes held a calmness betrayed only by the fierceness a father has for his child.

"Luke." He held out his hand, gave me a hearty shake.

"It's a pleasure to meet you." It was a heavy moment. I was stiff and awkward and making the kind of impression I hoped I wouldn't.

"You too," he said. A mild smile played over his lips, but his eyes scrutinized me. I let it be. A father should do that, I guessed. He relaxed a bit after sizing me up. "Thanks for coming here."

"Of course."

He looked out over the water. I watched him watch a boat for a moment. "Never been to the big city. Don't care for it much, but I guess it's okay to visit." He pointed. "Never been on one of those tourist boats there."

"You know what? Neither have I."

He turned to me, grinning like a little boy. "Then let's go."

He insisted he pay, and I wasn't sure what the custom should be. Being a Carraday, we usually paid for everything, but something told me I should let him, so I did. He pulled out a large, neat roll of cash and plucked two tens out. "I sure enjoy your food here," he said as we walked aboard.

We found a bench near the front. As we sat, I noticed it was difficult for him, like he knew the getting-up part was going to be harder.

I overestimated the conversation, I guess, because it really didn't start. Calvin was looking out over the water, seeming to enjoy the tour, as if he might've forgotten he called me and asked me to meet him here.

Apparently nobody told him that in New York, silence is practically a crime.

I cleared my throat. "When Faith and I were together, I used to think about having kids, and I'd always imagine having a little girl. And inevitably, I'd start thinking about her growing up to date guys and get married . . . and in the end, I'd work myself into a cold sweat with the fear that one day I'd be exactly where you are right now."

Calvin didn't even look at me. He seemed to be enjoying the peace of the water. "I didn't come here to grill you."

"I never touched another woman. Not last night. Or ever."

"We don't have to talk about that." He was looking at his shoes, and I realized, suddenly, that I might've said too much. Or maybe not enough. I wasn't sure, but Calvin was striking me as a man of few words.

I, however, had become the man who couldn't stop babbling. "And the whole time I was with Michov, I had no idea they were breaking the law." *Did he just smirk at me?* "I want you to know that." *Stop talking, for the love of all things manly.*

"You know something, Luke," Calvin began after a long

and uncomfortable stretch of silence that I was now certain was intentional, "I don't know you very well."

That's because I didn't get to keep spilling my guts like a moron.

"But as I sit here listening to you, I can't help but ask myself one question."

Now I was watching the water, kind of wishing I could drown myself because this guy had a way of looking right into my soul.

"If you're not responsible for anything, how can you be anything?"

I looked at him, forced myself to, and realized he wasn't raking me over the coals. That quiet calm that seemed to stir my soul like wind stirs leaves was intended for my good. I was pretty sure this guy was actually rooting for me. Could it be he was cheering me on, after all I'd put his daughter through?

I marveled at it and must've been staring awkwardly at him because his eyes darted back to the water, and I noticed his thumbs rubbing his knuckles like the skin might be dirty.

"There's something you should know," he said, and I braced myself because those words are hardly ever followed by good news. "I didn't come here for treatment on this cancer."

"What?"

"I've had a good run, son, and I'm not going to let them poison me so I can hang on for an extra month or two." He smiled. "I have someone waiting on me up there," he said, nodding toward the sky. "I miss her in a way that kept me unanchored to this earth for a very long time."

"Then . . . why are you here?"

"Because my daughter has a husband, and when I'm gone, she's going to need him."

"I want to be there."

He looked out toward the city, seemingly mulling his words like he wasn't quite explaining it right or maybe I was just not getting it.

"You and Faith, you're a couple of runners."

I started to nod but wondered how he knew we used to run together. Then it struck me . . . he wasn't talking about our athletic skills. He was talking about our propensity for hightailing it out of difficult situations.

"The two of you can't become a family yourselves if you're always running from the family you already have."

That stung, in all the right places. "I'm sorry I didn't go down to Carolina to meet you. I should've called you before we even got married."

He put a hand on my shoulder. "I'm not your family. Faith is."

"Just tell me where she is."

"That time is going to come. But before that, you need to figure out why the music stopped and make sure it keeps playing no matter what kind of noise your life brings in."

"I'm not sure I know what that means."

"I know. Just let me know when you do."

58

FAITH

"Hi, it's me."

I paced the sidewalk outside the hotel, clinging to myself as I turned away from the snapping north wind.

The surprise in his voice delighted me. "Hi . . . hey, how are you?"

"I've been better. Needed to hear your voice."

"How's your dad?"

"You wouldn't know he's sick. We're waiting for him to return from going out to the big city, I guess to do some sightseeing without the two of us."

Lee laughed. "Doesn't surprise me."

I weighed my words. And my motivation. Was I running

to Lee to get back at Luke? Was I comforted, expecting Lee to take good care of my dad when he returned?

Here was a man who sent me on to find answers for myself, without regard for himself or his feelings. If only Luke could've been that sensitive.

"You there?"

"I'm here . . ." I pushed the image of Luke and Maria out of my head. "I found the answers I was looking for."

"And?"

"It wasn't what I was hoping for, but life throws a lot of curveballs."

"Are you okay?"

"I've got to focus on getting Dad better."

"Don't forget about yourself."

I chuckled. "If I could just forget about myself, 90 percent of my problems would be solved." I tried not to shiver and wasn't sure it was even the wind. "When I get back there, Lee . . . it'll be for good. I'm staying."

He didn't say anything, I knew out of respect for my situation, but I could practically hear him smiling through the phone.

"Thanks for letting me work out what I needed to work out."

"Give yourself time to heal."

"Dad's brain and my heart. Throw in Olivia's gallbladder and we're a mess."

Lee cracked up. "Glad to see you haven't lost your sense of humor."

I glanced up to see an old man getting out of a cab, then realized it was my father. My heart dropped at the sight. The cab driver looked worried as he opened the door and grabbed his hand.

"Lee, can I call you later? My dad's back."

"Sure."

I hung up and hurried over. "Dad! What . . . how are . . . ?"

He waved me off as he glanced at the driver. "My daughter."

"Here, take my hand."

He grimaced, then scowled, then took my hand. I could feel his weight against me as we walked into the lobby. "Where have you been?" I asked.

"Took a ferry, saw the Statue of Liberty."

"Good grief, Dad. You had us worried sick."

"Didn't you get my note?"

"Kind of vague."

"Where's your sister?" He let go of my hand when we got in the elevator and rested against the glass that gave a view of the small restaurant below.

"Upstairs about to have a cow."

"Somehow I knew she'd show up."

"And I'm glad she did. You're a handful without the tumor. Your appointment is in less than an hour."

Dad nodded. Had I not seen how sick he looked before? The dark bags under his eyes. The red rims that held them up. The sunken cheeks and the shaky hands. The whole sight broke my heart.

The elevator opened and three squirrelly kids forgot their manners and bounded in. Dad grinned at them as he walked out, unassisted. He seemed to gain a bit of strength as we made our way back to the room.

Inside, Olivia paused midstride in what looked like vicious pacing. "Dad! Where have you been?" Her eyes were wide with wonder, her tone strained with concern.

Dad walked over to the chair by the bed and sat, looking utterly exhausted. "Girls, sit down with me."

"Dad, we've got to go. Your appointment—"

I cut Olivia off. "Let's let him rest for a few minutes."

"We can't be late for this. We barely got you in to see this doctor. The cab driver said it'd take about thirty minutes, *if* the traffic is good."

"Girls. Sit."

It was the tone he'd used since our birth to indicate we were to do what we were told. We both sat on the edge of the bed, our hands in our laps, our backs erect.

Dad took a long moment. Olivia was watching the clock, but I was watching Dad's eyes. I could tell something wasn't right.

Then he looked at us. "I'm going to break your hearts today."

Beside me, I felt Olivia hold her breath. I slid my hand under hers.

"Daddy, what are you talking about?" Olivia asked.

"I'm not going to get the treatment."

I looked at Olivia. Both our eyes watered. "But, Daddy,"

Olivia said, "we don't even know what the treatment is yet. That's why we're here, to see what—"

"That's not why I'm here," he said softly. He looked at me, then at Olivia, then at his hands. "I miss your momma."

I put a hand over my mouth to keep the sobs in, because there is nothing like seeing your own daddy weep. The tears streaming down his cheeks were like knives cutting through me.

"I know it must sound crazy to you. You're young, full of life, lots more life to live, but I'm okay with saying good-bye."

"Daddy, no . . ." Olivia had dropped to her knees, right by his feet. "No, you can't leave us."

"I can," he said, smiling through the tears. "The two of you will be okay. Now you have each other, and your families, and you're going to be just fine. Both of you." He looked squarely at me because he knew in my heart I was certain I would never be fine.

He took Olivia's cheek into his hand, and then I slid to the floor, by his knee, and wept, too. He pulled his fingers through our hair. "Hey, now, I'm not dead yet. I have a few good months left in me."

"It's not fair," Olivia said.

He smiled. "What? That I get to see Momma first?" His voice turned low and soothing. "I will always be with you, in your hearts. I promise. And we'll see each other again."

We laid our heads on his knees for a long time, and then Daddy, who always knew just what to say, lifted our heads. "Okay. Who's up for one of those greasy vendor hot dogs?"

I laughed but ached terribly. I remembered something Momma told me when I was very young. A rose is beautiful, but when it is crushed, the fragrance bursts out of it and you discover beauty you never knew it had. Every chance I got, I'd take a rose, crush it under my foot, then get down on my belly and let its smell envelop me. I'd close my eyes, lay my head sideways on the cement, and just breathe.

Momma was trying to tell me something I wouldn't understand for a long time. But she knew someday I would be crushed, and I am certain she hoped that I would remember the beauty in it.

59

LUKE

THERE WAS NO FANFARE as I walked up the courthouse steps. I was totally alone. It felt weirdly empowering because I knew I was pulling up my bootstraps, as Calvin had put it.

I hadn't told Dad and Jake. I knew they'd be both proud and conflicted, and I didn't want to put them in that position. So instead, I called on God.

In my briefcase there was only one document, but I carried it like it held the codes to nuclear bombs. It was my own personal nuclear bomb.

I'd requested we meet in the same room as before because this was my first of many full-circle moments. Right here, right now, I was going to start real change. If I could do this, I was pretty sure I could do anything.

But my legs were shaky underneath me, and I found myself a little apprehensive as I opened the door to the room. I had hoped I'd be the first there, but instead, the prosecutor whose bushy mustache greeted me before he did sat there waiting on me. He stood and shook my hand. "Mr. Carraday."

"Mr. Everett."

We both sat.

"I was very surprised to get your phone call. As requested, I kept it confidential. But why all the secrecy?"

I opened my briefcase and pulled out a folder, sliding it toward him. "I didn't earn this immunity."

Everett looked at the paper, then at me. I figured there were very few things that shocked a prosecutor, but I'd found one.

"But," I continued, "I will take your plea bargain."

"You're serious . . ."

"I'll be happy to tell you everything I know."

And so I did. For two hours, I answered his questions, staring mostly at the little silver recorder that sat between us on the table. Even as I spoke and answered questions, it confirmed to me that I was unknowingly involved, and maybe that's what I needed to hear. But it also confirmed that when the rumors started, I should've sought the truth. My other mistake was trying to hide it all from Faith, and she would be my next thing to make right. But first things first. I had to set my life in order before I could set ours.

I had absolutely no idea what this meant for my future.

But Calvin told me that the truth would set me free, and that no matter what, my character and integrity could recover from this if I took responsibility for the things I had done.

I dreaded the conversation I was going to have to have with my father and brother, but I knew deep inside they'd be proud of what I'd done. I wasn't going to be a runner anymore. If I had to run, I'd run to my family. And I hoped that family included Faith. I didn't just hope. I prayed.

60

OLIVIA

For mid-November, it was considerably warmer than usual. The clouds parted and the sparkly sun was high in the sky. We couldn't have asked for a more beautiful day.

Faith was putting the final touches on Silver, brushing his mane and tail, determined to bring back that silky shine he used to have when he was younger. Silver watched me from the side, blinking kindly at me, like he knew it was his day.

Dad stood nearby, relishing the moment. Even his head was tipped up a little, soaking in the rare November warmth. I'd dressed him in his favorite flannel shirt. He looked like he wanted to sell me a roll of paper towels, but that's how he liked to look. I couldn't talk him into his bolo. But I gave a nice trim to his hair.

"Looking good," Dad said, gesturing with the hand that didn't hold his cane. His words were slurred, just enough to be noticeable even to the girls. Nell glanced up at me, her eyes wide with worry.

"It's okay. He's doing fine." I said it with as much conviction as I could muster, but the lump came, as it did frequently these days, and I couldn't say much more. Instead, I patted her shoulder and tried to enjoy the day.

Down the long driveway, a cloud of dust circled Lee's truck as he pulled the horse trailer.

"Lee's here!" Vic said, running to meet him.

"Vic, stay back. Be careful." I sighed. I wondered if there was ever going to be a time in my life when I would be free of worry.

Lee slowed as he saw Vic, then parked the truck, getting out. He gave a long wave to us and a quick hug to Vic.

He ambled up, his thumbs locked around his belt loops, evidence that even if you leave for the big city, the country never leaves you. He joined me at the fence, leaning over the wood. "Look at you, Silver!"

Faith glanced up and smiled at Lee, but it was the cautious smile of a woman who'd decided to play everything safe. We'd spent hours on my back porch talking about it. I told her that if Lee was the one, then there was no use rushing things. He'd be there when the time was right.

My sister didn't need a man in her life right now. She had

a lot of healing to do, and the only thing I could do was be there for her when she needed me.

Looking forward to the fair had been a healing balm for all of us. It gave Dad a goal. We all knew he wouldn't miss seeing Silver shown at the fair. Not even a tumor could stop that. He'd started having trouble with his right arm and leg, and I knew things were shutting down, but each day he grabbed every ounce of happiness he could, squeezed the lemon dry like he was trying to make a big batch of lemonade.

"He ready?" Lee asked.

Faith stood. "I think he's going to protest if I brush him one more time."

Lee opened the gate and took Silver's reins. He guided him confidently, whispering calm into him as he led him onto the trailer.

"It's been ages since he's been in a trailer," Dad said, trying to get Lee's attention. "Keep him steady."

"He's doing great," Lee said. He shut the door behind Silver, then checked his watch. "All right, we don't want to be late for his big day. I can hold a couple of people in my truck."

"Me! Can I go, Momma?" Vic shouted, even though she was standing right next to me.

"Sure," I said, and she ran toward the truck.

"Me too?" Nell asked.

"Let's let Aunt Faith ride up there with, um . . . Silver. So he'll stay calm."

"Good idea."

"We'll ride with Grandpa."

"Okay!"

I took Dad's arm. Hardy was on the other side. He grumbled about not needing help but couldn't even get in the truck by himself. Nobody wanted to stare, but we all held our breath as he struggled to get in.

Then he smiled at all of us, that wild and wide kind of smile that kids get when their tummies are tickled on a tire swing. "It's a good day."

"It is, Daddy," Faith said as I slipped my hand into hers. "A very good day."

Forty-five minutes later, we were unloading Silver. Dad, Hardy, and Lee took him to the stables and the girls tagged along. Faith and I went to get Silver registered.

My eyes widened with the nostalgia of it all. I hadn't been to the fair since Momma died, despite my kids wanting desperately to go every year. Nearby, a man in white-and-red stripes called out, selling peanuts. Children rushed by, clutching plastic baggies with goldfish in them. A teenager nearly knocked us over as she tried to maneuver through the crowds with a gigantic giraffe she'd apparently won at one of the games. I looked at Faith. I knew the memories were overwhelming her, too. But we both smiled, knowing that soon memories would be all we'd have of our parents, and we were going to have to be okay with that.

"Do you ever feel old?" she asked me. "Sometimes I feel like I've lived two lifetimes already."

"You're more beautiful than ever." I winked at her. "And Lee sure is taking notice."

"Stop."

"He is."

"Train wrecks are hard not to notice."

"I guess you haven't heard from him."

"Just that one text, saying he was taking care of things. I'm still assuming that means he's drawing up divorce papers." She teared up. "That will be the worst day of my life."

"Well, it's not here yet. God can always work a miracle, you know."

She nodded and wiped her eyes.

"Anyway, Lee's a good guy. I've been watching him like a hawk, the way only a big sister can. He's a stand-up guy."

We found the registration table and stepped into line. Faith was staring upward, blissfully, as if she expected the sky to come down and kiss her.

"You okay?" I asked.

"Yeah."

"You're . . . staring at the air."

"The sky."

"The ozone layer?"

"I feel like something really good is going to happen today."

I tried to keep it in, but Faith was always the dreamer, and she had this enormous habit of getting her hopes dashed.

"Faith, you know it's highly unlikely that Silver is going to win, right? He's ancient. He walks with a limp."

"Magic happens."

Oh, boy. Well, I'd pick her up off the floor later, along with Vic and Nell, who were both certain he'd not only place, but get first. We'd have one big cry fest over some corn dogs and cheese fries.

Whatever happened, we had Daddy for one more day, and that was good enough for me.

61

FAITH

ALONG WITH THE HEARTY CLAPS of the crowd came squeals of delight from Vic and Nell, who were jumping up and down and bumping into everybody around them. Dad was standing next to Silver and looked as shocked as anyone, like maybe he hadn't heard right. I wished I'd had a camera to capture his expression.

I glanced at Lee, who was clapping as hard as anyone, then gave Dad the fist pump.

"Wow!" He practically slapped me on the back like we were teammates. "Silver was amazing! He didn't even limp. Did you notice it? It was like he knew this was his day, his moment. First place! Unbelievable!"

Silver had always been special, in an intuitive sort of way. I was sure he knew Dad was sick, probably long before any of us did. And he probably knew that this memory would serve us well over the coming years too.

As Dad accepted the congratulating handshakes of the people around us, I turned to Lee and pulled a small sack out of my bag. I handed it to him. "This is for you."

He reached into the bag. I was a little giddy with excitement.

"A vintage playbill for *West Side Story*," I exclaimed before he even had a chance to get it all the way out of the bag.

He looked surprised as he admired it for a moment. "Wow. What is this for?"

"I never thanked you."

"For what?"

"Getting Daddy into Sloan."

The delight on Lee's face faded.

"What?" I asked.

"I thought you knew."

"Knew what?"

"It wasn't me. It was Luke. Or at least someone in his family."

"What are you talking about?"

"He must have swallowed his pride, gone back to his father . . ."

"I. . . ."

"Didn't know. I'm sorry. I just assumed you did."

I pushed a cheery expression back onto my face. "Well

then, that's for all the other amazing things you've done for my family. And for me. I want you to know that I'm grateful."

"You're welcome," he said gently.

I looked carefully at this man, who'd been such a great comfort to me since I'd returned. He deserved way better than a woman who already had her heart tied up in a big, messy knot.

"Lee, I might've given you the wrong impression. I believe I gave myself the wrong impression. Others too."

He tried to interpret what I was saying, his eyes searching mine. "Impression about what?"

"That I wasn't going to fight for my marriage. I've realized that I have to. If it doesn't work out in the end, then it doesn't. But I have to give it as good of a fight as I can. That's what my momma would've done. I don't know if Luke will fight for me, but I have to fight for him."

"Faith!" I turned to find Daddy waving me down, beckoning me into the small arena. "Pictures!"

"I guess I better go get my picture made with the star of the show." I touched his hand. "I'm sorry."

"For the record," Lee said with that gentle, likable smile, "you always gave me the impression that you could handle whatever life threw at you, and it's thrown a heck of a lot."

"Thanks." We stared at each other for a moment. Was I throwing away a chance at a rooted, grounded life with a guy not unlike my daddy? I crawled through the rope fence and met Dad in the middle, my heart a little heavy with what might be before me. Hardy was snapping pictures like we were both standing by the NASCAR Cup winner or something. I squeezed Daddy tightly around the waist.

"Hey, I want to show you something. Walk with me?"

"Sure."

Daddy waved Hardy over to take Silver back to the stables, and he guided me through the crowds and into the streaming lines of the fair. We walked slowly, both relishing the time.

Suddenly Daddy pulled me aside and whipped out a five. "New York might have their pretzels, but we have our cotton candy."

"Pink?"

"You got it."

It was puffy like the clouds over us, and it tasted like pure delight, which was what we all had before Momma died. I guess we knew pure delight couldn't last, but we always hoped for more and relished it when it was around.

"My fingers are sticky," I laughed.

"You always managed to get it in your hair when you were little," Daddy said. "Even in your eyelashes!"

"I do remember the horrible task of trying to comb it out once we got home."

"What did your momma always say?"

"'But wasn't it worth it?'"

"Yeah."

"Yeah, it was."

We stopped and Dad pointed. In front of us was one of

three stages at the fair. A local country band was playing it up with their fiddles and tambourines. "Remember this?"

"My first show."

"Yep. Right there on that stage. I stood back and watched you sing your little heart out. No fear, I tell you. None. It was like nobody was watching, except you just kind of soaked up all that applause and it fired you up for another round. They loved you here. You got three standing ovations."

I leaned against him. "That was a lifetime ago."

"I guess so." A moment passed. "I'll be right back, okay?"

Before I could stop him, he was hobbling through the crowd, practically parting it with the cane they'd given him since his balance had gotten worse. Probably saw one of his fishing buddies.

I stood there waiting for him, listening to the band, my emotions quavering between the joy of the day and the heartache that would soon come. The band finished up and Dad still hadn't returned. I started getting worried. Had he fallen? Gotten lost?

Before I could worry much longer, I heard it. And I knew immediately it was no coincidence. "Someone to Watch Over Me" warbled through the old sound system that still hung by chicken coop wire from the small overhang I stood under.

What I didn't expect, however, was for Essie Mae to walk out on stage, wearing a brightly hued floral dress that cinched at the waist and spun lightly against her legs as she walked. She looked stunning. The crowd cheered her on. Who didn't love an old woman singing with that much charisma?

Suddenly Dad was by my side. He put his arm around me. "You did this, didn't you?"

"Maybe."

I smiled. The music had never stopped for Daddy. I could see that. His eyes twinkled with light as if he were somewhere back in time with Momma.

His big frame, hunching over more and more, still towered over me. And when he asked, "Sing it for me?" it felt like an honor.

"Of course I'll sing it for you," I said. We both smiled through our tears, understanding this would probably be the last time he'd hear me sing it.

My legs carried me briskly toward the stage. Essie Mae met me at the edge, handing me the microphone. I gripped it tightly, like Momma had shown me, and held it a half inch from my mouth. The crowd enjoyed the exchange between Essie Mae and me, but they couldn't quite understand the emotion behind it. Still, I knew they felt it, felt something special was going on.

I found Dad in the crowd. He was waving and looked like he might just break into a slow dance with someone nearby if his body could've handled it. I focused on him, sang it to him, gave him everything I had, enough to take him on to eternity. It felt good. It filled me deep in my soul, a place I'd barely acknowledged for years . . . the place where Momma's voice was, whispering her love to me.

I closed my eyes for a moment, took it in, literally sang my heart out. I didn't want this song to end, but I knew I had to find someplace deep within me to keep the music going. I knew it was what connected all of us, even across the chasm of death.

I found Dad again, and he locked eyes with me. I smiled, and he smiled too, but he kept nudging my gaze to my right, like there might be something over there I'd be interested in.

Momma had always taught me that there'd be lots of distractions on stage, and to keep my focus, even if I had to close my eyes. I wanted to, but Daddy seemed so urgent, as if the earth might collapse if I didn't look over there.

I couldn't imagine what would be so important, but I looked anyway.

And there he was.

62

LUKE

I WAS MORE NERVOUS than the first day I had to walk into that room with the SEC prosecutors. Maybe it was like those guys who propose to their girlfriends at a football stadium on the big screen. That takes guts. What takes more guts is knowing the person has hostile feelings toward you.

I kind of didn't want to interrupt the moment. I hadn't seen Faith sing like that before. She was a natural. She had the crowd in the palm of her hand. But this was my moment. My last chance.

So when she looked at me, like Calvin said she would, my eyes absorbed every minute detail of her face. Her frozen stare contrasted the small smile that turned into a small grin. I walked toward her and my heart was pounding like it thought it was drumming for the song. I extended my hand. It was shaking so badly I thought I might not be able to hold it out for very long.

To my great relief, she took it, and when she did, the shaking stopped.

"Dance with me."

The crowd was clapping loudly. If they only knew what all this meant. If they only knew I could very well be slapped right across the face.

"You hate to dance in public," she said, and that grin . . . oh, that grin. It still melted my heart.

"Not anymore."

I don't know who the little old lady was that suddenly appeared by our side, but as if on cue, she took the microphone, then pitched a thumb in my direction while looking at Faith. "Dance with him. Poor sucker looks like he could use a good dance from a hot woman."

We both laughed, and I drew her into my arms. I guided her down the front steps of the stage and we danced right in front, on a dirt floor that probably hadn't seen any dancing shoes for quite some time. A few other couples joined us, but at that moment, I felt like it was me, Faith, and the bright-blue sky.

Her face was nestled against my shoulder, right at the crook of my neck.

"Why are you here?" she asked.

"Because you are my wife, and I want you to come home."

She raised her head, her face close to mine, her eyes shining with hope and tragedy all at once. "I can't leave here and go back to New York."

"I didn't say New York," I replied, placing her hand on my chest. Surely she could hear how loudly my heart was beckoning her. "I said come home."

She nodded. Tears ran down her face.

"I'm sorry, Faith. I'm sorry for all I've done. My pride, my selfishness, my need to try to cover for myself rather than tell you the truth."

"I shouldn't have run." She sniffled. "I left you in the middle of a big mess because I only wanted the fairy-tale part of it."

"Well—" I smiled—"we're definitely no Disney movie anymore, are we?"

We laughed and I pulled her to me. The music continued, and I managed to tune everything and everyone out, except one young, strong-looking guy, standing under an overhang, watching us. Somehow he didn't seem like a stranger. Our eyes met, and a weird feeling shot through me, one of those times when you think maybe God talked to you, or maybe you're just crazy. But something told me this guy had watched over Faith while I was gone cleaning up my messes. His hands were stuffed in his pockets, and his expression seemed resigned. He gave me a short, definitive nod that said I was right where I was supposed to be and not to ever forget it. Then he disappeared into the crowd.

"You hear that?" Faith said suddenly.

My attention returned to her. "What?"

"The music."

"What about it?"

"It's ours."

I drew her in close, held on to her tight, danced her through the dirt and the sunshine. I glanced up once more to find Calvin smiling over us. He gave me a salute and a wink, then walked off in the direction of the stables.

My dad saved me. That dad saved our marriage.

I knew it now. Family grounded us, rooted us, nurtured us, and sometimes even saved us. In my life, they would never be taken for granted again.

63

CALVIN

I WAS SURPRISED when they told me it was the first day of spring. I was pretty sure I was going to kick the bucket sometime before Christmas. Weeks had passed that I'd barely been conscious for. That wasn't how I wanted to live, with large gaps of time missing in my life.

"Wilma. Wilma!"

I heard her hurried footsteps. "Mr. Barnett, you're awake!" I felt her grab my wrist, press her fingers into my veins.

I didn't have the strength to take it away, but I gave her the best stink eye someone could give without actually opening the eye. Except, suddenly, my eyes were open. Everything was blurry. "I'm awake, so I'm pretty sure that means my blood's pumping."

I could tell Wilma was giving me the stink eye back. "So this was what your daughter was talking about. Said you'd be an awful patient."

I looked closer at her, trying to make her out through the gray fog that had become my vision. Her voice was different. "You're not Wilma."

"I'm Dorothy. Wilma retired."

"I'm outliving my hospice nurses?"

"Retired, not dead."

"Same thing."

It looked like she put a cell phone to her ear, then dropped it to her side when we heard the front door open.

"I was just calling you," she said. "Calvin, your daughter Faith is here."

"He's awake?"

"Awake and talking and doing quite a bit of griping."

I could hear the smile in Faith's voice. "That's a good sign."

I couldn't explain why I was awake, but I didn't feel very much alive. My thoughts, my whole brain really, had seemed to shrink and shrivel, almost like I could feel it being sucked into a black hole of unconsciousness. But I was alive enough to know how much I hated having a big hospital bed in my living room. The girls thought it'd be nice, so I could hear the TV, get more sunlight. But it had to be an awfully imposing sight to walk in to.

I felt Faith's hand in mine. I tried to squeeze it, to let her know I knew she was there, but I couldn't hold my eyes open any longer and I couldn't talk, even though I wanted to.

"Daddy? Can you hear me? Daddy, I'm right here."

"His vitals are dropping again," Dorothy said.

"Can he hear me?"

"Yes, I believe he can."

"He was just awake. What happened?"

"Sometimes," Dorothy whispered though I could hear her fine, "right before someone dies, they'll have a surge of consciousness. Open their eyes. Even talk."

"Daddy, it's Faith. I'm right here."

I knew she was. I really wish she hadn't been because I didn't want her to see me like this. I didn't want this to be her last memory of me. The girls had held an almost-constant vigil by my bedside, and that was probably half the reason I couldn't get myself to shake this old body. I kept thinking if they'd go away for a while, I could slip out under the cover of darkness or something. But I was realizing I didn't have much control over this.

Open your eyes.

I was a stubborn old goat, which was probably the other half of the reason I hadn't croaked yet. I didn't like anybody telling me what to do. Lee had told me at Thanksgiving I probably only had a few weeks left, so I had to prove him wrong just to say I could, even though it was really defeating the purpose because I would've been happy dying months ago.

I managed to open my eyes again. She was watercolor in motion right before me.

"Daddy! Hi. Hi there." She lifted my hand, and it felt like she put it on a ball. "Can you feel him kicking? He's kicking really hard. He's very strong."

A baby? I hadn't remembered.

"We've decided to name him Calvin."

I closed my eyes, hoped she saw a smile on my face. What do you know about that? Calvin! I hoped that name would serve him well. And knew his family would serve him even better.

"Silver's doing great. We've been teaching Luke how to ride. He's kind of a natural, to tell you the truth."

Stubborn old mule. Knew he'd try to hang on longer than me. Wanted to see me out.

"I'm going to go ahead and call Olivia," I heard Dorothy say. "His blood pressure is dropping pretty . . ."

Words faded. Light faded. In their place, I heard the strong, majestic chords of the organ and the words to my favorite hymn, "How Great Thou Art," being sung by what sounded like a million voices, all belonging to me. I'd never heard anything like it. I wanted to be nearer to it. I wanted to sing it too. I desperately searched for a way to it.

Father, release me from this world.

I somehow managed to look up. I reached out.

And then there He was. And right behind Him, she was there too.

About the Authors

Rene Gutteridge is the author of nineteen novels, including *Misery Loves Company*, *Possession*, *Listen*, and the Storm series from Tyndale House Publishers and *Never the Bride*, the Boo series, and the Occupational Hazards series from WaterBrook Multnomah. She also released *My Life as a Doormat* and *The Ultimate Gift: The Novelization* with Thomas Nelson. Rene is also known for her Christian comedy sketches. She studied screenwriting while earning a mass communications degree, graduating magna cum laude from Oklahoma City University and earning the Excellence in Mass Communication Award. She served as the full-time director of drama for First United Methodist Church for five years before leaving to stay home and write. She enjoys instructing at writers conferences and in college classrooms. She lives with her husband, Sean, a musician, and their children in Oklahoma City. Visit her website at www.renegutteridge.com.

John Ward has over twenty-five years of experience in the film industry on both sides of the camera, in projects ranging from large studio blockbusters to independent films to cutting-edge emerging media.

He began his show business career at age twelve when his little sister, Jennifer, became Drew Barrymore's photo double for the film *Firestarter*. Within a few weeks of shooting, Drew moved in with the Ward family, and John was thrust into Hollywood. Catching the acting bug, John appeared in twenty-seven feature films and television episodes including *Teenage Mutant Ninja Turtles*, *Sleeping with the Enemy*, and *Matlock*, to name a few.

While continuing his acting, John attended the University of North Carolina, where he began screenwriting and directing films. While in school, he wrote and directed *Go West*, which was nominated for a Student Academy Award.

John wrote, produced, directed, and starred in *Enchanted*, which was sold to the Showtime and Starz networks. It also garnered John's admission into the Directors Guild of America as a director member at the age of twenty-five.

By the release of *Enchanted*, John had sold his screenplay *Cindy: A Cinderella Story* to Lakeshore Entertainment (maker of *Million Dollar Baby*, *Runaway Bride*, and *Underworld*). He continued his relationship there, writing an additional seven screenplays on the Paramount lot.

With a desire to return to film production, John began work on the Liquid DVD series in 2006. He wrote, produced, and directed the seven-film series for Thomas Nelson. The films parallel books of the Bible, giving them a modern context and feel. All seven DVDs (*The Ten: 1-5*, *The Ten: 6-10*, *Money Talks*, *Live at Five*, *Mirror Image*, *Fork in the Road*, and *Crossing*) debuted worldwide in September 2007. To date, Liquid films have been experienced by over 2 million people.

In 2009, John wrote, directed, and starred in his first faith-based feature film, titled *I AM*. The movie portrays the Ten Commandments, unknowingly lived out by ten different characters as their lives intersect on the streets of Los Angeles. Released by 20th Century Fox in October 2010, *I AM* made history by premiering on 10/10/10 to over 2,500 churches on six different continents to an estimated audience of 1.5 million people.

John currently serves as president of Bayridge Films, where he creates feature films and television as well as consults on fiction and other multimedia communications.

He and his wife, Christy, reside in Newport Beach, California, with their two children, Cali and Jack.

Discussion Questions

1. Faith and Luke leave their families in different ways. Why do you think Faith felt she needed to pull away from her family? Why did Luke? Was it necessary for them to leave?

2. How do you feel about Luke's brother, Jake, and his outbursts against Faith throughout the novel? Do you think his initial assumptions about Faith were justified? By the end of the story, has Jake redeemed himself for his previous behavior? If so, what is his saving grace?

3. Faith, feeling betrayed by Luke, returns to the familiarity of her hometown. Have you ever felt

overwhelmed by your circumstances and wanted to run to something comfortable? Do you see this instinct as positive or negative?

4. After his arrest, Luke must fight to put together the broken pieces of his life. He finally turns to his family, particularly his brother, to help him through this rough patch. Did you agree with his decision to go to Jake? When faced with personal disarray, who do you turn to?

5. Faith, the symbol of the prodigal daughter, returns home to find her sister managing their father's life. How does Olivia's treatment of Cal differ from Faith's? If you were in Olivia's position, how would you feel about Faith's homecoming?

6. There are many different kinds of betrayal in this story. Between husband and wife. Between sisters. Between brothers. Could you relate to the characters' thoughts and emotions in these situations? How do you react when faced with the betrayal of a friend or loved one?

7. Calvin, Faith and Olivia's father, decides against treatment for his disease. How do you feel about this decision? Have you or your loved one ever faced a similar choice?

8. During the last moments of her life, Catherine vacillates between fear and peace, between fighting for her

life and trusting that God has a plan. Have you ever found yourself in a similar struggle, where you felt unsure of God's plan? What was the result?

9. Catherine regrets that she will be unable to get a final message to her family, and later Faith imagines what her mother's final words would have been. If you knew your last moments were near, whom would you want to speak to? What would you say?

10. In the end, Faith has to choose between the husband who lied to her and the young doctor who obviously cares for her. Which man did you want her to choose? Do you think she ultimately made the right decision? Why or why not?

11. Which sister, Faith or Olivia, do you identify with more? Which brother, Luke or Jake? Which family did you most relate to, and why?

Interview

It's common practice for publishers to create interview questions for their authors so that you the reader can get a behind-the-scenes look at how the story came to be. But after working with these two creative minds, we thought it might be more interesting to see what they'd ask each other. We think you'll enjoy what transpired.

John Ward interviews Rene Gutteridge

JW: Your writing is so emotional. I haven't cried since the late seventies and you choke me up. Yet you're a mother and a wife with a totally normal life in Oklahoma. How do you process all these powerful emotions in your work and not be a basket case in your life?

RG: I think being a mother and a wife has created powerful emotions in me. It's one thing to love your own life and be sad or happy for yourself. It's quite another to love someone else fiercely, in a way that would cause you to give up your own happiness or contentment. There just isn't another kind of love that matches that. This is why God's love through Jesus was so powerful.

So why am I not a basket case in life? I can't claim that I'm not. Ask my husband. He'd probably argue I am very basket-case prone, but in a totally organized, administrative way. My basket-case moments are carefully worked around everybody's schedules.

JW: So you're given a screenplay from some dude in Hollywood (that would be me), and you're going to turn that into a novel. What ingredients were you looking for in that first read?

RG: I love a good story, no matter the genre. Years ago I'd written a family drama called *Troubled Waters*, so I was actually really eager to get back into that genre because I loved it so much the first time. I wanted to know and love the characters and I wanted emotion to be drawn out of me. I saw all of that early on in the script, so I knew I was going to like it. And I was so excited to see that the characters and story line were strong all the way through. I didn't have to read it twice to know I wanted to dive in and be a part of your vision.

JW: In *Heart of the Country*, we've got the battle between the two sisters . . . Faith, the prodigal artist who ran away to New York, and Olivia, the Steady Eddie who stayed home. Which are you?

RG: I'm Eddie. It is so difficult for me to break rules. I can't steal a pen from a bank. I totally want to be a rule breaker, but then I become a nonscheduled basket case. It drives my husband crazy. But I like structure, and rules create structure, so for me that is safe. Playing outside the rules is risky.

At the same time, one of the truths for me in the Prodigal Son parable is that the one who threw away the most experienced God's love and forgiveness on a deeper level. God's love is radical, and sometimes just going along, following all the rules, keeps us steady—but maybe not as useful as we could be.

JW: One character I feel you brought so much insight, depth, and magic to is Catherine. I'll always be grateful to you for what you found in her. What made you start digging there?

RG: Well, digging inside your script was a lot of fun, like a treasure hunt. I started thinking about the long-term effects their mother's death had on Faith and Olivia. But something made me also wonder what it might've been like for a mother to know she was about to become just a memory to them for the rest of their lives. Catherine was already so well-drawn in the script through the eyes of the other characters that I wanted to get to know her personally. And because of the nature of literature, I could do that.

JW: Which setting was easier for you to take on—rural North Carolina or New York? Why?

RG: Definitely North Carolina, though I had to adjust the region in my mind and get the Midwestern landscape out of my head, with your help. But I grew up in the country, so that is where I am most comfortable. New York City seems so loud and overbearing to me. For the New York scenes, I had to work to establish two characters who draw their comfort from a place that makes me feel uptight.

JW: Now be honest . . . you'll only hurt my feelings a little bit. Was writing from a screenplay a help or was it confining?

RG: It was terrific! I have studied screenwriting extensively and I love the craft very much. It was not in the least bit confining. In fact, it was like a playground to me. Part of the reason for that, though, was that you gave me a lot of freedom to create the magic in a novel. You understood the differences between the two and knew that whatever changes I needed to make were so the novel read well. Probably the most challenging part of the writing was the flashbacks in the script. My editors and I had to take a few stabs at exactly what to do with those, but that's the fun part, the experimentation.

JW: I still remember you calling me with the idea of writing the novel from the multiple first-person points of view. First, that was so heady it took me five minutes (and a Google search) to even follow what you were talking about. Once I got caught up to speed, I was blown away by its sheer brilliance. What is it about this story that made you think it should be told in that manner?

RG: I am not one for picking something unusual just for the sake of being unusual. But this story really lent itself to this style because of the strong characters. I couldn't pick whose story I wanted to be in. The thought that I could tell each story in first person struck me early on, and it just made total sense. It was more of a gut feeling than a logically thought-out idea, but I tend to write more from my gut.

JW: When you're writing, do you feel the desire to get it written as fast as possible—does it consume you? Or do you write for set amounts of time over a longer period? In other words, do you flip the switch between writing/imagination and the real world of carpools, making dinner, etc., all day?

RG: I definitely have set times I write. And I feel very strongly that I want to be present wherever I am. So if I'm with the children, I want to be there fully. Same with my husband and all the other things in my life. I do have a good on/off switch. But I steal pockets of time to think . . . driving, in bed at night. I let my mind wander a lot during those times and think about the characters. So much thinking is required to write realistic characters. If you don't know them well, your readers or viewers won't either, as you know. So we are more intimately acquainted with our characters than most people know or than we would likely admit.

JW: We both live in the space where art meets faith. What do you think makes a book or movie "Christian"?

RG: Everything I write will always be from a Christian point of view because I am the creator and that is my point of view. Calling books or movies "Christian" now has some meaning steeped in "brand," so it's sometimes hard to identify what that exactly means on a larger scale. But for me, I'm a Christian who creates art. However that looks to a marketer or on a bookshelf is for someone else to decide. I have to be true to who I am as an artist and as a Christian. That combination makes what I do unique to me, and it's true for all artists. Sometimes the results are hard for others to swallow and that makes them uncomfortable. That's okay too. I think art should rattle our cages and make us think about what we truly believe.

I think in our Christian artistic community, we can be awfully hard on our fellow artists when they're creating differently from ourselves. We all have the same basic vision and message, so I think we can settle back and realize that God is working in a variety of ways. What I think we do need to be held accountable for is our "production value," to borrow a term from the film world. We should always strive to be better—and to deliver the truth accurately but creatively—in everything we do.

JW: Tell the truth—weren't you secretly pulling for Lee to end up with Faith?

RG: Definitely! I had to be pulling for Lee because he had to be a viable threat to Luke. If he was just thrown in there as a stumbling block, he wouldn't have read as well. But to me, Faith could've ended up with Lee and a happily ever after. What won out was her deep commitment to her marriage vows, and that's the tie that binds.

JW: I know when I'm writing a screenplay, I won't allow myself to write a word until the story and characters "ferment" in my mind for a bit. What are the things you do before you write the first word of a novel?

RG: A lot of thinking. *A lot* of thinking. I'll take some notes here and there. I have an idea journal, where I keep track of things I want to put in the book. I discover a lot as I write, especially about my characters. But sometimes I'll be thinking on an idea for years before I actually begin writing it.

JW: Do you have people you talk with about what you're writing, or are you a Selfish Sally, hoarding it all in that brain of yours?

RG: Ha! That's funny. I'm now Eddie and Sally. I don't talk a lot about what I'm writing to anybody. For one, by the end of the day my brain is fried and I don't really want to spend any more time on it. Also, what I'd want to talk about—"I'm thinking about murdering character A"—comes across odd in a conversation with PTA parents. And I like that I have different aspects of my life. I have entire sets of friends who've never read one of my books, and that is totally fine with me. We have other connections that are just as strong, like parenting or our faith. Lastly, I think that it's hard to talk about the way we pour out our souls. Writing is a very intimate process for me, and I work through it almost entirely internally. So if I did talk about it, it would be with a fellow artist, an editor, or my husband—who also happens to be an artist, which works well.

JW: What do you think Jesus was trying to say when He told the Prodigal story? Did writing a novel based on it change or improve your understanding of both the parable and Jesus? If so, what did you learn?

RG: The thing that amazes me about Jesus' parables is all the layers that are present in what at first glance seems like a simply told story. And I love how the Holy Spirit can take a parable that you think is about one thing and apply it to your life in a totally different way. I've related to this parable in so many ways . . . as the prodigal, as the sibling, as the parent, as a person observing it all from the outside looking in. For this particular story, what I took away was how complex and simple God's love for us is, at the same time. He understands all of our layers more than anyone and saturates us with His love accordingly. But there is no bolder statement than the sacrifice He made to save us, which can be universally understood—under any circumstance, in any culture, through any language. So He is both intimate and far-reaching. Kind of mind-blowing.

Rene Gutteridge interviews John Ward

RG: Most writers like to be in their caves and crave solitude. But you're also a director and an actor—you work with a lot of people and have to bare your soul on-screen. So basically what I'm saying is that you're really odd . . . speaking strictly and mostly in the writing sense. What is quirky about your personality that makes you able to float from one personality type to the other?

JW: My funky LA friends say it's because I'm a Gemini, but I think I'm just bipolar. Seriously, it's funny you mention that because there was a time when I was just a screenwriter (no acting and no directing). I thought I was going to die! The walls of my little office started to move in on me. That was when I knew I had to return to the set. There's something about making a movie . . . once it gets in your blood, you're hooked. Being a director or an actor is like being a sailor. Eventually, you've got to get back to sea. If someone really twisted my arm—like *you*, Rene—then I'd probably say I'm a director and an actor who writes and not the other way around.

RG: I have to give you props. You really captured the heart and voice of women in your script. Since you're not a woman, how'd you manage that?

JW: That's a compliment I'm going to treasure for a long time! There's Atlantis, the Fountain of Youth, El Dorado, and man's search to understand the female mind. Honestly, I'm not sure how. . . . When my daughter was first born, I remember rocking her to sleep and thinking about the life she had ahead of her. The more I thought about life from her future point of view, the more I realized how hard it is to be a woman! I think that was the point when I had a real, true, vested stake in what it is to be female.

RG: Among many things, the theme of family reconciliation drew me to your story. Is this something you're passionate

about, and have you had your own personal experiences with family reconciliation?

JW: I was blessed with amazing parents, and my wife and I try hard to do the same for our kids. Still, when I was a kid actor, I worked with so many teen stars (some of whom died way too soon) who had utterly sad and destroyed family lives. I saw the pain that caused for *everyone* involved. It was a black hole at the center of their souls that seemed to suck away all joy no matter how much success they had. That seared into me the prayer that all families can find peace.

RG: In novels, we get to play inside characters' heads. But with a film script, you've only got visuals. So what are some of the tricks screenwriters use to help the audience feel the emotional angst and triumphs of their characters?

JW: You novelists make me so jealous because of that! In a movie, we really can't express the inner monologue very well. That's why we have to rely so heavily on the visual metaphor. In *Heart*, for example, there is the single horse in the field as a visual expression of Calvin's loneliness. There's also the use of music as a symbol of love. As Calvin helps Faith grow to the point that she better understands how to love, music returns and becomes more full. Things like that.

RG: I bet you know a lot of famous people, huh? Well, my good friend's sister's husband's brother used to work for Brad Pitt's brother. So that's only five degrees of separation. Beat that.

JW: Well, I'm zero degrees separated from Rene Gutteridge and one degree from Karen Kingsbury. So there!

Yeah, it's true that in Hollywood, famous people come with the territory. I think since I grew up constantly around really famous people, it kind of became normal for me. The only thing that bugs me is going through the checkout at the grocery store and seeing tabloid articles about someone I know. I turn into a crazy person as I point and pronounce, "That is *not true*!"

RG: Is it hard as the writer and director to step aside if an actor interprets a character differently than you anticipated? Or do you just clapper-board them until they do what you want? The latter sounds more fun, but that's why I'm just a cave-dwelling writer.

JW: First of all, no one let Rene near the clapboard.

Because I've been an actor since I was twelve, I have a keen appreciation for the freedom someone needs when they put their skin around a character. I think every director should look at their actors as collaborators in the character. I truly feel that I am in every scene with every actor—right there with them on camera playing the part—in every take. Their success is my success and vice versa. You can't make that relationship work if you're not willing to let the actors bring their ideas to the screen. Otherwise, they are just robots.

RG: What is the funniest thing that's ever happened on the set of one of your movies?

JW: A movie set makes summer camp look like chemistry class. It is a never-ending series of practical jokes and general tomfoolery. One of the all-time greats was when we were making *I AM*, and we had this really dramatic flashback scene where the actor was supposed to shave his head. His character's wife had been murdered, and it was part of a ritual to turn himself into a cold-blooded killer bent on revenge. Stefan Hajek, the actor who played the part (and one of my best friends), is notorious for his intensity—especially in scenes of high drama like this. *I AM* is a modern retelling of the Ten Commandments, so it was pretty intense, and we needed a lift . . . so I decided to put some almost-dead batteries in his electric clippers. As I said, "Action!" Stefan glared at the mirror, summoned up his most intense anger, and turned on the clippers into his thick, full head of hair—right at the forehead. The clippers made it about half an inch before the batteries began to fizzle, but he kept on digging it into his hair.

He never stopped trying to shave his head until we all burst out laughing. I think he still has a scar from that, and I know he hasn't forgiven me. Still, it was pretty funny.

RG: What is one misconception you think people have about directors?

JW: That we know what we're doing.

In all seriousness, the cartoon version of the director is the self-absorbed moron with that bullhorn, screaming, "Action!" The reality is that we're coaches. It's our job to help everyone else be the best they can be at what they do, from the actors to the cinematographers to the art department to makeup and wardrobe and so on.

RG: So be honest. When you learned your script was going to be turned into a novel, were you the least bit nervous about the process?

JW: I was intimidated! Novels are things that smart people write; screenplays are for people like me.

RG: What was the most rewarding thing about seeing your script as a novel?

JW: By far, it's the depth a novel can bring to the characters and the story as a whole. In Hollywood, we are trained to be lean and efficient. Every page is hundreds of thousands of dollars—at a minimum. This is the first story where *everything* in my mind and heart can be for public consumption. I love it, and I hope enough people read it so that we can do this for all of my movies!

RG: What draws you to the Prodigal story told in the Bible?

JW: As a storyteller myself, I am in awe of Jesus and His parables. Each of them is a masterpiece. Of all of them, I think the Prodigal is my favorite. It captures the essence of the heart of God and is the perfect portrait of His ability to heal all wounds. It completely refutes the pop-culture perception of God as judgmental. Here is the Father forgiving all and restoring His son with pure unconditional love. That's God.

RG: Why did you choose two prodigals for one story?

JW: I loved the idea of two prodigals being in a marriage together. Faith and Luke ran away from their families and wound up with each other. How could that ever work out? The answer is that it couldn't until they each went back and found healing with their families.

RG: Why do you think the Prodigal story has resonated for so long and with so many?

JW: We are all prodigals in one way or another. We all fall short and desperately seek the redeeming love of Jesus. When I became a parent, I really saw this story from the other side as well. Now I was a father, and as I felt the unconditional love I have for my own children, I had such a greater appreciation for the love God has for me.

RG: Were there other themes you wanted to explore through the subplots of characters like Olivia and Calvin?

JW: I wanted to create other portraits of God's redeeming love, particularly in marriage—although one of my favorites is Calvin's relationship with Luke. Here's a guy Calvin didn't even get to meet before his baby girl married him. There's no doubt he would probably feel more comfortable with Faith ending up with Lee—a good guy from his native North Carolina who he could relate to. Still, Calvin goes out of his way to help this wayward, rich Yankee-boy son-in-law repair the broken marriage to his daughter.

RG: Why did you choose to produce and direct faith-based films? Couldn't you be more successful by making films for a broader audience?

JW: *Good question. I ask myself that every day! I was blessed with a great career in secular Hollywood, but God kept tugging at me with one question: "Why do you take Me everywhere you go except to work?" I rationalized that for a long time, but in the end, He was right, of course. Now I believe that it's His calling for me to apply the artistry and grandeur that decades in Hollywood have taught me to telling His stories. It's not just about putting Christian thought onscreen; it's about creating emotion and being highly artistic and relevant in doing so. Artistry and subtlety are often overlooked in "Christian film."*

RG: Can you talk a bit about how you work with pastors, bloggers, social media, and the church to get audiences to the theater opening weekend?

JW: It's such an honor when a church or any group adopts your work and makes it their own. With *I AM*, we reached out to churches on 10/10/10 and offered them the chance to show this modern Ten Commandments movie for free on this "Day of Tens." We hoped maybe a couple hundred would do it, but we were shocked when twenty-five hundred said yes.

That's really how you can create change in the world. When your movie or book can create a moment and that moment can be picked up by people and transformed into a movement.

Social media is the coolest thing ever. Those who follow me on Twitter (@caliheel) are subject to hearing about my kids' every move, my alma mater UNC, and the daily comings and goings of my life in Hollywood, but what they give me is a relationship with them, making me and my work a small part of their lives. Nothing is cooler than that!

Also by Rene Gutteridge

THE STORM SERIES:
The Splitting Storm
Storm Gathering
Storm Surge

THE OCCUPATIONAL HAZARDS SERIES:
Scoop
Snitch
Skid

STAND-ALONE TITLES:
Listen
Possession
Misery Loves Company
Never the Bride
(with Cheryl McKay)
My Life as a Doormat
Troubled Waters
Ghost Writer

NOVELLA:
Escapement
(part of the 7 Hours series)

THE BOO SERIES:
Boo
Boo Who
Boo Hiss
Boo Humbug

NOVELIZATIONS:
Heart of the Country
(with John Ward)
The Ultimate Gift

www.renegutteridge.com

CP0664